EXTINCTION POINT: REVELATIONS

EXTINCTION POINT:
REVELATIONS

PAUL ANTONY JONES

47NORTH

Text copyright © 2014 Paul Antony Jones
All rights reserved.

Published by 47North, Seattle

www.apub.com

ISBN-13: 9781477817834
ISBN-10: 1477817832

Cover illustrated by Liam Peters

Library of Congress Control Number: 2013916756

Printed in the United States of America

For Karen

STOCKTON ISLANDS, ALASKA

CHAPTER 1

Emily Baxter stood at the frost-encrusted window and stared out at a distant horizon beyond the Stockton Islands rimed with thick, red clouds. The storm she and Rhiannon had fought so very hard to outrun had seemed, for a short while at least, to be intent on sweeping after the two women, following them to the safety they had fought so hard to reach. But the threatening clouds had slowed their steady march across the sky and finally stopped, far enough away from their island sanctuary that Emily felt able to relax, just a little; far enough away to begin to hope.

The same could not be said about her feelings toward the man who had convinced her to make the trip to this tiny group of frozen islands off the northern coast of Alaska; the storm roiling through Emily's blood was still a *long* way from subsiding. The deception that had led her on a trek thousands of miles to this place, that had cost lives, yet unquestionably saved her own and Rhiannon's, had dug itself deep into her mind and lodged there. Jacob Endersby, the man who had seemed to be her guardian angel as he helped to lead her across two countries under the guise of trying to save her from the horrible product of the red rain, had been a lie. Emily, Rhiannon, and Thor had reached the Stocktons exhausted, haunted, but thankful, only to find Jacob's motivation had not been as pure as he had led her to believe. Jacob was wheelchair-bound and trapped here in this icy prison, and Emily had been his only chance of surviving or ever getting off this rock.

There was no denying that Jacob had been correct in his assumptions about the alien invaders' intentions or their aversion to the colder climate of the north. But he had failed to mention that he was trapped in this place and had outright lied to her that he was a part of a group of survivors rather than the reality that it was just him, alone here and doomed to a slow death by starvation once his supplies ran out.

Jacob had pled his case to her, telling her that he had not thought she would believe him if he told her he was alone, that there was no ulterior motive other than to bring her to safety, but Emily remained unconvinced. And when she thought back to what she had endured . . . what she had *lost* and, God forgive her, what she had been forced to do during that terrible journey, it was all she could do not to leave him here.

And go where?

Where was there *other* than here? The storm had consumed everything within sight and now lurked at their doorstep like a hungry wolf.

But there was also no doubt in her mind that if she had not believed him she would have stayed in Manhattan and, most likely, died there.

And then there were Thor and Rhiannon; beautiful, confused, sad little Rhiannon. The child had been forced to grow up so very fast after first the death of her father and then the terrible loss of her little brother, Ben. Benjamin! His was a memory she would keep locked and unvisited for the rest of her life if she could.

Her head felt like it was full of tightly wound string that could unravel at any moment. But those emotions had to be set aside for now, there were more pressing concerns for her to worry about.

Not long after Emily and her companions had arrived at the research station, they had received a garbled radio signal, not from the International Space Station circling the Earth and Fiona Mulligan, its ever-watchful, but doomed commander. This new message had been from a British submarine, the *HMS Vengeance.*

At the sound of the static-broken radio signal, Emily and Jacob had momentarily forgotten their differences and rushed to the radio room. But the garbled signal had not repeated. And now, almost four hours after the first message had been received, there had been no further contact with the sub.

As the minutes slipped into hours, Jacob had finally said he had chores to do and left (due more to the angry stare Emily would give him every time he opened his mouth, than any real tasks, Emily thought). And as time wore on first Thor then Rhiannon had fallen asleep. The girl was slumped in a chair in the corner of the room, Thor on his side at her feet. But Emily remained awake, periodically pressing the talk button on the tabletop microphone attached to the large radio transmitter.

"This is Emily Baxter calling the *HMS Vengeance.* I'm here with three other survivors at the research station on the Stockton Islands. If you can hear me please respond." She spoke the words robotically now, the initial tone of excitement her voice had carried had moved to anticipation only to be replaced by one of desperation.

Thor gave a long, luxurious stretch of all four legs, arched his back, yawned, and looked up at Emily.

"Glad you're able to relax," Emily said to the dog, which immediately set his tail sweeping back and forth across the floor.

She rose from her seat at the radio and started over to where a slumbering Rhiannon was snoring gently. She was about to shake the girl awake when a crackle of static snapped her attention back to the radio. Emily rushed back to the desk, grabbed the mike in both hands, and thumbed the talk button. "Hello? This is Emily Baxter calling *HMS Vengeance*. Are you there?"

Another burst of static hissed from the speaker and then, as if he was standing in the room with her, a rich male voice burst from the speakers.

"Ms. Baxter, this is Captain Edward Constantine. I'm very glad to make your acquaintance. I hate to be—" The captain's speech was suddenly broken by a wracking cough. The radio went silent for a moment then his voice once again filled the room. "My apologies. My crew has an emergency on our hands and we badly need your assistance. Are you the person in command there?"

Emily hesitated for a moment before answering. "Yes," she stated firmly, "I'm the one you need to speak to."

■ ■ ■

The *Vengeance* had been laid up at the Canadian Forces Base Halifax in Nova Scotia for resupply and some well-earned R & R for the crew the day the red rain had swept across the globe.

"Most of my crew were ashore on leave when we got an order from the Admiralty to put back to sea immediately as soon as I had enough crew to operate the boat," the captain explained. "Only a handful managed to make it back in time. I cut it as close as I could, but we had only minutes, and orders are orders. The hardest thing I've ever done was leave my people behind. God help me.

Thirty-seven of us. That's all I managed to save, before we put to sea. Thirty-seven out of a crew of one hundred and eighty men."

Even over the low-fidelity radio, Emily could hear the pain of regret in the captain's voice. She wondered if she had that same tone in her own voice when she spoke.

The *Vengeance* and her crew had remained submerged, running radio silent, since that day, listening in disbelief as the world had died around them. Captain Constantine explained that the nuclear submarine could have stayed submerged for months if it had needed to, but two days ago a fire had broken out in the crew quarters. It had spread quickly, filling the ship with choking smoke. By the time the fire was out, four more of the crew were dead and another three had suffered serious injuries. Almost everyone else had suffered some kind of burn or smoke inhalation. The fire had damaged the sub's medical bay, and with the storm swirling above the waves, they had begun to look for somewhere, anywhere, that they could put ashore to tend to the wounded and bury their dead. That was when they had picked up on the radio conversation between Emily and Jacob.

"With your permission, Emily, we'd like to use your station facilities, if you have the room for us?"

"Of course," Emily said without hesitation. "Do you know our location?"

"We have your coordinates on our charts. You can expect us within the next two hours. I'll sound the boat's horn when we put ashore, so you'll know to expect us. And Emily, thank you. Over and out."

"Over and out," Emily repeated awkwardly, trying but failing not to smile at how odd the words felt.

Emily turned from the radio. Jacob was sitting stone-faced in his wheelchair at the doorway. "You don't think it would have been a good idea to ask me if they could come here, before you invited them?" he asked.

"No," said Emily, flatly. "No, I did not."

"Jesus, Emily. Did you stop to think about how their presence is going to impact us? We only have so much fuel and supplies to last. I really can't allow you to—"

Emily felt her blood rush to her head as she took a step toward Jacob, her hands bunched into tight fists at her hips. "*You* are not in a position to *allow me* to do anything," she spat. "You dragged us here for whatever reasons you had, and while I'm still not entirely clear how I feel about that, while we *are* here you will have no influence over my or Rhiannon's life. Am *I* clear?"

Jacob held her gaze for a moment, his own face flushing red from either anger or embarrassment, then he swiveled his chair and stalked off in the direction of his room saying nothing.

The argument had woken Rhiannon and she stared up from her chair at a red-faced Emily.

"Come on," she told the girl, "I need your help."

"What? What for?"

"We're expecting visitors. We need to make sure we are ready for them."

"Visitors? Who?"

"I'll explain later, just grab your coat and follow me."

With a huge sigh Rhiannon pulled herself up off the seat. "That was comfy," she said as though she had just been asked to give up her bed for the night.

"There will be plenty of time for sleeping later; right now you need to get your butt into gear and follow me."

Emily tracked Jacob down in his bedroom.

"The other buildings," she asked, "are they heated? Capable of holding the injured?"

"Yes," Jacob said, the sullen tone in his voice making it obvious he was cooperating under duress. "Each building has its own generator. You'll need to fire it up though. I've had them all turned off since . . . well, you know, since everyone left. The generator is in the small outbuilding adjacent to each of the living quarters. There should be more than enough fuel to power them for the next day or so."

"Okay, I'll find it."

"But Emily, I'd suggest you leave one building turned off."

Emily looked at him questioningly, expecting another attempt to re-exert control.

Jacob glanced sideways at Rhiannon, sighed, and spoke. "For the morgue, they'll need somewhere to put the bodies."

"Bodies?" Rhiannon asked. "What bodies?"

■ ■ ■

Emily found the generator where Jacob had said it would be and fired it up. Seconds later she heard the whine and rumble of the big industrial-strength heaters on the roof sparking into life, circulating the cold air out and replacing it with warm.

The inside of the second building was still above freezing thanks to the layers of thick insulation squeezed into the wall spaces, but only just. Within a quarter of an hour, though, the air was warm enough for Emily and Rhiannon to drop the hoods from their parkas. Ten minutes later the coats were off and draped over the back of a chair.

The two girls did a quick walk-through, moving from room to room. This building's layout was similar to the one Jacob had claimed as his own, but it had a larger meeting area with four smaller office areas leading off of it. There were also several other rooms that served as sleeping quarters, the beds nothing more than hard-looking mattresses on a metal frame.

"The bigger room will work as a makeshift first-aid and hospital area. We can put the more seriously injured in their own rooms. What do you think, Rhiannon?"

The girl nodded enthusiastically. Rhiannon was obviously thrilled about the new arrivals. "Do you think there will be other kids?" she had asked, unable to keep the excitement out of her voice.

"Maybe," Emily had replied cautiously, not wanting to dampen her enthusiasm. She didn't think there would be many children serving on a modern hunter-killer submarine.

The main room had chairs and tables that needed to be moved to make space for their new guests. They stacked them out of the way against a far wall, then moved into the sleeping quarters and manhandled six of the ten beds out into the cleared room. Rhiannon found clean blankets and bedding in a storage locker and brought them to Emily.

"Good job, kiddo, now see if you can find the first-aid kits around here." Emily had no idea what supplies the sub crew would have with them, but she figured every little bit would help.

The girl disappeared down the corridor and was back five minutes later carrying two large boxes with the distinctive red cross embossed on their lids.

"Will these do?" she asked.

"Perfect. Put them over there on the table." Emily pointed to a foldout table with some of the supplies they had brought with them from the other building. It also held a large coffee machine that was already sending a steady signal of steam and the aroma of freshly brewed coffee into the air.

They were almost finished making up the beds when a deep bass ululation rumbled through the walls of the makeshift hospital.

It could only be the horn of the sub, which meant their company would be arriving soon.

Emily stationed herself at a north-facing window, blotting away the condensation that had collected on the inside of the glass with the arm of her sweater, and watched. From her vantage point she could look out past the other buildings and have a clear, almost unobstructed view of the land to the drop-off that led down to the northernmost beach of the island. For minutes nothing but the occasional whirligig of snow moved between her and the distant edge of the world, but beyond that, a scarlet wall of angry clouds, shot through with deep purple layers, rolled and tumbled, filling the sky. The red storm—it lurked like some mighty beast, prowling the horizon, waiting for a chance to pounce.

Then, in the distance, Emily saw a silhouette emerge over a bank of snow. At this distance, the newcomers looked like a single entity, but as they drew closer the silhouette resolved into individual shapes and she could see it was a procession of parka-clad individuals, their heads bowed against the freezing wind as they trudged across the snowy ground toward the base. At the front of the procession were several men carrying the injured on stretchers; Emily counted eight stretchers in all. Behind them, each shouldering a large military backpack similar to the one Emily had used, came several sailors, wobbling as they tried to keep their balance on the treacherously uneven ground. And rifles, Emily noted somewhat nervously, all the figures carried rifles.

"Here they come. I have to go and meet them," Emily told Rhiannon. "Can you finish these up?" She nodded at the remaining beds still left unmade, sheets and blankets stacked neatly beside them.

"I'm on it," Rhiannon said in her singsong voice, and Emily felt a surge of pride swell in her chest. The kid was really turning out to be something.

Slow to button her parka as she stepped out of the building's exit door and crunched down onto the snow, Emily felt the freezing hand of the ever-present wind push its way between the layers of her clothing, grabbing at the exposed skin it found there. She quickly zipped the rest of the jacket up and flipped the hood over her head. *Dear God, how does anything survive in these conditions?* It was a thought worth pondering, especially as she had no idea just how long she and Rhiannon would have to call this place home.

Looking up from fastening her jacket, she could see the snaking line of British submariners had almost reached the edge of the base, but they were angling toward the other building, following the lights from Jacob's room. Emily took a few steps away from the side of the building so they would be sure to see her then began waving her arms back and forth above her head.

A few moments later she saw the lead stretcher-bearer stop and look at her. Whoever was beneath the parka turned his head and yelled something to the people behind him; she could see the white puffs of frozen breath spill out from the hood, then he changed direction and began trudging toward her.

The wind was beginning to make itself known again, picking up frozen crystals of snow and twirling them across the ground. Standing still wasn't a good idea, she could already feel the knife-edge of cold cutting through the thermal armor of the coat, stabbing its way through the other layers of clothing, looking for the warm flesh below.

In the few minutes it took the sub crew to stumble their way to the building, the wind had whipped itself into a fury, gusts roaring between the boxlike buildings, rattling the triple-paned windows and whipping the antenna at the center of the camp back and forth until the guy-lines supporting it twanged and sang. Emily had to lean against the outer wall of the building for shelter or risk being blown over. It wasn't that the wind was even that strong, it just seemed to switch direction in a heartbeat, as though it too was being pulled and pushed by some unseen force. The particles of snow and ice that flurried through the air only added to Emily's disorientation.

The first member of the crew appeared out of the wind-whipped snow like a Bedouin nomad emerging from a sandstorm. Emily could not make out whether the form belonged to a man or a woman, their gender hidden beneath the layers of the white parka, their eyes hidden behind a pair of snow goggles, and from their nose down, some kind of facemask covered their lower face.

"Hello!" Emily yelled, but her voice was torn away from her by the wind. Instead, she beckoned the crewman toward the doorway, pulled the door ajar, and leaned into it to stop it being ripped from her hands.

"Inside," she yelled. "Through the second door."

The figure dipped his head and stepped through the door, carefully maneuvering the stretcher and its blanket-covered patient through the narrow doorway. The blankets and the injured sailor beneath it had been secured in place by what looked like straps or belts. Rhiannon's face appeared around the edge of the far door; she opened it wide enough to allow the figures to stagger inside one after the other.

Over the next few blood-freezing minutes, the procession of half-frozen survivors made their way past Emily into the safety of the building, each clad from head-to-foot in the same all-white, military-style parka, facemask, and goggles. By the time the final one yelled into the hood of Emily's parka that he was the last of them, she had counted all thirty-six survivors, including the injured carried on the stretchers.

Thankful to get out of the cold, she followed the figure through the door and closed it behind her, making sure the airtight door was fixed firmly in place, then followed the figure down into the anteroom off the corridor.

"That's everyone?" Rhiannon asked as Emily stepped through.

Emily nodded and Rhia closed and secured the secondary door behind them. "I showed them where the beds are already," the kid said.

Emily gave the girl's shoulder a squeeze and shot her a smile as she dropped the hood from her parka, her lips still too cold to talk.

The last of the crew were disappearing from the anteroom into the main area she and Rhia had prepared. Emily followed them through into the makeshift hospital area. Thor was still sitting in one corner, his tail wagging slowly back and forth as he watched the procession of newcomers enter the room. His tail beat faster when he saw Emily.

Emily and Rhiannon waited patiently out of the way in the doorway, watching as the crew worked with military efficiency.

The newcomers wasted no time settling in. The injured had already been transferred from the stretchers to the waiting beds and the room was a commotion as the sailors dumped their backpacks and shed their cold-weather clothing. Medical supplies were pulled from packs as commands were shouted back and forth, order slowly being exerted on the chaos.

Bandages covered the injured, some had their chests wrapped; another had both hands covered in thick wadding that made him look like he wore boxing gloves as he was gently helped beneath the sheets of a bed; a woman, one side of her face wrapped up, watched Emily as she waited her turn to be transferred over. The gaunt-faced girl managed a weak smile, which Emily returned. Only six of the beds were occupied. She had counted eight stretchers, which meant two others must have been transferred to the side rooms she had prepped for the more seriously injured.

A tall man with a military crew cut directed the group from the center of the room. He looked to be in his early forties, a little taller than Emily, and with a week's worth of dark-brown beard shot through with gray covering his lower face. He walked to the bedside of each of the injured, chatting with them briefly, smiling, joking too, judging by the smiles, and reassuringly touching their hands or arms before moving on.

"You must be Emily," he said when he was finished with the last of his injured crew. He smiled widely and held out a hand, realized it was still gloved, and quickly pulled it from his fingers with his teeth. "I really can't thank you enough for this."

"It's nothing," said Emily as she shook the proffered hand. "This is Rhiannon."

"Captain Edward Constantine," the man replied, "and I am very pleased to make your acquaintance." He held his hand out to Rhiannon, who flushed bright red as her tiny hand was swallowed up within his.

"At some point, I'd like to arrange a burial service for the members of my crew who died."

"Of course," Emily replied. "I'm sure we can arrange something with Jacob's help."

"Jacob? Ah! Of course, he's one of the scientists here at the station?"

Emily stifled a bitter laugh: "He's *the* scientist. He's also wheelchair-bound, so you'll have to excuse him not being here to greet you."

Another man, broad shouldered and obviously fit beneath the layers of his military uniform, approached them.

"Sir," he announced.

"Jimmy. I'd like you to meet Ms. Emily Baxter. Emily, this is Sergeant James 'Jimmy' MacAlister of the SBS, and my head of security."

"You're the lass we owe for all of this? Well then I'm doubly pleased to meet you," MacAlister said through a smile in what Emily guessed was about as thick a Scottish accent as she could imagine. He was only a few inches taller than her, with what could only be described as a craggy face; thick eyebrows sat above a pair of soft brown eyes that hinted at a hidden level of mischievousness.

"What's an 'SBS'?" Rhiannon asked curiously.

"Special Boat Service," the captain explained. "British special forces."

"We're like your Navy SEALs," Jimmy chimed in. "Only better looking," he added, his face split by a playful grin. "Yeah, much better looking," he agreed with himself.

Emily smiled politely and coughed, and even Rhiannon giggled.

"What? You don't agree, young lady?" Jimmy said, directing a ten-megawatt smile at the little girl that caused her to flush an even brighter shade of red and burst into a fit of nervous laughter.

"If you're quite finished making an impression, Sergeant," the captain said with a hint of his own smile, "I believe we have some injured who could use your help?"

The soldier's playful demeanor dropped away and he instantly snapped to attention, followed by a brisk salute. "Sir!" he said, twisted on his heels, and was gone, but not before he gave Rhiannon a playful wink and a farewell, "Ladies."

"You'll have to excuse Jimmy, modesty is not his forte. He's a hell of a soldier but a bit of a charmer, I'm afraid," the captain said, his voice taking on a tone of obvious affection for the man. He took Emily by the elbow and maneuvered her toward the door. "He left most of his troop back in Nova Scotia. They were a tight-knit bunch and he's taken it pretty hard."

Emily nodded. Everyone had lost someone because of the red rain. "Can you spare a few minutes to come and meet Jacob?" she asked.

Captain Constantine scanned the room, which had settled into a less frenetic scene. "Everything seems to be under control," he said, more to himself than Emily. He caught the attention of one of the nearest sailors.

"Sir?"

"Ms. Baxter has asked me to accompany her to the other building. If you need me, you know where to find me."

"Sir!" the man nodded his understanding.

Emily glanced to the back of the room where Thor still waited patiently. "Thor, come," Emily said. The big dog was instantly at her side.

"He's a beautiful dog," said the captain, admiring the malamute as he joined them, sniffing the captain's boots and trouser legs.

"I owe him my life," Emily said matter-of-factly. She reached down and stroked the side of Thor's head.

"Well I hope we'll have the time for you to tell me all about your adventures, Ms. Baxter. Please, lead the way."

Emily zipped her parka shut then made sure Rhiannon's was also secured, flipping the girl's hood into place, followed by her own.

"Call me Emily," she said finally as she turned and headed toward the exit that would take them back out into the storm.

■ ■ ■

The squall had grown even more furious, whipping between the buildings so violently that it felt like multiple pairs of hands trying to push Emily over. She felt a sense of dread begin to permeate through the layers of clothing and chill her bones. If the red storm, which seemed to have slowed to a stop at the edge of the Arctic Circle, was once again pushing in on this tiny island, then there was nowhere left for them to run to. The effect of the cold on the creatures she had crossed paths with had been obvious: They either died or fell into some kind of hibernation, but she had no idea if the storm would be affected in a similar way. Surrounded on all sides now, she and the other survivors would *have* to hunker down here and hope that whatever changes the storm brought with it would at least leave them alive when it passed. *If* it passed.

"Use the guide rope," Emily yelled to the others, pointing at the thick, red rope strung between the buildings that would ensure they did not stray off track in the blinding snow. Visibility was down to just a few feet. She pulled Rhiannon in front of her and headed in the direction of the main building where Jacob was still waiting, the light from its windows appearing periodically as a faint orange glow through the dense sheets of snow. At least there was no red mixed in with the dove-white flakes.

Even Thor seemed eager to get back inside. He loped on ahead through the storm, pacing impatiently at the entrance to the main building when they finally caught up with him.

Once inside they brushed off the snow and ice that had collected on their shoulders and around the hood of their parkas, allowing the warm air to revitalize their chilled skin.

Jacob was waiting for them in his room.

"Hello Captain," he said, stretching a hand out in greeting. "I hope you'll excuse me not getting up."

Constantine gave a good-hearted chuckle and gripped the man's hand in his own. "It's a pleasure to meet you. Emily told me a lot about you in our radio conversation."

Jacob shot Emily a sharp look, but a second later the smile was back. "None of it bad, I hope?"

"All good, I can assure you," the captain said, giving no indication that he was aware of the tension between them, but he quickly eased the subject away from Jacob. "I was just thanking Ms. Bax . . . Emily for your help, Jacob. My crew and I are indebted to you, more than you could know."

"Well, I can assure you that your thanks should go entirely to Emily, Captain. She's the one in command . . . apparently," said Jacob with a smile and no hint of sarcasm. Before anyone could reply, Jacob wheeled himself out of the room. "If you'd follow me, please," he said politely over his shoulder. He led the way to a larger conference room farther along the corridor, and gestured for them to take a seat.

"Can I get you a drink?" he asked, holding up a half-full bottle of whisky.

The captain declined politely.

"So, how can we help you?" Jacob said once they had all taken a seat and he had a half-filled glass of whisky in his hand.

"As I explained to Emily, we had originally planned on staying submerged for as long as we could, but the fire has basically scuppered that idea," said the captain. "What we'd like from you is a place for our injured to rest while they recuperate. Only so long as this damn storm lasts, then we can repair our boat. And of course, we would like to make arrangements to deal with our dead."

"And after that?" Jacob said abruptly, a smile still fixed disarmingly to his face.

"Well, that rather depends on you and how long that storm holds out for. If you'd like to come with us when we leave, we have more than enough bunk space for all of you."

"And where exactly do you plan on heading?" Emily asked. She tried to hold back the note of uncertainty she felt edging into her voice.

"As soon as we are able we'll reestablish communication with the nearest naval base and have them send out a rescue vessel."

Emily felt her heart sink. "Captain, you said you'd maintained radio silence since the red rain fell, right?" He nodded, a question forming on his lips, but Emily ploughed on. "So you have no idea what caused the deaths or how wide spread the devastation is?"

The captain's questioning look was replaced by one of uncertainty. "We assumed it was some kind of viral outbreak or maybe a highly organized and effective terrorist attack. You have information that would indicate otherwise?"

Emily sighed. In the confusion of the past six-or-so hours, Emily had not even considered the possibility that the British submarine crew would have no inkling of what was really happening in the world left behind after the red rain. And why would they? They had been submerged since the rain fell and maintaining radio silence. There was no way they could know.

"You'd better have that drink, Captain," Emily said. "Because I've got a hell of a story to tell you."

■ ■ ■

Captain Constantine sat in a chair and listened as Emily spoke, his chin resting on the interlaced fingers of his hands, eyes never leaving Emily for an instant, never interrupting her as she recounted the harrowing details of the events leading up to and during her trip. She chose to leave out Jacob's outright deception (although she was tempted not to) and skipped over the more painful parts of the story after she met Rhiannon and her family; there was no need to stress the poor kid out.

When she was done, Constantine continued to stare at her, a look of wariness behind his steel-gray eyes. Understandable, she supposed as she returned his stare; Emily knew he probably possessed a highly tuned bullshit detector after years of navy service, but he must also be a highly intelligent pragmatist to have achieved the position of Captain of a nuclear submarine. It wasn't like they handed out those positions to just anyone, after all. Still, his inscrutable gaze made her uneasy.

"You know," he said, finally unfurling his fingers from beneath his chin. "I think I will have that drink after all."

Jacob poured two fingers of whisky into a glass and handed it to Constantine. The captain downed the whisky in one go and set the glass aside, smacking his lips in appreciation.

"I hope you will forgive my bluntness, Emily," the captain said, "but apart from your own eyewitness account, do you have any other proof—not that I am questioning your honesty, of course—but do you have any physical evidence to back up your account. Photos maybe?"

Not for the first time since leaving Manhattan did Emily give herself a mental kick in the ass for not thinking to take her camera. She had left it behind with almost everything else she owned in her apartment, an unforgivable sin for any journalist, but all the more so considering the incredible sights she had witnessed. There had been mitigating circumstances of course; like trying to escape from a city whose population had turned into an alien menace, but still. A couple of pictures of the aliens or even some video footage would have made explaining what had happened so much easier.

"No, nothing tangible that I can give to you or show you. Not unless you're willing to travel back to Fairbanks with me at some point."

Rhiannon had taken the seat next to Emily, sitting quietly while the adults talked. "Emily wouldn't lie," she said, suddenly interrupting. "I saw the monsters too. They murdered my daddy . . ." Her cheeks flushed almost as scarlet as the storm clouds surrounding their tiny island, her bottom lip quivering as she struggled to find the words, ". . . and my baby brother. They would have killed me too if Emily and Thor hadn't saved me."

Rhiannon's voice trailed off when Emily laid a comforting hand on the girl's arm. "It's okay," Emily said, smiling reassuringly. Rhiannon leaned in closer to Emily, a trickle of tears moist against her cheeks. Emily glanced at Jacob for some support of her story.

"Perhaps if we can get in touch with Commander Mulligan, she could at least tell you what she saw," Jacob said.

"Commander Mulligan? Is she a member of your military?"

"She's a Brit, like you," said Emily.

"Oh!" said the captain, suddenly brightening, "You mean *that* Commander Mulligan, of the International Space Station fame? You've been in contact with her?"

All contact had been lost with the commander of the ISS and her crew, a consequence of the wild electromagnetic activity created by the huge storm that had blanketed North America, and Emily explained this to the captain.

"She'd be able to confirm what *she* saw on the first day, but not what I saw." Emily leaned toward the sub commander. "Captain, I've gone through this experience once already with Simon, Rhiannon's father; our lack of knowledge of just how dangerous the world had become cost him and his son their lives. I understand that you have a crew to worry about, but I have nothing to gain by lying to you—this is no longer our planet, and the sooner both you and your crew come to terms with that fact, the longer we all will live."

"She's telling the truth," insisted Rhiannon.

Jacob nodded his agreement as he sipped from his glass.

"I believe you, Emily. At least, I believe that you believe what you saw was real. And, given the lack of evidence to the contrary, I think it would be foolish of me not to assume that you know what you're talking about. But surely there could be other reasons. I mean, aliens?"

"Of course there *could* be other explanations," said Jacob, finally coming to Emily's defense. "It's *possible* that the creatures Emily encountered were the result of some genetic experiment gone awry. It's *possible* that the red rain and the storm are both just some natural beat within the ecosystem or some geological event. But Occam's razor favors Emily's account; the simplest answer is probably the correct one. Factor in that she is the only person we are aware of to have come into direct contact with the red rain and lived to talk about it, then logic seems, at least to me, to dictate that she is telling the truth. In short, listen to what she's telling you, Captain."

Constantine now regarded all three individuals sitting in front of him with a laser-sharp focus, his eyes moving from person to person, lingering momentarily as he considered them with an air of quiet intensity.

Eventually, he simply nodded. "If you will excuse me," he said, standing and offering Jacob his hand again, "I have dead I need to bury."

■ ■ ■

Given their circumstances and the storm that now lurked menacingly on the horizon, Captain Constantine eschewed the traditional burial at sea for his men. Instead, they chose a spot at the easternmost tip of the island. Four graves, shallow given the toughness of the frozen ground, lay in a row before the gathered mourners, each marked with a rough headstone denoting the name, rank, and date of death of the grave's new occupant. Even though the wind had quieted somewhat, the temperature was still fifteen below, cold enough to freeze the tears in the mourners' eyes. The group of crew members and Emily and Rhiannon stood quietly, shuffling from foot to foot to keep warm as Captain Constantine read a brief eulogy for each of the dead men; then, in his deep baritone, he read from a small, well-thumbed book of poetry clasped awkwardly in his gloved hands.

When he was finished he closed the book and slipped it back into his winter coat. Without another word, chilled and with a tangible sense of depression clinging to the air, the group left the dead to their new home and crunched their way back to the station.

CHAPTER 2

"Knock, knock."

Captain Constantine and Jimmy MacAlister glanced up from their conversation to see Emily and Rhiannon standing in the doorway of the makeshift office he had chosen, hidden away at the back of the hospital building. The desk had a collection of maps, a laptop computer, and notebooks brought from the *Vengeance* strewn across it. The captain and MacAlister had been poring over the maps when Emily interrupted them.

She felt her cheeks flush as Jimmy's face broke into a wide smile when he saw her. "Sorry to disturb you, but do you have a moment, Captain?" she asked.

"Of course, come on in. Excuse the mess."

"No, thank you," Emily said to the offer of a chair from MacAlister. "We're beginning to feel like the proverbial fifth-wheel around here," she began. "Your crew have been working around the clock over the past forty-eight hours, they look exhausted. There must be something that I can do to help?"

"Me too," chirped Rhiannon. "I want to help too."

The captain chuckled. "That's what I like to see, enthusiasm in the youth of today. Let's see: Sergeant MacAlister, is there anything that Emily and her young assistant can help with around here?"

"Aye, skipper. I think we have a few job opportunities available," the soldier said with an even broader smile than usual. "Emily. Rhiannon. If you would like to follow me?" MacAlister escorted Emily and Rhia back up the corridor to the main hospital area.

"This fine gentleman is Amar. He's in charge of making sure our injured are given the attention they deserve. Amar, meet Emily and Rhiannon. They've been kind enough to volunteer their time; do you think you can put them to good use?"

"Hello," said Amar with a tired smile. He was a tall, good-looking man, no older than Emily and with distinct West Indian features. The medic sounded as exhausted as he looked but he managed to add a smile and a nod.

"I'll leave you in his capable hands, then," said MacAlister. He looked as though he was about to add something else, but instead turned and headed back toward the captain's office.

"Okay ladies, here's how you can help . . ."

■ ■ ■

Over the next few days, Amar taught Emily how to monitor and change the dressings on some of the less severely injured.

The crew was desperately short of medical personnel and Amar quickly began to refer to Emily and Rhiannon as his "Angels." The sub's surgeon had been ashore when the rain fell, along with most of the trained nursing staff, so the job of surgeon/chief nurse had fallen to Amar. Until the rain had arrived, he had been a nurse but now found himself the only qualified member of the crew with anything more than general first-aid training. Since the fire he had spent his time supervising the injured while trying to impart as much of his medical ability to the other surviving crew. Now he could at least grab a few hours of welcome sleep while Emily and Rhiannon watched over his patients.

The extra pairs of hands allowed him to direct more time to the three more severely injured members of the crew. Their injuries ranged from second-degree burns to the most severe, a crewman who had fractured his skull during the fire. He'd been in a coma since then.

"All I can do is make him as comfortable as possible," he told Emily as they stood over the injured man. "If I had access to a hospital or a qualified doctor, he might stand a chance. Here . . ." his gaze swept around the small room, "there's little hope he'll make it." The frustration Amar felt at not being able to help his colleague was palpable. "Thank God we at least have more morphine available than we need."

Rhiannon on the other hand quickly became the crew's surrogate mascot. She spent her time flitting from patient to patient, fetching water and meals for them, and listening intently and with wide eyes to the crew as they spun tails of the exotic-sounding ports of calls they had stopped at during their tour of duty aboard the *Vengeance*. She seemed particularly taken with one of the more badly injured patients named Parsons and would spend hours reading a dog-eared copy of *Alice in Wonderland* aloud, his burned hands unable to turn the pages.

Thor seemed especially happy with all the extra attention he was receiving too. To the extent that Emily had to speak quietly to the captain; his crew was surreptitiously feeding the dog treats and leftovers when she wasn't looking, and he was starting to put on some extra pounds. The captain would make sure that stopped, he promised her, much to Thor's chagrin, he was sure.

The only person who didn't seem happy was Jacob. He was as good as trapped in the other building, the snow too deep for him to make it through in his wheelchair, but Emily got the impression that even if the path had been clear between the two buildings, he would have found some other excuse to stay where he was. The arrival of the crew of the *Vengeance* was a fly in the ointment for whatever plan he had had, she supposed. Her feelings toward him were still a confusion to her, his motivation for bringing her here to this desolate island duplicitous at best, but still, if he hadn't done what he had done . . . she didn't even want to think about what would have happened to her and Rhiannon. Maybe one day, she would be able to forgive him. For now, she kept her distance from him.

■ ■ ■

The young sailor in the coma died in the middle of the night two days later. Amar discovered him the following morning and they buried him in the cold ground next to his comrades that same day.

His death seemed to hit the crew especially hard, as if their defenses had been down, and Emily felt a distinct numbness begin to settle over them.

And, as she walked with them back to the tiny cluster of buildings, Emily realized she didn't even know the kid's name.

"Gregory," MacAlister had told her bitterly when she asked. "His name was Gregory."

CHAPTER 3

Emily had to lean hard on the second door leading outside before it would open. The temperature had dropped even further and bands of ice and snow had formed around the rim of the doorway, freezing it shut; she heard it crack as she leaned her shoulder into the door.

Stepping out into the glacial air, she felt her breath freeze instantly, stinging her nostrils and lips.

At least the wind had finally relaxed its hold on the island, leaving the air feeling thick and heavy in Emily's lungs. But when she looked to the south she sucked in a painfully deep gulp of the freezing air; the skirt of cloud hemming the horizon was so much darker now, like thick pools of congealing blood. The intertwining seams of purple stitched through the storm's body twisted and tumbled to form cauldrons of spirals that coiled and melted their way into each other like the beads and colored glass of a child's kaleidoscope.

What little light that made it through the clouds covered the island in a pall of perpetual twilight. It created a dull dissimilarity with the pristine white of the snow. Emily's eyes tried but failed to compensate for the painful contrast, and she quickly felt a dull throbbing headache form in her forehead as she squinted from beneath the shade of her outstretched hand.

She hoped it was just her imagination, but the cloud to the west seemed closer. It was hard to tell from ground level as the buildings obscured her view.

She stepped down off the ice-covered steps and crunched through the knee-deep snow, walking awkwardly around the side of the building while using the exterior wall to steady her balance as she high-stepped through the snow to the opposite end.

Fifty feet beyond the cabin a hillock rose sharply up to a blunt plateau high enough to give a clear view over the roofs of the camp's buildings. Emily's breathing came in short, rapid pants as she climbed to its top, the air collecting like rubble in the bottom of her lungs. At the hill's summit she had an unobstructed 360-degree view of the island.

It stilled her heart, petrifying it in her chest.

The ring of clouds circling the horizon on every side had crept closer, constricting the hole of hazy sky above the survivors' sanctuary.

Emily's gaze skittered across the curve of the island, and out to sea where a shining mist descended from the cloud base and melted into the sluggish sea: rain! Sheets of it were pummeling the waves out there. She could see a slick of red forming on the ocean's surface, slowly spreading with the swell. It was the same in every direction she looked, a slowly tightening noose around their necks.

A gust of wind thumped against her, pushing her back a step. A second gust buffeted her sideways. She tottered for a second, almost losing her balance as her legs tangled at the knees. She had a sudden disquieting notion that the storm *knew* she was observing it, and it was letting her know it saw her, watching her right back, this insignificant bug crawling on the surface of the world it had conquered.

From the west, another strong gust rocked her then rose to a constant blast that threatened to push her off the summit. Steadying herself, she sidestepped down the hill toward the camp just as the snow began to fall again, but this time the crystal-pure white of each perfect flake was stained with red.

CHAPTER 4

The survivors gathered in the large room, sitting on the floor in small groups, talking quietly amongst themselves. Occasionally, one of them would stand and walk to a window and look outside.

Emily had observed that whoever was doing the looking inevitably fell into one of two groups: The first would quickly glance through the frosty window, not taking more than a second to assess the situation and wander back to their seat, as dark of mood as when they'd first stood. The second group would linger for well over five minutes or more, staring out that window as if they were willing the bloodstained clouds poised just a few miles off every corner of the coast of their island sanctuary to dissipate.

Both groups left the window disappointed every time.

There was a third group too. The one Emily fell into: those who watched the watchers. That had always been her way, that deep drive to observe and understand had had a large part to play in her becoming a journalist. But she wondered now, as she sat, her butt on the floor, her back against the wall, whether she should attribute that calling to nature or nurture.

Emily shifted her legs, disturbing Rhiannon who, head in Emily's lap, moaned softly in her sleep. "Shhhh," Emily cooed, stroking the girl's hair until she sensed the child was asleep again. Thor lay nearby, stretched out, his head resting on his front paws, eyes wide open, watching Emily and Rhiannon with an unblinking gaze that seemed accepting of everything that was happening around him.

Emily had brought the news of the red-tinged snowfall and the tightening of the storm's stranglehold on the island to MacAlister. He in turn had relayed it to the captain. Both men had gone outside to check her story for themselves, and both had returned grim-faced.

"Emily, I think it's probably best if you and Rhiannon stay here with us for the duration, don't you think?" MacAlister had suggested and Emily had readily agreed. She did not want to be alone through whatever might be coming. Once had been enough. But the excited chatter of the sailors as they had learned of the encroaching storm and seen the red-tinged snowfall had quickly devolved into worried murmurs, and finally, as the hours wore on, almost absolute silence.

Emily had begun to wish she had done as Jacob had and requested a room to herself. She had not seen him but once since Constantine and his crew had arrived. But Emily thought that Jacob's hermit-like attitude was more from the habit of loneliness (or possibly the stash of whisky she knew he'd smuggled across with him) than from a shirking of any need for social interaction.

Occasionally, MacAlister or the captain would wander between the groups, chatting with the sailors. They were the epitome of stoic, she thought as she eyed MacAlister. He took a knee next to a lone sailor who had isolated himself off hours earlier, his hands clasped around his drawn-up knees as he silently stared at the opposite wall, his head bobbing slowly back and forth as if he listened to some inner song. Within minutes of MacAlister talking with him, the kid was back with his shipmates.

He was a good man, MacAlister.

The hours wore on, darkness came, and with it a howling wind that tore at the roof and walls of their shelter, rattling the windows and denying everyone sleep. The wind-driven snow had long blocked any view through the windows, tinting the glass with its pink stain, but that did not seem to deter the "window checkers," who would still occasionally stand and wander over to look, even though they could see nothing now.

By the time the second morning crept almost unnoticed over the camp, the mood had dropped as low as the temperature outside, and Emily began to feel a new nervousness settle over the group.

"Cabin fever" was not a phrase you heard very often in these modern times, but Emily thought she could detect a sense of paranoia attaching itself to the men. It was a knifepoint of anxiety pushing through the thin skin of civility still left; the thick blade, the part that would do all the damage, barely concealed beneath the surface.

Later that day MacAlister insisted that the two girls take over his room, which they did with a sense of relief. Earlier, a fistfight had exploded seemingly from nowhere, and Emily felt a skinny rat of worry begin to gnaw at her insides. As it was, it was all she could do to stop Thor from attacking. His barking and the men's yells had alerted MacAlister, and he had quickly stepped in and banged some heads, stopping the fight before it got past a black eye and a few raw knuckles. But Emily doubted that even MacAlister's imposing reputation and martial ability would be able to brace the emotional wall holding back the swelling fear that threatened to wash over the men for long.

For the second time in the last twenty minutes Emily checked the Glock on her hip, relishing the sense of security as her fingers played over the weapon's butt in the holster. The move to MacAlister's quarters would be a good idea, she decided.

You're a regular Calamity Jane, Emily Baxter, she thought with a hint of disdain as she followed MacAlister down the corridor past Jacob's temporary quarters to the tiny room Mac had claimed as his own.

"Here you go, ladies," he said, holding the door open for them.

"Where will you sleep?" Rhiannon asked, her face still flushed from witnessing the earlier fight but, and Emily could not help but feel a surge of pride over the growing toughness of the kid, no tears had been shed.

"Oh, I think it best that I stay out there where I can keep my eye on the rabble for the foreseeable future," he said. "You ladies relax, and make yourself at home. I'll check in with you later."

As he closed the door behind him, Emily reached out a hand and placed it on top of his.

"Thank you," she said, fixing his eyes with her own.

MacAlister smiled and nodded, and then was gone.

CHAPTER 5

Emily was teaching Rhiannon how to play poker with a deck of cards donated by Parsons—and was already down three straight hands to the damn kid—when Jimmy MacAlister knocked loudly on his door, pushing it ajar before she could tell him to come in.

"Are you decent?" he blurted out through the gap, but didn't wait for an answer before he stepped inside. "Sorry, ladies, but you need to come see this. Come on." He grabbed Emily's hand then Rhiannon's and pulled them to their feet. Thor jumped up and leaped along beside them, barking excitedly, eager to join in whatever new game his humans were playing.

"What's going on?" Emily said, half-protesting, half-laughing as she and Rhiannon were led down the corridor toward the exit.

"You'll see," he said cryptically.

As they passed Jacob's lab he spotted them. "What's going on?" he asked.

"That's what Emily said," Rhiannon laughed as they passed his door.

Jacob shook his head in bemusement, then swiveled his wheelchair away from his desk and followed after them.

MacAlister led Rhiannon and Emily through the anteroom and straight to the door, finally letting go of their hands as he reached for the handle to open the exit.

"Hey!" Emily objected, bracing for the sudden rush of freezing air. "Let us get our jackets on before you open that."

"Won't need 'em," the Scot replied and pushed the door open. The anteroom was flooded with bright daylight.

Emily gazed out through the open doorway. She could feel the cold air but she could also *see* all the way over to the other buildings and beyond even. She edged forward until she was standing in the doorway.

The blizzard that had pinned them to this island was gone.

"Finally," Rhiannon sighed as she squeezed in next to Emily. Thor pushed his way between them and bounded off into the snow, barking as he plummeted through the newly fallen powder.

MacAlister stood behind the two women, then all three stepped aside to allow Jacob to edge up to the open door.

"Notice anything different?" MacAlister asked.

"Besides the absence of the ninety-mile-an-hour winds and the blinding blizzard?" Jacob asked, his voice buoyed by a sense of sarcasm. "Not really."

"Look beyond what you can see," MacAlister said in his most mystical voice, his eyes wide and his hands fluttering at the side of his head.

Emily ignored the cold and stepped down the steps into the snow. Slowly she turned, trying to take in everything: The sky above her head was clear of all but a few wispy white clouds, the sun beat down on her skin as it burned brightly in a blue sky that stretched off to the vanishing point in the distance.

To the *clear* horizon, Emily realized.

"Oh my God!" she whispered, her hands flew to her mouth, not daring to believe what she was seeing. "Oh my God. Oh my God. Oh . . . my . . . God." Her eyes raised skyward, and she twirled around, looking for all the world like a child intent on making herself dizzy.

"What is it, Emily? What do you see?" Jacob called out.

Emily skipped back to the door and the waiting survivors. Truth was, she wanted to dance her way back, but the snow was still too deep for that. But already she could see the telltale wet glistening of a thaw.

"Careful!" said MacAlister.

"Careful, my ass!" she yelled out, grabbed MacAlister's face with both her hands and, before either knew what she was doing, planted a smacker on his lips. She felt her face blush as the look of surprise on MacAlister's face turned into a broad grin. To cover up her own embarrassment she grabbed Rhiannon and pulled her down into the snow with her.

"It's gone," she yelled, kicking waves of snow with her hands at the two men in the doorway as if she was in a pool.

"What is?" Jacob yelled back, frustration in his voice.

"The red storm," Rhiannon yelled back. "The red storm is gone."

■ ■ ■

No one knew when the alien storm had finally released its stranglehold on the planet. The only thing they did know was that when they looked out beyond the curve of the island, in every direction to the thin line where the sky met the sea, the blood-red clouds that had stained them for so many days were gone, vanished as though they had never been there. It had not simply faded away or subsided, there was no slow diminishing of its fury, nothing. It was simply gone, as if God himself had, with the sweep of a hand, brushed it from the skies.

Emily, Rhiannon, and Thor joined the crew of the *Vengeance* in the courtyard between the buildings, a white fog of hot breath collecting above their heads. Two crewmen carried Jacob and his wheelchair from his room, swaying from side to side as the two sailors carefully picked their way over the melting snow, like he was some ancient pharaoh. As they set him gently on the snowy ground, Emily looked down at the man who had brought her here. He looked about ready to cry, and Emily felt something shift inside her. It was as if, with the passing of the storm, her anger for him had also diminished . . . at least, a little.

It was still freezing out here, no way would they be ditching their coats just yet, but now that the blizzard had stopped, standing still for any period of time no longer meant you ran the risk of being frozen into a human Popsicle.

And the view. My God, the view was breathtaking now that she finally had a chance to take it all in. A crisp white blanket of snow with a top layer of rapidly melting ice particles that scintillated in the light lay across the undulating ground of the island, stretching off in all directions seemingly until it met the blue of the sky. But Emily knew the island sloped away just a few thousand feet from where she stood, dropping gradually down until it met the Beaufort Sea. As Emily listened carefully, in the spaces between the excited chatter of the assembled group, she could hear the waves breaking against the shoreline in the distance.

Everything looked so normal.

Emily had tuned out the chatter of the survivors milling around the entrance to the hospital block, but now she allowed the voices to fade back in again.

". . . what's it mean? . . ."

". . . you think it's safe now? . . ."

". . . can we leave? . . ."

At a nod from Emily, the two sailors flanking Jacob raised him up again and followed Emily into the hospital building, depositing him in the corridor of the sailors' quarters. Emily took the wheelchair's two handles and began pushing Jacob toward the main room where the rest of the survivors now waited.

Jacob swiveled his head around and looked back at Emily with curiosity.

"Don't start getting used to it, just yet," she told him.

He looked at her with his sad eyes, the words almost forming on his lips, but instead he smiled. He faced forward again. "Onward James," he laughed, with a pretty good imitation of an English accent, before adding "and don't spare the horses."

What had been the hospital area was now filled with the sub crew. They sat on the beds or stood together in small groups talking excitedly. *Everyone looks ten years younger,* Emily thought as she entered the room with Rhiannon, MacAlister, Jacob, and Thor.

MacAlister squeezed Emily's elbow and nodded toward the front of the room where Captain Constantine and another man were talking.

"Duty calls," Mac said and zagged across the room to join the men. Emily aimed Jacob toward the front, maneuvering the wheelchair through the tangles of bodies.

Captain Constantine's deep voice cut through the chatter. "Alright. Alright. Quiet down everyone. I know today has brought some very exciting developments, but we still need to maintain discipline." He waited for all eyes to be on him and all mouths to stop moving before he continued. "Alright, that's more like it. While it does seem that the storm has abated, we still don't know what's changed out there. Now, I know that you're all eager to get off this rock—no offense to our gracious hosts—but the simple fact of the matter is that we have no idea what this latest development means for us. And of course we're not going anywhere until we repair the fire damage to the boat.

"I'm sure you all have a lot of questions, but neither I nor the good people of this station have any answers for you just yet. However, as soon as we have any clue as to the sudden disappearance of the storm, I can guarantee you will be the first to know about it. In the meantime . . . Mr. MacAlister?"

"Skipper?" grunted MacAlister.

"I want you to get some eyes on the inside of the boat to assess the damage. When you have a good idea of how bad it is, I'll need you to organize two cleanup crews: twelve hours on, twelve hours off, so we have a constant presence on the sub. Am I understood?"

"Yes, skipper!" MacAlister replied.

"In the meantime, I want all of you to remain as calm and as professional as you have been up until this juncture. Am I understood?"

The crew responded in unison: "Sir!"

"Alright then. You are dismissed. Mr. MacAlister, carry on."

Immediately MacAlister began barking orders at the crew. Within minutes he and three men had collected tools and supplies from the stash they had brought ashore and headed off in the direction they had originally arrived from.

"I think I'm going to head back to the radio room. Now that the storm's over, maybe I'll have better luck contacting the ISS again," Jacob told Emily.

"Great idea," said Emily, "but I still need to speak with the captain first." She caught the eye of one of the two men who had carried Jacob across the snow and he agreed to round up another helper and get Jacob back to the other building.

"Captain?" Emily caught Constantine as he headed back to his office.

"Hello, Emily. Wonderful news, isn't it?" he said, smiling warmly at Rhiannon.

"Have you given any more thought to what I told you about what could be waiting for us out there?" said Emily.

The sub captain's eyes narrowed slightly and she saw him blow a puff of air out before replying. Exasperation. Well, at least she knew how he really felt.

"I've given it as much thought as a man stranded on an island with no way to contact the outside world can," he said, his face softening again. "But now that the storm has blown over, I've got Jacob and MacAlister trying to establish contact with anyone that they can reach on the base radio. We'll at least know if there are more survivors out there that can help us."

The captain turned to walk away, but Emily grabbed his arm.

"One more thing, is there anything else I can do to help you and your crew?"

The captain considered her request for a moment. "Quite honestly, Emily, you and Rhiannon are of more use to us watching over the remainder of my crew who are still hospitalized. If you don't mind continuing to help out here, it means I can pull a couple of the crew from hospital duty and get them on the cleaning crew instead."

■ ■ ■

Emily shrugged off her coat then helped Rhiannon out of hers, the little girl chattering excitedly as they made their way back to their rooms.

"Do you think we'll be able to go back home? Or maybe there'll be others out there like us too." She fired the questions off one after another, barely pausing for breath between each of them. Emily nodded noncommittally at each of them and added a "maybe" to each. But at the door to her room Rhiannon finally paused. "Do you think the monsters will be gone now?" she said, her voice barely audible over the sound of the warm-air vents.

Emily placed both hands on the girl's shoulders and knelt down until her face was level with Rhiannon's. It was so very easy to forget the kid was only thirteen, but when Emily stared into her eyes, she could see the traumatized child still hiding just behind those blue orbs, a reflection of Emily's own inner fears.

"Listen, kiddo. I don't know what's going on out there, but I promised you when we were on our way here that I would *never* let anything bad happen to you, do you remember?"

Rhiannon nodded.

"But the truth is, I just don't know what's out there anymore. But guess what? Now we have all these other people who are going to help keep you and me safe. So, don't you worry, okay?"

Rhiannon nodded and Emily watched as her frown turned into a smile again. "MacAlister likes you," the kid said from nowhere.

"No way?" Emily replied with mock shock, nudging Rhiannon gently with her shoulder.

"Does too," said Rhiannon.

Emily stood, her knees cracking in protest.

"Yeah, well, I quite like him as well," she said, and ushered Rhiannon down the corridor toward the radio room.

■ ■ ■

Emily heard familiar voices floating down the corridor as she and Rhiannon headed to the communications room. One of them was definitely Jacob's, the other MacAlister's, but the third was too faint for her to make out.

MacAlister smiled when he saw Emily and Rhiannon in the doorway.

Only when Emily stepped into the room with the two men was she able to hear the voice clearly.

"Fiona?" she blurted out just as Rhiannon let out a happy cry of "Commander Mulligan!"

The microphone must have been open because the commander of the International Space Station immediately replied. "Emily! Rhiannon! It's so very good to hear your voices and know that you made it to Jacob safely. I was so worried about you both. The storm blocked all radio transmission from us to you. I . . ." She paused as if wondering whether she should bring up the next painful subject. "I am so very, very sorry to hear about Simon and Ben. I wish . . . well, I just . . . I'm just *so* sorry."

"It's okay," said Rhiannon, her voice barely loud enough to be picked up by the radio's microphone. "They're both with Mommy now."

Emily pulled the girl closer to her, rubbing her hand up and down her arm.

"Commander, it's good to hear your voice too. I'm assuming Jacob has told you about our new arrivals? The crew of the *HMS Vengeance*?"

"Yes, yes, wonderful news in so many ways, Emily. And it's good to know that a little bit of Great Britain made it through all this."

"Their timing could not be better; it looks like the storm we outran has disappeared. How does it look from the ISS?" Emily continued, steering the conversation away from Rhiannon's deceased father and brother as succinctly as she could.

"The commander and I were just discussing that very thing when you walked through the door," said MacAlister, his smile broadening even more. "Emily, the storm seems to have vanished . . . worldwide."

"Everywhere?" Emily said, astonished.

"That's correct," said Mulligan. "We noticed it beginning to dissipate about six hours ago. Its disappearance was almost as strange as its arrival."

"What do you mean, strange?" asked Emily.

"Storms usually take days or even weeks to really lose their full power, but this one was gone in a little over two hours," said the commander. "It was almost as though it disintegrated, bit by bit. From what we could see up here, the edge of the storm just began to dissolve toward the center until there was nothing left, as though the original process was being reversed, only at a much faster rate. I'd tell you it was the strangest thing I've ever seen, but I've seen some very odd things these past few weeks."

"So that's it? Everything is back to normal again?"

There was no reply from the space station.

"Commander? Are you still with us?" Emily asked, even though she could hear the astronaut breathing slowly over the radio.

"There's something else," said Fiona. "While the storm has vanished, it appears to have changed everything on a global scale. I can't see any sign of Earth's indigenous flora, nothing is green down there anymore. It's all red. Everywhere."

Emily knew that she should feel something at the commander's shocking revelation, some kind of surprise or remorse at the passing of the final vestiges of the world that had existed since life first sprang forth on this tiny rock. But the truth was that she felt none of those things. She had suspected that when, or rather *if* the storm ever subsided, the world would be a very different place, transformed and as different as its former human rulers had been when they crawled from their cocoons after the red rain. Even Rhiannon seemed to have accepted that the world was no longer theirs. Only Jacob, who had witnessed the demise and eventual transformation overtaking the world from this distant, isolated island, seemed taken by surprise at the commander's words.

"Nothing? It's all gone?" he said, aghast. His skin was slowly fading from pink to a waxy gray, in spite of the warmth of the room.

"Yes" was the answer from miles above their heads. "While I obviously can't be certain this far from home, I see little other possibility for the changes we are seeing."

Jacob's voice became momentarily childlike, almost a squeak. "What are we going to do?" he asked, his eyes wide. He was asking her, Emily realized. Why was everyone asking her what to do? Being a mother figure was not in her survival plan, and she sure-as-shit didn't fit the job description.

Emily laid a reassuring hand on Jacob's shoulder. "We're going to do what we've always done: continue to survive." It was the best reply she could come up with under the current circumstance.

Jacob stared up from his chair at her with watery eyes. "How? Can you tell me that, Emily? We have a limited amount of food and nowhere to go. So, how? How do we make it, exactly?" His voice held no malice, she knew, but Jesus, she expected a little more backbone from the man who had dragged her ass out here in the first place.

"We have allies now," she said, looking at MacAlister. "We have the *Vengeance* and her crew. And once they get the sub fixed we have a way off this island." She tried to sound as positive as she could.

Jacob laughed, an ironic grating snicker. "Well that's just wonderful, but *where* do we go? You heard the commander, nothing out there is the same anymore."

"Anywhere," she said. "We go anywhere. Because if we stay here, then we've given up and the one thing I've learned about myself is that I *never* give up. *Never.*" She paused and sucked warm air deep into her lungs, calming her nerves. "Look, we are all there is right now, but the chances have to be good that there are other survivors out there, other submarines, maybe ships, bunkers. People are like roaches, we have a way of surviving even the worst of situations. We *will* find a way to survive this."

"And that about sums us up, doesn't it: bugs. We've been on the receiving end of a fucking galactic pest control effort and we're the survivors." Jacob paused in his diatribe for a moment, closing his eyes tightly, a vein pulsing periodically in his temple. He sucked in a deep breath of air before he began talking again, this time there was less of a panicked edge to his voice. "Jesus! I'm sorry, Emily." He forced a bleak smile as he tried to pull himself together. "I'm just so sorry for all this. Truly."

"We'll find a way," Emily said gently, laying what she hoped was a reassuring hand on the man's shoulder. "Commander?"

"Yes, Emily? Is everything okay down there?"

Now there was a question. Everything was far from fine, but compared to the crew of the ISS, trapped in that tin can circling the world, the survivors encamped here on the Stockton Islands were just peachy-keen, thank you very much.

"We're fine, Commander, just ironing out some problems is all." An idea had begun to form in the back of Emily's mind, hell, she might even classify it as a plan. "Tell me, Commander, apart from the obvious changes to the landscape that you can see, is there anything else you can tell us? Do you still see cities? Any other sign of human life?"

There was a delay before the commander replied. "It's hard to be exact, but we see some cities along the coasts of most countries that appear to be somewhat unaffected by whatever this red . . . stuff . . . is. But it's really rather difficult to be sure from up here. We haven't seen any distinguishable signs of any human activity though. If there is anyone else alive down there, they're keeping quiet about it."

"Okay, okay. That's good."

Everyone else in the room looked at her as if she had lost her mind. "Good?" said MacAlister. "By what stretch of the imagination can that possibly be classified as 'good'?"

"Bear with me on this: Look, every alien life-form I encountered—from the spiders right through to the trees they constructed—seemed to me to be a small piece of a much bigger . . . machine, or . . ." she hesitated, looking for the right word to describe the sense of what she had seen, "or a part of a plan, yes, part of a plan. I mean, think about the progression we saw: The rain created the spider aliens, they made the trees, the trees made the dust, and the dust created the storm. Now that the storm is done, doesn't that mean that whatever-the-hell plan was being implemented is probably done too? Ding! Ding! Ding! The timer on the stove is going off, because everything down here is cooked to perfection. I mean, that makes sense right? Tell me if I'm wrong?"

"It makes a strange kind of sense, I suppose," said Jacob. "When you described your experiences to me there seemed to be a very definite progression of effects. Even the creatures that attacked you in the woods outside Valhalla could have been there protecting or maybe tending to the things growing in the white orbs. And the alien that attacked you and Rhiannon's family—" Jacob paused and glanced at Rhiannon, measuring his words carefully, "—from the way you described the creature, it seemed very purposeful in its actions. It obviously had some kind of rudimentary intelligence, at least enough to be able to mimic the speech patterns of its prey— I mean, Rhiannon's father. The fact that it didn't just kill Simon outright, instead using him as a lure for the children and you, does suggest that it was following some kind of program or plan. Yes, I think you might be on to something, Emily."

She hadn't given that much thought to the motivation behind the takeover of the planet, and truth be told, there could be any number of reasons for the actions of the alien that had killed Simon and Benjamin, starting with it was just downright fucking evil, but Jacob's theory of its motivation seemed as possible as any other. After all, every alien she had encountered had seemed . . . single-minded in its actions, designed for a very specific, even obvious, task.

"So, if the storm has truly ended and whatever changes it was designed to make have run their course, then the world should at least be safe again, right?" she said with a little more hope in her voice than she actually felt.

"Define 'safe,'" said MacAlister. "Just because the aliens you encountered may have executed their programmed plan, doesn't mean they aren't still out there, either in their original form or maybe they've changed again. Or that there isn't still another stage yet to come."

Emily shook her head at that. "No, it's over. Everything about this event has been so efficient, so incredibly neat, so precise in its execution. Whatever is behind this, its plan has succeeded. I can feel it."

Jacob considered her words for a time. "If you're right, then maybe *we* can start over again. Assuming the commander is correct and at least the coastal cities are free of this red 'stuff,' then there must be years' worth of food and supplies left in some of those cities. All we have to do is find it. Who knows? Maybe we can find an island, preferably one that's a little warmer than this one, and settle down. If there are other survivors out there, we can find them, and with enough determination and the right men . . . and women," he added quickly, "we can start all over again."

It was a beautiful dream, the idea of a second chance for humanity, a chance to get it right this time, but was it a plausible plan? The only way to find out would be to try, but they were painfully short of options: stay on this island and last as long as the food did or travel with the *Vengeance* and see what was waiting out there.

But what that really boiled down to was a simple choice: give up or forge ahead.

It was all starting to make sense to Emily, but as she said her farewells to the commander and headed back to her room, there were still far too many unanswered questions eluding her. But she needed two answered most of all: Why? Why had all of this happened? And if all the events *had* been part of a plan, then whose plan was it?

CHAPTER 6

Commander Fiona Mulligan tried to quash her growing excitement, she had to remain professional after all, but damn it, the news that there were other survivors, and a submarine crew of all things, was just so wonderful.

There was a chance for them up here. Some of them, at least.

She had a secret that she had held back from Emily, not wanting to cause her anymore undue distress than the poor girl had already gone through, but now that the *Vengeance* had shown up, she had new hope.

Mulligan shifted her body and maneuvered herself with practiced skill through the narrow spaces between modules, floating down to the Destiny module. For the third time since she had said good-bye to Emily earlier that day, she repositioned herself in front of the round observation port. Through the window she had a clear view of the rest of the station's modules. And there it was. Their last and only chance. Locked onto the side of the space station, between the two Heat Rejection Subsystem radiators, was another spacecraft: a single Soyuz-TMA escape vehicle.

The Soyuz-TMA was a specially redesigned version of the Russian spacecraft used to ferry loads, supplies, and crew back and forth to the ISS. But this iteration of the craft had been specifically reengineered by NASA to act as an emergency escape vessel from the ISS. Normally, there were two of these space lifeboats docked with the station, enough to accommodate all of the crew. But just two weeks before the red rain had arrived, a life-threatening injury to an astronaut had proved too much for the medical facilities available at the station, and with no resupply craft scheduled for several months it meant one of the spacecrafts had been used to return the critically ill astronaut back to Earth. No replacement craft had ever arrived.

After the rain came, there seemed little reason to even consider the capsule. The commander and her crew had discussed it, of course, but the single escape pod could accommodate only three astronauts; the remaining would be forced to stay on the ISS, doomed.

The craft was programmed to land on the steppes of Kazakhstan in central Asia, but it was feasible to override that programming and to use the manual guidance system to navigate the spacecraft for the majority of the two-and-a-half-hour trip back to Earth to any location. This latest edition of the Russian craft, while designed specifically to place the astronauts safely on land, did have the capability for a water landing. It could last up to three hours at sea before the crew either were rescued or abandoned it, forced to take to the inflatable emergency life raft.

And right there had been the sticking point for the crew.

Even if they did make it back to Earth safely, with no recovery crew to pick them up, whether they splashed down in the middle of the ocean or managed to survive a landing somewhere in that strange spread of red that now covered the majority of land, they would still face almost certain death.

Her crew had chosen to remain together.

Emily, she was such a sweet girl, so strong, but she had faced her own trials and problems, so Commander Mulligan had chosen not to tell her about the one escape route they had. There had been no reason to trouble her even more than she already was, but with the arrival of the *Vengeance* and its crew, there was a chance for half of her crew to escape.

When she got off the radio with Emily and Jacob she had immediately called her crew together and told them the news.

There had been arguments about who should go and who would stay. Her crew, as always, had made her proud, each volunteering to remain behind, insisting that someone else should take one of the three precious seats available, but eventually, they had resorted to the time-tested short-straw pick. And, with only one spot left, it had come down to herself and Muranov, the Ukrainian astrochemist, and two straws (actually, plastic toothpicks). Muranov had drawn the short one.

The commander had insisted that the Ukrainian take her place on the Soyuz, but he had refused.

"My family is gone," he said in his heavily accented English. "I stay here, join them when I am ready."

And so it was settled; they had a way off of the station and back to Earth. Now all she needed to do was persuade Captain Constantine that the three of them were worth risking his crew and craft to collect.

CHAPTER 7

They began work on repairing the submarine that very same day, right around the time the first of the most seriously injured crew was back up and on his feet, to cheers from his remaining, still less badly injured colleagues. His name was Parsons and he was the Chief Engineer for the boat. Emily assumed he had a first name, but nobody ever seemed to use it. Hell, for all she knew Parsons could *be* his first name. After a quick meeting with the captain, he emerged from the office and immediately rousted up three of his men, flexing his burn-scarred hands.

The fire had gutted several areas before the crew had managed to get it under control, and, while those areas had been destroyed beyond repair, a preliminary survey by Parsons showed there was no permanent damage to any of the submarine's critical navigation, weapons, or propulsion systems. The real problem was the smoke damage. It was everywhere. With such a severely diminished crew onboard to fight the fire, watertight doors that should have been closed had remained wide open and the smoke had quickly penetrated throughout the boat, coating everything in a sticky black tar that gunked up controls and obscured vital computer screens. It was all going to have to be cleaned off before the craft was seaworthy again.

Parsons was a short, gruff Welshman with a thick beard and a habit of yelling at anyone beneath his rank, and occasionally, a few above him. He reminded Emily of the belligerent dwarf from *The Lord of the Rings* movies, but he had developed a soft spot for Rhiannon during his recuperation and would slip the little girl chocolate bars from a private stash he kept in his cabin. He had taken to calling her his *little cariad*, which he said was Welsh for *love*.

The cleanup took just under a week to complete. The *Vengeance* had to undergo a seaworthiness test, and then, if everything was "shipshape and Bristol fashion," as Captain Constantine put it, they would be ready to leave at a few hours' notice.

"We're just going to take her for a short jaunt out to sea, make sure there are no holes or leaks," said the captain straight-faced. "Would you like to come along?"

Emily laughed. "I think I'll take a rain check until you're sure the submarine's not going to spring a leak and sink."

"Oh, but that's exactly what we're supposed to do," said the captain, smiling broadly this time. "Sinking is what that sub does best."

CHAPTER 8

Hours later Captain Constantine and his selected crew members returned from the sub's test run and met with the rest of his crew in their quarters. The boat had a few minor kinks that needed to be ironed out but otherwise she was seaworthy, he explained, to a rousing cheer from the assembled men.

"She's ready to put to sea whenever we are," Parsons added. "So you lazy buggers had better not get used to this cushy life or you'll have me to answer to."

There was a smattering of laughter at the comment, but Emily wasn't sure Parsons was joking.

"And that leads me to the next item, and why I've invited our hosts to join us in this meeting." The captain gestured to Emily, Rhiannon, and Jacob sitting at the table across from the crew who were either standing or sitting on one of the now unoccupied hospital beds.

"I don't need to tell any of you that our situation would have been far more . . . uncomfortable, if it had not been for the kindness shown by our new friends, and for which I would like to officially thank you on behalf of both myself and my crew."

A round of cheers and applause rose up from the assembled crew and Emily found herself smiling while she hugged a beaming Rhiannon to her side. Even Jacob, who had taken to secreting himself away for long periods, and, Emily suspected, begun drinking on a regular basis, had joined them. Looking embarrassed, and a little too pale, he raised a hand in acceptance of the crew's thanks.

"It was never our first choice to remain here on this island," the captain continued, "but given the circumstances and the information we've received from both Emily and Commander Mulligan of the ISS, I think it's time for us to discuss what we will do next."

The captain paced back and forth in front of his men, stroking his beard as he spoke.

"We have enough supplies to last us for several months, but after those supplies are gone we are going to be up that proverbial creek without any kind of a paddle. So, bearing that in mind, we need a plan for survival. So, if we are to survive . . . if the human race is to survive . . . then we *must* work together and we must do so smartly, with a plan. And that means we have to leave here and find somewhere where we can regroup, recuperate, and reorganize. I know we all hold out hope that there will be other survivors, but we have to assume that, for the foreseeable future at least, we are alone. And, while you are all still members of Her Majesty's Royal Navy, and subject to my command, this is not a decision I can make alone. It's your lives that are at stake, and humanity has become the rarest of resources on this planet. So, I ask for all of you to speak your mind. Speak freely."

There was a moment of silence as the crew looked at each other, unsure of just how much they could say. Finally a lanky seaman toward the back of the room Emily thought might be named John stood up.

"Sir. Why not just stay here? No offense to Miss Baxter, but all we have is her word for what's going on out there. Who's to say she's not lying—again, no offense, Miss—but we don't know her from Adam. Don't you think we should check out other options first?"

Emily smiled at the young sailor, he couldn't have been more than twenty. "No offense taken, but it's not just my word, is it? You've all heard from the captain and MacAlister what Commander Mulligan has seen happening," she said.

"And what options do you think we should aim for exactly?" the captain asked. "Where do you think we should go?"

"Well," the sailor hesitated, "if these aliens are as affected by the cold as she says, then maybe we should stay right here? Or maybe stay in Canada at least? I mean, didn't Miss Baxter say that they couldn't survive in the cold?"

"That's not entirely correct," Emily said. "From my experience, all the cold seems to do is slow them down. Extreme cold seems to stop them in their tracks, to the extent that they are unable to thrive, but the same applies to us, right?"

"Emily's correct," said MacAlister. "And think about it for a second: Where would our food come from? We can't grow anything here and there's only so much food we can scavenge from the area. So that would mean regular trips out to locate supplies. We'll need to become self-sufficient as quickly as possible, which means we have to find somewhere we can support ourselves. There's no guarantee we'll find anywhere that'll support us, but we have to try. Besides, if you're going to meet your maker, wouldn't you prefer to do it in the sunshine?" Jimmy gave the room one of his devastating grins and Emily couldn't help but smile right back.

The man had a way of making even the most depressing of positions seem hopeful.

"Sergeant MacAlister is correct . . . for a change," said Constantine, with a smile of his own. "We have to look at the big picture, long-term planning. If we are *it* for the human race—and God help us if we are—then we have to be smart. We need to find somewhere we can be safe and start afresh, grow our food, and settle down. Raise families and begin over."

"Yeah, but if there really are aliens out there still, what then? How are we supposed to defend ourselves?" the sailor pushed.

"Son, we have a nuclear bloody submarine at our disposal," the captain said. "I think we can handle a few aliens, don't you?"

This brought a roar of agreement from the crew.

"So, let's see a show of hands then. All of you in favor of finding someplace warmer than this island, hands in the air."

The vote was unanimous.

Captain Constantine smiled like a happy father at his crew. Emily doubted that he had ever had any worries how the vote would turn out. In the time she had spent with them, it had become obvious that his crew had nothing but respect for the older captain of the boat. Most of them were still on the right side of twenty, by the looks of them, so the captain really was a father figure to most, she was sure.

"So, now the only question is where? Any suggestions?" asked the captain.

"Emily," the captain said, turning his attention to her; he held a single sheet of paper in one hand. "We have put together a list of naval bases that we think would be prime candidates to at least set up an initial base. What we would like you to do is speak with Commander Mulligan, give her the coordinates of each site, and have her reconnoiter them from her rather unique advantage point for us. What we would like to know is how viable they are, given the spread of the alien plant life."

"Of course," said Emily, "I'll get right on it." She took the sheet of handwritten notes from the captain.

"Sergeant MacAlister. Would you be good enough to start organizing our departure plans? I expect us to be ready to depart as soon as we have confirmation from Commander Mulligan on an appropriate location."

"Yes, skipper." Mac turned to face the crew, waiting impatiently for their next order. "Alright you lot, you heard the captain. Let's get this show on the road, shall we?"

The crew was on their feet and immediately moving with a practiced familiarity toward their allotted tasks.

"Ms. Baxter. Mr. Endersby. If I may have a few moments of your time?" The captain asked as the rest of the crew cleared the room.

Emily walked with the captain while Rhiannon pushed Jacob as Constantine ushered them to his office, closing the door behind them.

"I know you had your own plans, and that we did not factor into them, but I want to officially extend you an offer to join us. There's more than enough room on the sub for you, and, to be perfectly frank, we could use the extra sets of hands."

"Are you offering us a ride?" Jacob asked.

The captain nodded. "If you're interested . . .?"

"Yes?" said Emily, looking at Rhiannon. The little girl nodded enthusiastically. "Yes," Emily repeated to the captain. "You can count Rhiannon and me in." All eyes turned to Jacob, who looked unsure.

"I suppose I have little choice," he said eventually. "Yes, I'd like to come along too."

■ ■ ■

Emily managed to establish a crackling, static-filled communication link with Commander Mulligan.

"These connections seem to be getting worse," the commander told Emily. "I think the degradation of the Earth's electronic communications systems is finally starting. We may not be able to stay as connected as we have been once the satellites begin to fail."

"I understand, Commander. You have a fallback option?"

"The station is equipped with an amateur radio system that doesn't need any kind of relay or satellite system, but it does require line of sight with whoever we are talking with, so you won't lose us altogether when everything goes down, but communication will be a lot more sporadic, I'm afraid."

"I understand. Commander, the captain has asked if you would be willing to survey a few locations, naval bases that he thinks would be viable locations for us to begin afresh from. Is that feasible for you right now?" Emily wasn't sure how the commander was going to react to her request, it felt odd to Emily asking someone who was doomed to certain death to help them find a place to live.

But Mulligan did not hesitate. "Of course I can do that," she said. "What are the coordinates?"

Emily read the list of six candidates to her.

"It's going to take a full twenty-four hours for us to hit all of those locations but I don't see a problem. Now, Emily, I have a question of you, well, actually it's more of a request for Captain Constantine."

"Of course," Emily replied. "What is it?"

A long silence settled over the link, and Emily began to suspect the connection had been dropped.

"We have a way off this coffin," Commander Mulligan said eventually, her voice surprisingly calm for the news she delivered, "and we need the *Vengeance* and its crew to pick us up when we splash down."

For the first time in forever, Emily Baxter found herself speechless.

"Let me explain," Mulligan said and began to tell Emily of her plan.

■ ■ ■

"My God," Captain Constantine said after Emily relayed the news Commander Mulligan had passed on to her. "But they only have the one Soyuz escape vehicle? So just three of the crew will be able to make it off the station? . . . My God!"

"They drew straws," Emily said. "The commander says that they are confident that between the adjusted programming of the Soyuz's navigation computer and the craft's manual controls they can pretty much put the escape craft down anywhere they need to. The problem comes once they land; it has to be a sea landing, so they will need to be picked up within a couple of hours."

"And that's where we come in," said MacAlister, matter-of-factly.

"Yes," said Emily. "The commander has requested that you rendezvous with the Soyuz and pick them up."

Captain Constantine looked squarely at MacAlister. "It's a risk," he said, "but I don't think it's an exceptional one. If the commander can navigate the escape craft close to whichever of the new destinations we pick, then I think it's feasible. Yes, I think it is very feasible. Tell the commander it's a go. We'll await her instructions."

"I'll tell her," said Emily, her face wearing the biggest smile she thought it had ever had. "And Captain . . . thank you."

. . .

Despite the space station being several hundred miles above her head, Emily thought the sigh of relief she heard from Commander Mulligan was palpable enough that she could feel it all the way down here on the ground.

Her call to the ISS was a hurried one, the connection between the Stockton station and the space station seemed to have noticeably deteriorated over just the past few hours.

"Wonderful, wonderful news, Emily," the commander said. "Please thank the captain on behalf of myself and my crew. I don't know how I can ever repay him or you."

"You can thank him yourself when you meet him. As for me? I already owe you my life so, please, think nothing of it."

"Listen, as much as I hate to be the bearer of bad news, I've made some progress on the search for a new home for you. It's not good I'm afraid."

Two of the six potential locations were completely overrun by the creeping red vegetation she'd seen moving across the land, Commander Mulligan explained. The new plant life was spreading at an unprecedented rate. And if this was any indication of how bad the infestation was elsewhere, then the plan might have to change dramatically.

"I'm sorry, Emily. I'll keep looking until we know for certain, you have my word."

"I know you will, Commander. Thank you, and please be safe," Emily said by way of a sign-off.

"You too, Emily. You too."

And with that final comment, the commander's voice vanished back into the ether.

CHAPTER 9

The news was better the next morning.

"Point Loma, California," Commander Mulligan told Emily excitedly. "That's where you need to go. There's a large incursion of the red vegetation in the surrounding areas and into the base itself, but the main structures in the area seem to be more or less free. Of course, at the rate this plant life seems to be spreading, I can't guarantee that it will remain that way for very long."

The naval base at Point Loma, from what Captain Constantine and MacAlister had explained to Emily, was a collection of naval support groups, training facilities, and berthing for several submarines, among other things. Located on a peninsula of land across a bay from San Diego, it seemed like the perfect place to pitch their tent.

"Commander, we really can't thank you enough. I know the crew will be ecstatic to hear this news."

"Just convince them to move quickly, Emily. Time is of the essence for all of us."

■ ■ ■

Once Emily notified Captain Constantine of Point Loma's viability, things moved at a breakneck pace and, within a seemingly impossibly short time, their refuge at the Stockton Islands was stripped bare and emptied of all salvageable material and supplies, which in turn were transported to the *Vengeance*, waiting offshore.

And in just under two hours from the time Emily first passed on the information, she found herself standing on the snow-cleared pathway just outside the building she had called home since arriving at the Stocktons, waiting as two sailors carried Jacob out into the still-freezing air.

"This is so surreal," Jacob said to himself. "So very surreal." A plastic supermarket bag was clutched tightly to his chest, and Emily could make out what she was sure was the outline of a whisky bottle within it.

"It's for the best," she said as he was carried past her, not sure if she actually believed her own words.

But what else was there to say? They were giving up the safety of this place for the unknown, yet again, and more uncertainty. She looked back at the building and deserted camp one final time then took Rhiannon's hand in one hand and Thor's leash in the other and started after Jacob.

RED WORLD

CHAPTER 10

The *Vengeance* cut silently through the Pacific Ocean, heading south just twenty miles off the west coast of North America. As the submarine pushed ever closer to the equator, the temperature of the water surrounding it gradually climbed, echoing the growing excitement of the crew as they drew, mile by mile, nearer to their destination.

Just over three thousand nautical miles separated the Stockton Islands off northern Alaska from Point Loma, California. At an average speed of twenty knots it was going to take the crew of the *Vengeance* just under a week to cruise down the West Coast.

Life onboard the submarine was incongruous for Emily. The crew, safe in their familiar surroundings and with the familiarity of routine to take their minds off the almost uncountable variables that were at play around them, carried on as if all was normal.

Rhiannon too had settled into a routine of reading from a collection of old paperback novels—Emily supposed every book was now *old*—and watching British TV shows on the sub's entertainment system; typical teenage stuff and Emily did not begrudge her this brief period of normalcy. It was a chance for the kid to just float along on the current of life for a little while, buoyed by the friendly faces and the easy pleasures of life that come with being thirteen and possessing few skills other than being young.

Hell! Even Thor seemed more than content to lounge the hours away in Emily's room or occasionally wander through the corridors with one of the crew who wanted a little canine company. Thor was good therapy for everyone.

So why was *she* finding it so difficult to relax? Emily knew she should take full advantage of this time of almost assured safety being onboard—or was it *in*board for a submarine?—the *Vengeance* afforded her and just chill out, even if it was only for a little while. But she just could not seem to sit still for more than a half hour before she found herself restlessly wandering the corridors, looking for something to do or for someone to talk with.

But finding someone to converse with was almost impossible. Shorthanded, the crew were pulling double- and even triple-shifts. So Emily found herself alone for most of the time.

So, for lack of anything else to hold her attention, she set herself to the task of conditioning herself. Abandoning her bike riding back in Stuyvesant, followed by the long drive to Alaska, and then spending those long weeks on the road and holed-up in the Stocktons had sapped the strength from her legs. The submarine had a well-equipped gym, it even had a stationary exercise bike she tried a couple of times, but it just wasn't the same as *her* bike, wasn't as thrilling as feeling the air rushing by her as she hurtled along the empty roads and lanes of the East Coast. She missed that, missed the freedom.

So Emily took to jogging through the passages. Running laps back and forth between her room and the engine room until the sweat soaked her back and chest, and until the almost constant nagging sense of anxiety she felt in the pit of her stomach was drowned out by the thumping of her heart and the thrum of her blood through her veins.

Each evening, the few off-duty crew not needed in the command center or ordered away from their positions by the captain congregated in the galley for dinner. The ship's cooks were all dead so the job of preparing food fell to a different crew member each evening.

Emily quickly found out that a lot of the submarine's would-be culinary masters were as suited to food preparation as she was to a career as a professional singer, and she was about as tone deaf as you could get. To say the evening meals were a surprise (pleasant or otherwise) would be a grave underestimation of the word, but at least there was beer, albeit tightly rationed to a single bottle a day to ensure no drunkenness. To their credit, the sailors seemed to grasp the implications that even a single hungover member of their crew could be disastrous when there were already so few of them to go around. Even so, Emily was sure that on more than one occasion a sailor had had a little more than their assigned bottle, either substituted in from a friend or maybe from some secret stash they had managed to smuggle onboard.

On the third day Emily had become tired of the smell of undercooked bacon and overcooked eggs that the crew seemed to relish so much and nominated herself as the de facto cook for the rest of the trip to Point Loma.

"Do not get used to this," she told the smiling line of sailors as she ladled out beef stew on her first night. Inevitably, they did and Emily found herself falling willingly into the comforting routine provided by the need to feed so many hungry mouths. It surely was not any kind of step forward for the cause of feminism, but it made her feel useful in an environment where she was out of her depth and felt herself to be more of a distraction than a help.

Compared to the preceding weeks, life aboard the *Vengeance* was the equivalent of a cruise around the Caribbean, but that nagging fear still chewed at her when she was alone.

But as time passed onboard, Emily felt the numbness begin to dissipate. She found herself smiling more, and the restless, ever-present need to keep moving, so long ingrained in her as she travelled across the country, began to be replaced by something new: not quite peace, but a sense of calm that she had not felt in a very long time. And there was something else too. Something she hadn't thought she would ever experience again: a sense of belonging.

And then there was MacAlister. The more time she spent in the company of the Scot, the more she found herself looking forward to the next time. On more than one occasion over the past two days, as she pounded through the corridors, she had found herself casually plotting ways to run into him.

"Don't be such a damn fool," she said aloud one evening as she sat in her bunk thinking about him.

"What?" said Rhiannon. "I didn't do anything."

"Oh, no, not you sweetheart. Sorry," Emily apologized, feeling her face blush in embarrassment.

The truth was she suspected he might be doing the same. Every night, despite his almost constant requirement to be present in the command room, she would find him waiting in line for food and they would spend a half hour just shooting the breeze while they ate their food together. Nothing specific, nothing heavy, just talking about where they grew up, favorite foods, old friends, and the little gems that mark the trail of a person's walk through life.

Or of course, he could just be hungry, she supposed.

"He likes you too," said Rhiannon.

This time it was Emily's turn to say, "What? Who?" while try-ing to give Rhiannon her best I-have-absolutely-no-idea-who-or-what-you're-talking-about face, only to be met by a knowing smile. "Jesus! Is it that obvious?" she admitted.

"Umm hmmm! I see him looking at you when he sees you're not looking," Rhiannon said, adding a "He's so dreamy" that ended in a huge flamboyant sigh and flutter of her eyelashes before she promptly cracked up into one of her patented fits of evil cackling.

"Hey! Don't make me come over there," Emily warned in an equally playful voice. After a long pause she added, "But he is kind of cute, isn't he?"

CHAPTER 11

The *Vengeance* burst through the ocean surface; first the conning tower appeared, the huge fin-shaped tower slicing through the water, seconds later the sleek, matt-black body emerged, water roaring from its deck, sunlight glistening off the ribbons of spray cascading from the hull.

In the belly of the submarine, Emily waited with Rhiannon for the *Vengeance* to stabilize. When the rocking finally stopped, she rolled off her cot and opened the door. In the corridor sailors were already making their way toward the upper decks, their excited chatter elevating Emily's own sense of excitement at finally discovering firsthand what had happened to the world.

"Stay here," Emily told Rhiannon and Thor, then slipped outside and followed the sailors.

A metal ladder ran up through the hollow center of the sub's conning tower from the main deck of the submarine. At the bottom of the ladder Emily and the rest of the crew gathered in the corridor, milling nervously as Captain Constantine and MacAlister climbed the metal rungs to the observation deck at the top.

A few minutes passed and then Emily heard the sound of MacAlister's standard issues against the metal rungs of the ladder as he descended.

"What's it look like, Sergeant?" asked a crewman, as MacAlister stepped off the ladder, eager for information. Emily could not read Mac's face; it was blank, impassive.

MacAlister ignored the sailor and spoke directly to Emily. "Come on up," he said, offering his hand to her. "The rest of you stay here."

"Jesus, Sarge—"

"No more lip out of you. You'll get your turn," MacAlister snapped. "Wait here until either the skipper or I call you up top."

The sailor looked displeased but fell silent under Mac's stony stare.

Emily caught the briny scent of the Pacific Ocean wafting down to her as she pulled herself rung-over-rung up the ladder then up onto the flat observation deck at the top of the conning tower. Although her view was still blocked by the security wall that spanned the circumference of the tower she could still hear the *whoosh* of waves breaking over the deck of the sub below, gently rocking the vessel as it pitched and rolled with each swell.

They had surfaced a half mile offshore of Point Loma, California.

"It's a safe enough distance for us to make a quick exit if we need to," Captain Constantine had told Emily minutes before the sub's ballast tanks had been blown and the sub began its ascent to the surface. "And far enough away that we won't appear to be a threat if there's still anyone alive in the base. Don't want to be sunk before we even get a chance to see what's going on, now do we?"

Emily's eyes squinted painfully in the bright California sunshine. She couldn't see a damn thing after spending so long in the artificial light of the submarine. She allowed her eyes a few moments to acclimate, filtering the light through the flat of her hands while she listened to the crashing of the waves and absorbed the warmth of the sun.

"My God!" she exclaimed when her vision finally cleared enough that she could see past the scintillating crest of the breaking waves.

She was staring out over a bluff, a clutch of buildings squeezed together, too distant to make out any real detail, but she could see radio masts and satellite dishes jutting out from some of the buildings' roofs. To the right of the buildings, the land slipped gradually down to a harbor. Another submarine was moored to a quayside; it was canted away from her, its conning tower pointed inland and its curved underbelly exposed. A long jagged crack, about thirty feet in length, zigzagged along the exposed hull. She could see waves hitting the side and flowing into the interior.

Everywhere was silent, deserted. Not even a gull riding the warm thermals rising over the land disturbed this still-life portrait of a place deserted, abandoned. Emily took it all in within the first few seconds, but beyond the waves, past the rock-strewn beach and buildings with abandoned vehicles still visible in the parking lot, lay another world: an *alien* world.

A red world.

"Here," said MacAlister, "take these." He handed her a large pair of binoculars. Through their powerful lenses the distant shore seemed just feet away, and with it came the realization of how profound a change had been wrought across the world.

Where once there had been palm trees, neatly trimmed stretches of grass, roads, oak and California ash, now lay an alien jungle. Giant red fronds and creepers snaked their way over every foot of exposed surface, thick lush leaves sprouting from thin stalks (if they looked thin from half a mile away, they would be anything but, she realized). They waved in the slow breeze, wafting inland from the ocean. The alien vegetation clung to every wall, wound its way over roofs and around antennas. Leafy creepers threw long tendrils across blacktop, snaked through broken windows like thieves, cracked concrete, and levered up slabs of sidewalk until the ground looked like an 8.0 temblor had rocked the coast the naval base was built upon.

The submarine she had spotted earlier had not escaped the red vegetation; although the deck was angled away from her, Emily could still see a latticework of thick ropelike feelers spilling over the edge of the quay, obscuring the front of the hull under its swaying leafy camouflage. Red vines wound up the conning tower and dripped toward the ground like lank red hair, swaying in the breeze.

Mixed with the smell of the ocean, ozone was another less inviting one. Even at this distance from shore the aroma wafted back to the *Vengeance*. It smelled like mold and burned hair. There was also another less distinct, but more easily identifiable odor of something disturbingly familiar to Emily: ammonia.

"My God," Captain Constantine mumbled, his voice barely above a whisper, his head unable to turn away from the line of red that stretched along the coast into the distance. "We might just as well be on another world."

Emily ignored him, focusing the binoculars beyond the base, tracing the line of the coast. Wherever she looked, what should have been clear land was obscured by the same red vegetation. It covered all but a scant few buildings within the Point Loma base but seemed not to have made it to the beach anywhere along the coast surrounding the base, as though the sand-covered, pebble-strewn beaches delineated the alien world's dominion.

Within the ocean of red flora, she could see the occasional alien tree surging into the air above the red canopy. They reminded her of the alien trees that had taken root after the red rain, but while what she looked at now were just as large, they also lacked the constructed uniformity of those first invaders; these were more natural, more recognizable as simple trees, yet undoubtedly not of this planet. They towered over the rest of the jungle. And that was *exactly* what this was, she realized: a freaking *jungle*!

Somehow, over a matter of just a few days, the red storm had raged through the old world and changed *everything*, converting it from what it had once been; reshaping, reorganizing, recreating it into everything that now lay before her.

Emily felt a bitter laugh escape her as she stared through the binoculars. Finally she understood what had occurred on their insignificant little rock: God had visited this planet and he had found it wanting, so he bent it to *His* will. And if it wasn't God, that was okay, it might just as well have been. Because the intelligence, the technology, the sheer amount of raw power that had been harnessed to achieve this transformation was so far beyond anything imaginable it could drive you insane just thinking about it.

"Emily?" Captain Constantine's voice sounded as though it was coming from a very long way away. "Emily!" he said again, louder this time, touching her shoulder. She allowed her arms to drop the binoculars to her waist and turned to look at him.

"It seems you were correct all along," he repeated. "Do you have any suggestions?"

"We need to get Jacob up here to see this," she said. "We need to get him up here right now."

■ ■ ■

Two crewmen carried Jacob up into the sunshine of the sub's conning tower and then supported the climatologist between them so he could get a good look over the edge of the conning tower's observation deck.

"Ho-leee shit!" he hissed when he saw the transformation of the mainland. His eyes grew wide. Thanks to many long months cooped up in the Stockton research station, Jacob's skin was already the wrong side of ivory, but Emily was convinced she saw him turn, as Procol Harum had so eloquently put it, a whiter shade of pale. "Holy shit! I mean . . . I never thought . . . Jesus! This is . . . this is just astonishing." The sense of awe in the scientist's voice was tangible.

"Here," said MacAlister, handing Jacob a second pair of binoculars. The scientist glassed them back and forth over the base, then up into the jungle growing behind it. His index finger moved rapidly back and forth over the focus knob as he zoomed in as far as the magnification would allow, then out again as his head jerked, zigged, and zagged across the horizon.

"It's everywhere," he whispered, more to himself than the others who were watching him. He studied the coast for another ten minutes, *oohing* and *ahing*, with the occasional "Fascinating!" thrown in for good measure as his eyes caught some new feature or form within the explosion of tangled vegetation littering the landscape.

By that time the two sailors holding him were beginning to wilt in the sun.

"So, Jacob," Captain Constantine said eventually, growing impatient for some kind of input from the scientist and his seeming obliviousness to the welfare of the sailors, "do you have *any* idea what we are looking at here?"

Jacob reluctantly dropped the binoculars and equally reluctantly ordered the two sailors holding him to turn around so he could face the others. He thought for a moment before replying, "Ideas? No, I have no *ideas*, but I do have a theory."

"Well, what is it? Spit it out for God's sake would you, man?" said the captain, a tight smile crossing his lips as he refused to be baited by Jacob's truculence.

"We've been terraformed," Jacob said eventually, quietly, his voice flat, as if the words he had just spoken were wrong in some way, as though they did not quite fit the space within the air they had to occupy. "Our planet has been repurposed, reconstituted, and retooled. It's the only possibility." Jacob's hands swept across the red landscape. "I mean, just *look* at all of this."

Nobody spoke.

"It was always a possibility, I suppose," Jacob continued. "I mean, we've talked about it for years as a possibility for colonizing Mars and eventually other planets, but we are . . . *were* . . . nowhere near it as a possibility technologically. And this, this is light-years beyond how we theorized we could do it. I mean, it's simply amazing."

"Mr. Endersby," the captain snapped, as his patience finally wore thin. "I have no idea what the hell you are talking about. So how about you explain it to us, how should I put it, less scientifically adept people: What exactly are we looking at?"

Jacob eyes fluttered to the other survivors gathered on the observation deck, moving from one to the other as though he had only now noticed them.

"Let's get below," he said finally, as if the words he had previously said had never been spoken. "I need a drink."

"Good God, man. Would you just tell us what you think?" the captain said, finally beginning to lose his temper with the man.

"Captain. What I need right now is a stiff drink, and I think when I tell you what you want to know, you're going to need one too. Besides, this is for your ears and for you to tell the crew, so just have these two oafs carry me down and I'll be happy to explain everything. Okay?"

For a second, Emily thought the captain was going to order his men to toss Jacob into the sea. His face flushed a bright crimson. This was probably the first time anyone had spoken to him in such a manner in a very long time, if ever, and she would bet her last dollar that no one had ever spoken to him in such a manner in front of his crew before.

Captain Constantine sucked in a deep breath of the ocean air, his gaze never leaving Jacob, until finally he nodded to the two sailors carrying him. "To my cabin," he said brusquely. The sailors disappeared with Jacob back down the tower.

MacAlister posted two armed guards on the observation deck before descending down the conning tower. Emily and the captain had gone below ahead of him and they had been met by the throng of crew eager to learn news of what waited for them beyond the outer hull of the sub.

"As soon as I know more, I will let you know," the captain was saying, his voice raised to be heard over the barrage of questions. "Right now, I do not have enough information. Mr. Endersby is about to brief us and when we know, you *will* know. Now get back to your posts."

Emily could tell from the look on the men's faces that they were not happy, there was even some barely concealed anger on the face of one or two of them. They quieted down when MacAlister stepped off the final rung and eyed them all with an ice-cold stare.

"You heard the captain. Don't you all have somewhere else you're supposed to be?"

The group of sailors slowly dispersed, but not without a few furtive glances at the conning tower ladder and the daylight leaking in from above.

■ ■ ■

The two sailors carried Jacob to the conference room and placed him a little roughly in his wheelchair before waiting to be dismissed by the captain.

When the door closed behind them, the captain spoke, "Okay, in small words so you will be sure we understand *exactly* what you are talking about, Mr. Endersby: What can you tell us about what's going on out there?"

Jacob had parked himself next to the captain's small wet bar. Emily watched him pull a bottle of Glenlivet whisky from the shelf and pour himself a shot, downing it in one sharp gulp. He poured another then raised the bottle toward the others but no one wanted to join him. Jacob shrugged.

"Perhaps after you've explained what's happening we might feel the need to partake, but right now, all I want to know is what you know," Constantine said.

Jacob wheeled himself to the head of the conference table, carefully balancing his glass between his knees. He took a swig of the whisky and began to explain.

"Our climate, our planet, along with every form of life on it, has been co-opted. Every major ecosystem appears to have been manipulated toward supporting some other form of life. In short, we've been terraformed."

"Terraformed?" Emily questioned, her eyebrows furrowed. Constantine and MacAlister looked on with equally questioning expressions.

Jacob wheeled himself back to the wet bar and poured another shot of whisky, spilling some on the surface as he observed the blank expressions on the faces watching him. He sighed deeply and continued.

"We've been invaded," he said, his words beginning to slur around the edges. "You know, like in the movies. Planetary engineering." He gulped down another mouthful of whisky. "*They* sent the red rain and transformed humanity and most every other life form on this rock into self-assembling biological machines. No need to ship complicated machinery here, like we'd have to do, just send in the red rain and use the indigenous species as the building blocks. Have them follow an encoded blueprint for making bigger, more complex organisms, and *poof*! Out with the old and in with the new."

Jacob sank the remaining whisky and stared at the empty glass.

"They used those biological machines to build the equivalent of atmospheric processors, the trees Emily saw. And in just days they accomplished what would have taken *decades* for us to have even theoretically achieved. I mean, it is genius. Pure fucking genius. No, it's bigger than that; it's fucking God-like. They didn't even need to come here themselves. Jesus! It's just magnificent."

Jacob tipped the empty glass toward his outstretched tongue; when he realized it was still empty he poured another shot into it, this time spilling more on the wet bar than he got in the glass.

While Jacob was speaking, Emily had watched Mac pace back and forth, his normally unfazed demeanor obviously stretched thin by what he was hearing. "You're telling us Earth has been taken over by an alien race?" she said when Jacob paused to refill his glass.

Jacob shook his head and polished off the shot. "Not *by* some alien race, *for* some alien race. The only question now is who *they* are and when we can expect them to show up." He paused, then laughed as he reached for the bottle of whisky again. "Wait, that's two questions," he said, his words slurring into one.

MacAlister moved to Jacob's side and took the bottle from his hands. "I think you've had just about enough, mate."

Jacob looked up at the soldier. "I think you could be right," he said, before letting out a long braying laugh.

"So the rain, the creatures I saw, the alien trees?" Emily said.

The effects of the drink were quickly robbing Jacob of his faculties and his words were becoming indistinguishable.

"That, my dear, dear Emily, is the interesting part. This is just a theory, mind you, so don't you hold me to it in the morning—" he let out another long laugh "—but *I* think that the rain was some kind of biological super nanotechnology. How it got here, I have *nooooo* idea, but it took every carbon-based life form on this planet, disassembled it molecule by molecule, and then reassembled it in whatever shape it wanted."

Jacob jabbed at the ceiling with the index finger of his left hand. When he next spoke his voice was conspiratorial. "It gave us what you saw out there. A new world. *Their* world." He stared at his hand still pointing at the ceiling. "I mean, do you have even the slightest inkling of what that means? Whatever did this to the world is so far ahead of us technologically, it might just as well be God." He slowly lowered his hand to his lap and turned to face Emily. "I do not feel so good," he said, his face suddenly turning a shade of green.

"Don't worry," said MacAlister with a sigh, "I'll take care of him. Come on." He began pushing Jacob out of the room toward the scientist's cabin. "I'll get him to his room."

"We should all be afraid," Jacob yelled as the Scotsman wheeled him away. "We should all be really fucking afraid."

■ ■ ■

"He'll sleep soundly tonight," said MacAlister when he returned from taking Jacob to his room. "I expect he'll have a bit of a hangover in the morning, though."

"Let's assume his theory is correct," Emily said, picking up the conversation where they'd left off before the interruption. "Does it really change anything for us?"

"Our primary objective has not changed. We still need to find a place to pitch our tent, so to speak. Point Loma seems to me to be as good a place as any to do that, wouldn't you say?"

"From what Commander Mulligan has told us, the chances of finding anywhere unaffected by the storm seem pretty slim and growing slimmer by the day. And if Jacob is right we might be running out of time faster than we know," Emily said. "And since we're already here . . ."

The captain nodded. "Mr. MacAlister, I'd like you to take two men you know can handle themselves and go take a look around our new home. Report back to me if we need to call in a fumigator or not."

"I'd like to go ashore with them," Emily interjected.

"Not this time," MacAlister replied. "Leave it to the experts for now."

"But—" she began to object.

"No buts, Ms. Baxter," said the captain. "My men know what they're doing and you would be nothing but a liability at this point, I'm afraid. Please just let them do their job."

Emily couldn't argue with his logic, but the itch to get off the submarine, to stretch her legs on solid ground again was surprisingly strong, even to her. Or maybe it was something else? Even though MacAlister was a professional soldier and had undoubtedly survived numerous firefights and life-threatening situations during his time in the Special Boat Service, she found herself worrying about him. She was the only one with any direct experience of just how alien the world out there really was and how dangerous the creatures that wandered through it could be. And she still was not convinced that even with the evidence they had all seen topside that anyone *really* believed her warnings.

"Alright then, let's get this show on the road shall we?" MacAlister said, with a clap of his hands and an eager smile, signaling the discussion was over. He moved toward the door.

"MacAlister!" She grabbed the man's elbow as he walked away. "Be careful. It's more dangerous than you can possibly imagine out there."

Emily had expected him to fire back with one of his huge grins and dismiss her warning; instead his face became almost unrecognizable, cold even, grim, and for the first time she saw the warrior who lingered just below the surface of the gentle, funny man she had come to know. When his smile did return it was accompanied with one of his trademark corny quips: "Don't worry, my middle name is danger." He paused as the smile spread into the grin she had expected. "Actually, it's Colin, but if you tell anyone I'll never bloody talk to you again."

And with that, he was out the door.

■ ■ ■

MacAlister picked two sailors to accompany him.

Emily watched nervously from the observation deck of the conning tower as the heavily armed men hauled a large, black rubber dinghy onto the deck, attached a powerful-looking outboard motor to it, and dropped it into the water alongside the sub.

MacAlister gave her a thumbs-up before leaping into the boat after his men and speeding off toward the beach.

For the next two hours Emily watched as MacAlister and his men methodically moved from building to building, securing each one before moving on to the next. By the time they completed their initial search of the final building, it had become obvious that the base was completely deserted.

MacAlister's voice crackled over the radio: "Area is secure and ready to accept its new tenants."

Captain Constantine nodded silently then adjusted the radio frequency: "Attention all hands: Security team and shore parties, make your way to the deck immediately."

MacAlister and one of his team stayed on land, positioning themselves on the rooftops of the two tallest buildings, watching over the compound, their weapons held at the ready while the third sailor brought the dinghy back to the sub.

The *Vengeance's* crew emerged from the belly of the submarine via a hatch that exited onto the deck, chattering excitedly as they shaded their eyes from the bright California sun. But as they spotted the extraordinary transformation that had taken place on land, Emily heard a wave of expletives from the milling crowd of sailors followed by a stunned silence as each new pair of eyes inevitably became fixed on the distant shoreline.

The captain addressed his dumbfounded men from the conning tower. "Alright! Pull yourselves together," he called out. "You'll have plenty of time to stare when you are on shore. In the meantime, you have a job to do, and I expect you to do it. Now get on with it."

At his command, the sailors' training kicked in and one after another they returned to their allotted tasks. Within minutes a large pile of supplies in waterproof containers had piled up on the deck. A second dinghy was manhandled up top and dropped into the ocean next to the first.

A security team, heavily armed and looking as nervous as Emily felt, took the first boat back to shore. They headed to a building near the center of the compound identified by MacAlister's team as the best suited to become the survivors' new living quarters.

By the time the second boat full of sailors hit the shore Emily, Rhiannon, and Thor were next in line, their backpacks and a couple of boxes of supplies resting next to them on the gently dipping deck of the sub.

"Where's Jacob?" Rhiannon asked.

"He's asleep," Emily lied. "He'll be coming over later." The truth was, Jacob was still in his cabin, still drunk from earlier, but the captain had told Emily it was probably better to just let him sleep it off.

"Good," said Rhiannon, her dislike for Jacob patently obvious. There was little love lost between the teenager and the scientist, at least from Rhiannon's side of the equation. Jacob was going to have to work very hard to ever gain her trust again.

■ ■ ■

The dinghy bounced and dived over the surface of the ocean, wind fluttering Emily's and Rhiannon's hair out behind them like streamers, spray dousing all of them with cool seawater in the few minutes it took to cover the half mile between the sub and land. The boat rumbled and rocked as the sailor ran the flat-bottomed boat up onto the beach.

"That'll be five quid, please," he joked as he cut the engine.

Emily jumped ashore, her feet sinking into the wet sand. "Put it on my tab," she said and began transferring their bags onto the beach.

Now that she was actually ashore, Emily could see that the buildings of Point Loma, in typical military fashion, were actually packed far more densely onto the spit of land than they had appeared. She, Rhiannon, and Thor followed the sailor who had brought them ashore along a concrete path surrounded on both sides by eerily alien red bushes and creepers that twisted and tangled with each other like frozen snakes. The concrete path had fractured in places, and more than once they had to carefully maneuver over raised broken slabs of concrete that had been cracked open and pushed up by the thick roots burrowing beneath the path.

A sea mist, thick and gray, obscured the majority of the bay that lay to the east and northeast of Point Loma. Emily could just make out the westernmost tip of Coronado Island and its naval supply center and airport, but the fog was so thick that everything beyond that was hidden beneath its pall. Somewhere northeast of where they walked, across the bay and beyond Coronado Island, lay San Diego.

There was no trace whatsoever of anything green, no plant or tree that she could recognize. If it had not been for the manmade buildings ahead of her and her escort, Emily would have felt as though she truly had just set foot on an alien world.

"The captain has asked that you don't touch any of the plants," the sailor said as he helped first Rhiannon and then Emily to step over a particularly thick cord of root twisting up through the broken concrete path.

"You don't have to worry about that," Emily said as she passed him the bags she carried and then swung one leg then the other over the looping twists of the plant, carefully avoiding any contact.

Where there should have been grass was now a short leafy almost lichen-like plant, its stubby fronds blanketing the ground like a shag-pile carpet. There did not seem to be a square inch of dirt or sidewalk that wasn't coated by it.

No matter where she looked, the same lurid red landscape filled her vision. And that smell! The wet air was redolent with an inescapable mustiness that spoke of wet rotting vegetation. There was still a definite scent of ammonia mingled in with it, but the aroma seemed to Emily to be fading, residual even, as though it was being washed away by the ocean winds soughing against her body and rustling the leaves of the plants.

Rhiannon did not appear to be as disturbed as Emily by the weird vegetation that had taken root around them. Her age maybe? Or her limited experience of the world that had been here softening the impact, perhaps. Or maybe her youth gave her the advantage, made her more fatalistic, more accepting of the inevitability of this takeover. Whatever the reason, the girl seemed happy to be off the submarine and feeling the warm California sun against her skin.

Emily had to agree: It felt fine with a capital *F* to be in the sunlight again. After so many weeks of subfreezing temperatures, this weather was like a welcome warm caress from a lover.

The office building MacAlister had chosen as their base of operations, uncreatively labeled Building One, lay behind a security fence of chain-link topped with curls of barbed wire that encircled the entire compound. They had to walk through a security post, the only entrance through the perimeter that Emily could see, to get to Building One. It was a squat, gray, three-story box sitting close to the edge of the beach. Two hundred feet of open space lay between their new home and any other building; at least, the space *would* be clear once the tangles of red vegetation that had overtaken the area had been cleared away. Beyond the office block's seaward-facing rear, Emily could just make out a deep wall of boulders, each easily weighing a ton or more, that followed the edge of the cigar-shaped spit of land Point Loma was built upon and dropped down for a hundred feet or so to meet the ocean. A dark stain, about fifty or so feet from the top of the wall of boulders, marked the high-tide point. There was no sign of any seaweed caught on the rocks, but there was a lot of wreckage that had become trapped in the gaps between the boulders; broken plasterboard, cans, what looked like a window frame, and, halfway up the wall, the rear half of some kind of boat, maybe a fishing trawler, had found their final resting place, at least until the next high tide found them again and washed them elsewhere. Flotsam and jetsam left by the storm, no doubt. Strangely, there was also no sign of any of the invading plants on those rocks. In fact, the growth of lichen seemed to stop a few feet back from the top edge of the boulders with only a few sporadic spots of red scattered over the top layer of rock.

"It gives us a good defensible position with a clear field of fire if the *you-know-what* ever hits the fan," said MacAlister by way of greeting as he met Emily and Rhiannon at the main entrance of the building. He took their bags from them, dismissed the sailor, and led Emily, Rhiannon, and Thor inside. "There are more than enough rooms on the second floor that we can each get our own living quarters. I've got men up there now, clearing out the office equipment and filing cabinets to make room for some cots." MacAlister led them down a corridor and up a flight of stairs to the second floor. From somewhere on the same floor came the sound of furniture scraping along floor and the voices of men talking amongst themselves.

"It's probably best if we all stay in the same building for now. At least until we know what we're dealing with out there. Then we can start looking at spreading out to the other buildings . . . give each other a little elbow room." MacAlister stopped in front of a plain gray door. "This one's yours," he said as he nudged it open with his butt and carried Emily and Rhiannon's bags inside, dropping them next to two cots already set up in the otherwise empty room. "It's not much, but it's cozy in its own way."

"I think we'll manage," said Emily, smiling.

"Well, I'm in the last room at the opposite end of the hall. If you need anything . . ." The Scotsman smiled and left.

Thor sniffed around the room a few times, then settled down in a corner, panting as he watched the two women unpack what few belongings they had.

The room was about twelve-by-twelve and Emily could see the marks on the industrial-weight carpet where the four legs of a desk had sat and an area where the rollers of a chair had flattened the weave. With no air-conditioning to cool them, their new room had the same musty dampness to it as outside. Emily doubted opening the single window would do much to alleviate the problem as she wiped sweat from her forehead. She supposed they would get used to it, but after the perfectly maintained environment of the submarine, this stifling heat and smell made for an unpleasant welcome.

"Home sweet home," Emily said sarcastically.

Rhiannon raised her eyebrows in mock judgment and began emptying the contents of her rucksack onto her bed.

■ ■ ■

Once unpacked, Emily and Rhiannon joined the rest of the survivors gathered outside the entrance to the building. Captain Constantine was in the middle of giving an update when they arrived. MacAlister and Parsons stood behind him. The Chief Engineer gave Rhiannon a friendly wink when he saw her.

"Mr. Parsons and a couple of crew have located the camp's emergency generator; it seems to be in working order, so we should have power up and running within the next few hours. For now, we need you all to lend a hand clearing the vegetation from the paths and around the buildings. Starting with our new home. While there doesn't seem to be any problem with handling this stuff, minimize your exposure, people. Wear the goggles and gloves that we've handed out. Keep those long-sleeved shirts buttoned up, am I understood?"

A chorus of "Yes, sir," echoed up from the group.

"Now grab your weapon of choice, and let's make this place livable."

A selection of chain saws, fire axes, and machetes had been brought in from the submarine and scavenged from a tool shed MacAlister had identified during his reconnaissance mission. They were laid out on a nearby table. The tools were being doled out by MacAlister.

"What can we do?" Emily asked him as she and Rhiannon walked up.

"Well, if you feel like lending a hand, you can take one of these and start clearing away the vines on the side of our new home. If you chop them at the base and give 'em a good tug, the rest comes away pretty easy," MacAlister said, handing Emily and Rhiannon a pair of goggles and gloves each, then a machete to Emily and a large, plastic fifty-gallon trash bag to Rhiannon. "Careful of that blade, it's sharp," he warned.

"No shit," said Emily.

Emily and Rhiannon walked over to the west side of the building and took a moment or two to inspect the outer wall. A tall red creeper extended from a bulbous trunk at the base of the plant, twisting up the plane of the wall. Every few inches thin shoots had sprouted off the main stem, digging into the rough stucco of the wall. The vine spread out in a web across the side of the building, shoots curling and bundling on the sills of windows, looking for purchase on the glass. A thin clear membrane, wet and shiny, surrounded the inner dried-blood-black core of the plant.

"Step back a bit," Emily told Rhiannon as she raised the machete above her head and angled it down at the base of the plant just above the bulb. She brought the blade down hard into the plant and felt it dig deep with a wet slurp. Two more chops and she was able to separate the main body of the creeper away from the bulb with a swift kick from her sneaker-clad foot.

A viscous red fluid dripped from the detached end of the vine like a severed artery. Emily took the jagged edge of the detached plant in her gloved hand and began pulling the creeper away from the wall. She pretty soon discovered the most effective way to separate the plant from the side of the building was to give short, sharp tugs that pulled the tiny fingers from the stucco with a popping sound.

Emily pulled the final foot of vine free from the wall and watched it fall to the ground next to them. She picked up the severed end and examined it. It hung loosely in her hand like a dead snake. The plant was made from a thick fibrous material, obviously vegetable based, but with three lengths of root wound around each other at its core. Each root was covered by an outer skin that glimmered with a shifting pearlescence.

"It smells *bad*," said Rhiannon, wrinkling her nose at the pungent smell of rotten eggs the bleeding end gave off. "Everything smells different now."

Emily began chopping the fifty-foot length of vine into smaller chunks. Rhiannon stuffed the chopped parts into the bag MacAlister had given her. An hour later and they had managed to rid the entire west fascia of the building of all signs of the red creeper. Emily tried to pry out the root bulb, but she could not budge it. Getting that sucker out of the ground was going to take a pickax and a lot of sweat. She drank deeply from a canteen of water she had brought with her and wiped sweat off her forehead. Her eyes stung and her muscles ached but *Good God*, it felt *so* good to be doing something physical again.

"You could lend a paw too," she told Thor. The dog had taken up residence in the shade of the building, panting heavily. This warm weather was not going to be comfortable for the Alaskan malamute. His thick coat was not conducive to this kind of temperature. She would have to track down an electric trimmer or a pair of shears and give him a haircut at some point. Emily emptied half of her water into a plastic bowl and set it in front of the dog. He lapped at it eagerly then sat back down in the shade.

By the time night fell at the end of their first day at Point Loma, the crew had managed to put a fair dent in the overgrown area out front of the building and also cleared several of the surrounding buildings of the insidious creeping vines. The same success could not be said of Parsons's attempt at getting the base's emergency generator up and running though.

"The damn thing is just too gunked up with that red crap," Parsons told the group as they gathered in the reception area that evening. They had turned the area into a makeshift refectory, handing out hot meals cooked on the sub and then taxied back to the hungry crew at the base. "It's going to take another four or five hours to disassemble and clean it out and then a couple more to put the bugger back together again."

Rhiannon had helped take food out to the sentries posted around the base on rooftops. Now she stepped through the door and Emily saw her eyes brighten at the sight of the sub's Engineer. Emily had felt concerned enough at Parsons's attention to

Rhiannon that she had taken MacAlister aside and expressed her concerns.

"Parsons had a wife and daughter back home in the Rhondda," Mac had explained. "His girl would have been about Rhiannon's age. Lovely little thing, she was. I think Rhia reminds him of her."

Rhiannon grabbed a sandwich from the counter and sat down next to the Engineer. "Hi!" she said.

"Well, if it isn't the prettiest girl in the whole wide world," said Parsons cheerily.

Rhiannon blushed at the gentle compliment, but Emily could see that the girl was taking some pleasure in the fatherly attention the man lavished on her and she smiled at the kid.

Jacob had been given a room on the ground floor that allowed him some freedom to move around. He'd spent what little of the day had been left after his drinking spree working with a loaned sailor unpacking and putting together the radio equipment he had brought with him. A large dipole radio antenna had been fixed to the roof of the building. They'd have radio communications again as soon as the power was up. For the first time since Emily had known Jacob he was smiling freely. The man had lost some of the tension and seemed to have relaxed considerably since coming ashore. He was sitting across from her now listening to the conversation as it unfolded, apparently suffering no major hangover.

The discussion around the table focused mainly on the plants they had spent the day clearing from the compound. There were at least twenty varieties within the confines of the compound alone, someone remarked. None of them recognizable as indigenous Earth species. Jacob had examined specimens they had collected from some of the creeping vines and plants. One in particular was proving to be a particular hazard: There was an abundance of squat plants that grew close to the ground, sprouting broad drooping leaves which measured just over two feet in length. The leaves were razor sharp along the edges and a few unlucky crew members had already suffered deep cuts and lacerations when they had tried to pull them out or unsuspectingly stepped close to one hidden by taller plants.

"If I hadn't seen all this with my own eyes, I would never have believed any of it," MacAlister said. "I mean, it's just so damn . . . out of this world."

"At least we haven't seen any of the spiders," said Rhiannon through a mouthful of half-chewed sandwich. "They scared me."

In fact, no one had reported seeing any signs of life since stepping ashore. But that didn't mean there couldn't be something out there in the alien jungle lying just beyond the chain-link perimeter fence of the compound.

"Ah, you don't want to worry about a few spiders," said Parsons, "I'll keep you safe, *cariad*." He placed a friendly arm around the girl's shoulder and squeezed her gently to him.

"Do *you* think there's *anything* out there?" Captain Constantine asked Emily. "Any of those creatures you saw when you were traveling still exist?"

Emily's hand fluttered subconsciously to her shoulder where the creature that had attacked her in the forest outside Valhalla had left her scarred.

"I don't know," she replied. "I don't see any of the trees that made the dust, so I think the spider aliens have probably served their purpose. But the other monsters? Who knows? They could be out there right now for all I know." The word "monsters" sounded so childish in her present company, but that was what they had been. Scary fucking monsters and the sooner everyone realized it the safer she would feel.

MacAlister nodded his understanding. "We've got a tight guard on the compound. You can rest easy tonight."

The conversation faltered for a moment, a silence slipping in between them until MacAlister announced, "Okay, who wants a refill of their cuppa?" He pointed at his half-empty mug of tea.

Emily nodded and handed her own empty mug to him. Tea, she decided, was beginning to grow on her.

▪ ▪ ▪

The screams started just after sunset.

At first Emily thought it was Thor dreaming, whining as he relived some personal nightmare, but when the wailing grew louder and the sound of panicked human voices joined it, a sudden jolt of adrenaline cleared her sleep-addled brain and she was awake.

"What is it?" Rhiannon's voice, tremulous and low, whispered from beneath the sheets of her cot.

The wailing came again before Emily could answer; a strange mixture of high-pitched screeching with a deep intertwined staccato bass thrum that sounded like a badly out-of-tune cello. Emily looked down at Thor at the side of her cot; he was awake, his ears up and eyes wide open, head cocked to one side. He seemed more curious than perturbed, unlike the voices yelling back and forth to each other beyond their door.

"I don't know," Emily answered when the wailing died away again, "but I'm going to go find out. You stay here and look out for Thor. I'll be right back." Emily grabbed her pistol from under her pillow and headed toward the door.

The wailing call rose again. This time it sounded much louder and closer, rattling the glass in the windows. Emily did an about-face and headed back to where she had left the Mossberg shotgun leaning against the wall. She checked it quickly and walked back to the door.

"Stay put," she told Thor as he rose to follow her, but he instantly sat back down at her command. She slipped through the door and into the corridor, pulling the door closed behind her. Several bleary-eyed sailors were pulling on shirts and firing questions at each other. Flashlight beams cut through the darkness, turning the faces of the sailors into ghoulish masks. No one had any answers but each of them held a weapon in his hand as they moved from their rooms and headed toward the stairwell. She followed behind them, pushing her way through the group, down the stairs and out into the courtyard.

A three-quarter moon punctured a cloudless sky dappled with stars. The moon's ghostly light was bright enough for Emily to make out a collection of human shapes gathered just outside the entranceway.

"Emily, you should stay inside," said MacAlister when he spotted her exiting the building, the light from his flashlight illuminating her and the other sailors behind her. He glanced disapprovingly at the shotgun in her hand and the Glock pistol strapped to her hip. "Do you sleep with that under your pillow?"

She ignored him. "What is it?" she asked. "What's making that sound?"

"We don't know exactly what—" He stopped, cut off halfway through his sentence as another wail split the still night air. It was so much louder out here.

Emily felt a cold shiver run down her spine at the memory of the creature on the floor above her apartment back in Manhattan. "You need to be really, really careful," she said to MacAlister. "We don't have any idea what we're dealing with here, but I can guarantee whatever is making that noise won't be friendly."

"You, Collins," MacAlister said pointing at a sailor behind Emily. "Get up on that roof and tell me what you see." He tossed a walkie-talkie and a pair of night-vision goggles to the sailor, who ran to the building he had indicated. "The rest of you, follow me."

Emily slipped in beside MacAlister as he led them in the direction they thought the cry was coming from. The night air was chilly and Emily could feel gooseflesh rising on her skin beneath her thin T-shirt. Flashlights cut through the blackness of the night like searchlights, but as they reached the western perimeter fence MacAlister hissed an order: "Lights off." Instantly all were extinguished. The group fell silent and waited for their eyes to acclimate to the darkness.

From the radio in MacAlister's hand came the voice of the sentry he had ordered to the rooftop. "There's movement northwest of my location, sir. I can't make out what it is but there's definitely something out there." The voice was a low, calm whisper.

Emily stared in the direction the guard had said he saw something, her eyes trying to penetrate through the darkness. She tried to picture the area beyond the wire fence from when she had first come ashore: a gentle hill that gradually rose toward the sky, covered in thick alien plants that towered twenty feet or more into the air, perfect cover. She could hear the forest of swaying plants soughing and rustling in the breeze just a few yards beyond where she and the others now silently crouched, weapons at the ready. Her eyes searched the blackness again . . . nothing . . . wait! Something *was* moving in the darkness. What *was* that?

Halfway up the hill Emily could see multiple points of light weaving through the tall plants. The lights rose and dropped, up and down, tiny pinpricks of intense luminescence about the size of one of those laser pointers people loved to tease their pet cats with. There were hundreds of them, glowing orange then green then red, flowing silently between the stalks and stems of the plants.

"What the fuck is that?" someone whispered over Emily's shoulder.

"Quiet," MacAlister whispered, his eyes focused on the lights as they moved from right to left across their field of vision.

The lights continued to undulate, burning so brightly that Emily could make out their glow even when they were obscured by the thick leaves of the plants they moved behind. They stopped abruptly, and the wailing again echoed through the night. The moment the cry faded away, the string of lights began to move once again.

Out here, without the walls of the building to baffle the sound, the cry had sounded plaintive, melancholy even, as though whatever creature the voice belonged to knew it was the last of its kind, doomed to wander the earth alone.

Or maybe, she had it all backward, maybe it was just the *first* of its kind, Emily thought.

A silence-shattering *crack* exploded from high up and behind where the group was crouched. It was followed immediately by a bright orange flash that left a ghostly outline of its glow on the back of Emily's eyes. The entire group jumped in unison at the sound of the single rifle shot.

"Who's firing? Cease fire! Cease fire!" MacAlister yelled into the radio just as a second shot from the same location shattered the silence. "Collins, cease fire."

Emily saw the lights freeze, then almost faster than her eyes could follow, the cloud of lights coalesced into a single stream and swarmed toward the rooftop where the shots had been fired from. The lights flowed over the fence and Emily caught the faint shadowed outline of something sinuous and dark flowing through the air with them. Three more shots followed in quick succession as the lights landed on the flat roof of the building where MacAlister had sent his man. A silence-filled moment stretched out for seconds as the lights ebbed and flowed then they surged forward in a wave of brilliance, quick as a striking cobra. The night was punctured by an unmistakable scream of agony, shrill and screeching. Then silence descended again as the man's shriek was abruptly cut short.

The lights twisted and turned in a vicious twirling storm right where Emily judged the rifle fire had come from, the afterimage of the muzzle flashes still glowing in her eyes.

And then the lights reversed their trajectory and flowed back over the fence and into the forest. Emily watched as they streamed up the side of the hill. Abruptly, they blinked out of existence.

"Oh, fuck!" said someone in the dark beside her. "Fuck me sideways. What the fuck *was* that?"

No one answered him.

The group was up on its feet almost as a single entity, racing toward the building where the screams had come from, and Emily found herself swept along with them.

Emily almost screamed when she felt a hand grab hers in the darkness. "Stick by me." The sound of MacAlister's voice was an anchor in the chaos.

They followed the sailors into the building and up the stairs. On the top floor, the group slowed and raised their weapons, covering the corridor and the access door leading out to the flat roof beyond. The door was ajar, creaking eerily as it moved back and forth in the breeze.

"Collins?" MacAlister called out as he moved forward, placing the flat of his hand against the door. There was no answer. MacAlister pushed the door slowly open, then stepped out onto the roof, his rifle raised to his shoulder as he swept the barrel back and forth across the deserted rooftop. The other sailors followed quickly behind him, fanning out across the roof, providing cover for every potential angle of attack.

Emily allowed them a few seconds to position themselves then followed behind the last sailor, her Mossberg at the ready.

"Collins?" Emily heard MacAlister yell out again, then, "What the . . . ? Oh, Jesus!" A flashlight flicked on, illuminating MacAlister's standard issue boots.

He was standing in a wide pool of blood.

■ ■ ■

They found no sign of the sentry's body or any of his equipment. And judging by the amount of blood that had pooled on the roof, Emily did not think there was much chance of locating Collins alive, either. Apparently MacAlister shared her grim reasoning. Flashlights illuminated the darkness of the roof they stood on as sailors shone their lights over the sides of the building and down onto the ground surrounding it, searching for any clue as to where their comrade had disappeared.

"I want everyone off this roof right now and back to the main building immediately," MacAlister said once he was sure Collins wasn't lying injured nearby. Emily could hear the restraint it took not to yell the command. "And switch those damn lights off. We're too exposed up here."

"But sir, what about . . . Collins?" a voice from the darkness asked.

"He's gone and there's nothing we can do for him. Right now we need to get back to the main building and make sure it's secure. If there are any more of those things out here I don't want them getting access to it. We'll organize a search party for Collins in the morning."

"But, sir—"

"No buts. We don't have nearly enough light; we have no idea what that thing was, and no way of tracking it. No, we get off this roof now," MacAlister commanded.

Emily followed the shadows and sound of scuffing boots back to the exit door and down to the ground floor. The group jogged quickly across the open ground and back to the safety of their building.

"Everyone in?" MacAlister asked the guard standing just inside the exit doors.

"You're the last, sir."

"Good. I don't want you to move from this position until I send someone to relieve you, am I understood?"

The sailor nodded, his head bobbing nervously.

"And if you see *anything* at all out there I want to know about it immediately. You do *not* engage it. You come and get me or the skipper. Got it?"

Another nod from the sailor.

MacAlister positioned a pair of guards at the door to each floor, then told everyone else to head back to bed. "There's nothing you can do, and it's going to be another long day tomorrow. We're going to need to organize a search party to try and find Collins so I need you all alert and ready."

When Emily quietly opened the door to her room, Rhiannon was still awake, her worried face illuminated in the glow of a battery-powered LED lamp. Thor was sitting on the cot next to her, his tail thumped loudly as Emily stepped into the room.

"Is everything alright?"

Emily sat next to Rhiannon, stroking Thor's head. "Everything is just fine," she lied. "Just a false alarm."

"I heard gunshots."

"It was just a mistake, nothing to worry about. Now, come on. It's late and I don't know about you, but I need my beauty sleep."

Rhiannon seemed to accept the lie and, before Emily had even removed her clothes for bed, she heard the girl's breathing change to a slow, steady rhythm as sleep overcame her.

Emily switched off the lamp and climbed between the sheets. She lay staring into the darkness, running the strange event she had witnessed earlier over in her mind again.

Those lights had seemed to be linked together, almost as if they were part of the same creature, or at least, operating as a single entity.

This world, this truly *new* world, was waking up, she thought. Humanity's crown had been stripped from its head and they had been cast out into the red wilderness as naked and vulnerable as every other creature that now walked this planet. More so, in all probability, because none of them had any idea what the rules for this new world were, and those rules had most assuredly changed . . .

. . . and every soul under the roof of this building was as vulnerable as the next.

CHAPTER 12

Early the following morning the whirling mist between Point Loma and the rest of the world had turned into a deep, impenetrable fog. It hung in the air, sucking in all the light from the rising sun, turning the world a depressing gray.

Captain Constantine and his men were already up and assembled when Emily joined them in the refectory. He had split the remaining crew not tasked with guarding the compound into two search parties. One led by him, the other by MacAlister. Emily could tell from the looks on the men's faces that they held out little hope of finding their missing comrade. Everyone present on the roof last night who had witnessed the attack had also seen how much of Collins's blood had been left behind after the man was plucked into the darkness. There was little doubt as to his fate. If the man had still been alive last night, there was no way he was going to have survived for more than a few minutes before he bled out. Constantine was just going through the motions for his men's sake.

"Good morning, Emily," MacAlister greeted her when he saw her coming through the door. His eyes were bloodshot, dark rings of puffy flesh below them. He did not seem his normal nonchalant self. Understandable, after all, he had lost one of his men on his watch, and she was sure he was taking it very personally.

"Hi," she replied. "Is there anything I can do to help?"

MacAlister shook his head. "We're going to push into the area where we think Collins was taken. The captain and his group are going to reconnoiter the buildings on our side of the fence. Probably best if you stay here in camp."

"Are you sure that's a good idea, going out there?"

"We have a missing man. We have to at least try and bring his body back . . . assuming we can find it."

"Okay, let's get a move on," the captain said, leading the way through the door. "Team A with me. Team B, fall in behind Sergeant MacAlister."

Emily followed MacAlister and his men as far as the gate on the west side of the camp. The fog was already burning off, she noted, as she stopped at the security-fence line, lacing her fingers through the links of the chain.

MacAlister took his men and moved off around the perimeter, heading in the direction of where they had seen the wave of lights disappear the previous night. Overnight, the red jungle had taken on a new menacing overtone. Not that it had changed in any way, of course, it was just that now they all knew *something* lurked in that thick mess of leaves and vines, roots and trunks. Something new to this planet.

MacAlister and his team edged their way cautiously through the thick fronds and plants of the jungle's perimeter just beyond the security fence, using the barrels of their automatic rifles to push back the leaves. In seconds they had disappeared from her view, with only the occasional movement of one of the tall fronds to mark where they were heading.

Emily felt a pang of worry stab at her gut. What if that thing was waiting for them in there? What if it knew they were coming? She was surprised at just how concerned she was for the Scotsman. She had not realized until now how attached she had grown to him. Her affection for the man was all the more surprising considering the circumstances of their predicament. With the human race on the brink of extinction, affairs of the heart were still as distracting as they had ever been. Life had been *so* much easier before the end of the world, she decided.

Okay, this is getting ridiculous, she thought. *What am I going to do? Stand here all day pining?* No, there had to be something she could turn her hands to while they were out looking for signs of their fallen comrade. She needed to keep occupied, to keep moving. Idle hands are the devil's tools and all that.

Reluctantly, she released her hold on the fence and headed back to Building One.

■ ■ ■

Emily occupied her mind by helping the remaining sailors chop through the plants still covering the space between Building One and the surrounding offices. They had managed to remove a good-size swath of the weeds between them when there was a yell from the sentry stationed at the main gate.

Emily looked up and saw MacAlister and his men stepping back into the base. She let out a long sigh of relief at sight of him and then mentally kicked herself for allowing him to get under her skin so damn easily. *Sneaky bastard*, she thought. She had always been a sucker for a man in a uniform, and when you threw in the accent . . . well, she guessed she could be forgiven for caring.

Emily dropped her machete and began walking over to meet them.

"No sign of Collins," MacAlister was telling Captain Constantine as she drew closer to them. "The vegetation is so dense in there it might just as well be the jungles of Borneo. We could have walked right by him and never known it."

"We are going to need to push that forest back if we want to maintain any kind of security around the perimeter," the captain said, his hand methodically stroking his beard as he spoke. "Suggestions?"

"It's going to take forever to chop that stuff down, it's just far too dense and I wouldn't be able to guarantee anyone's safety while they were beyond the fence. Hell, I can't even guarantee their safety this side of the wire, but I don't see we have much in the way of a choice. I'll start organizing teams once we're done with clearing inside the perimeter."

"Why don't we just burn it?" Emily suggested.

"If we had access to flamethrowers, or some napalm even, that might work but we don't carry anything like that onboard the sub," said MacAlister.

"But there's a fuel depot on the other side of the compound," said Emily, pointing to the aboveground fuel tank she had recognized when they'd first arrived. "Couldn't we just siphon it off and burn the vegetation line back?"

Both men looked in the direction she was pointing.

"It's risky," said the captain. "Keeping it under control is going to be difficult. All it's going to take is a stray ember on one of these roofs and we could have a major problem on our hand. And fuel is going to be at a premium from this point onward, who knows if we'll find more anytime soon."

"If we put bodies on every roof we should be able to cover any risk of fire, so long as we choose the right time," Emily explained. "And there's a pretty consistent breeze coming in off the ocean that should push the fire and smoke away from us . . . probably."

MacAlister and the captain stared wordlessly at each other as they silently thought over Emily's suggestion.

"What do you think?" Constantine asked MacAlister.

"It'd have the added advantage of potentially driving back anything . . ." MacAlister paused as he searched for the right word ". . . *undesirable* that's shacked up in there too, skipper. It could certainly take care of two problems.

"The vegetation isn't dry," he continued, "so that should go a long way to helping keep the chance of the fire spreading down to a manageable level. If we concentrate on small areas at a time, and have a crew ready to catch it before it spreads, we should be okay." He shrugged and nodded, "Yeah. I think it could work."

Captain Constantine considered the options. His hand was stroking his beard again in what had become an obvious tell of concentration to Emily.

"Alright, I'm convinced. Let's give it a shot, shall we?"

"Good thinking, Emily," said MacAlister as they walked across the newly cleared area of the camp. He smiled and gave her elbow a light squeeze.

Emily felt herself flush bright red. "Goddamn it," she muttered under her breath, but enjoyed the warm tingle she felt anyway.

■ ■ ■

Two crews, most of them bare-chested and soaked in sweat by what had become an afternoon that hit the high seventies, cut a six-foot-deep firebreak around the edge of the west fence.

One crew chopped away at the stubborn trunks and branches, another made sure the debris was moved clear of the slowly forming firebreak.

Emily helped cart off the debris and stacked it in piles along the beach. Rhiannon busied herself bringing water to the men.

The gap between the fence and the new edge of the jungle would give them enough space to keep the fire from leaping to any of the closer buildings. Captain Constantine ordered sailors onto each roof with at least two handheld fire extinguishers apiece that they collected from the buildings. Two "floating" pairs of sailors would be on standby, ready to mop up any stray fires that might flare-up around the camp.

If the worst happened, and the fire managed to get a toehold within the camp, they were all under orders to retreat to the beach and the safety of the sea.

When the break was completed all personnel not in MacAlister's "pyromaniacs"—his name for the three-man team that would be setting the fires—were to retreat to a safe distance. They moved to the seashore where they could still have a decent view of MacAlister and his men as they set the fire.

MacAlister laid a line of gas from the start of the break then twenty feet out along the edge. As he walked back he doused the foliage and leaves with a second jerrican of gasoline. He emptied the last drops from the last jerrican and tossed it away, checked the wind direction one final time—it was good, blowing northwest, away from the camp—then lit a makeshift torch made from a broken broom handle wrapped with gas-soaked rags. MacAlister ducked as the flames from the torch flared dangerously close to his face. He held the burning torch at arm's length for a few moments to ensure it was completely lit, then took two steps closer to the jungle and tossed it into the gas-soaked vegetation.

There was a bright flare and the front of the jungle bloomed with orange flames that sped along the path of the accelerant laid by MacAlister, who was quickly backing away from the conflagration. The flames leaped from plant to plant, and curling tongues of orange fire crept up thick trunks, consuming leaves and branches.

In seconds, what had been a lush, impenetrable jungle became a maelstrom of flames that leaped ten feet above the highest point of the canopy. A thick cloud of red-tinged smoke rose from the fire and then whirled into a funnel that began reaching toward the heavens, twisting and roiling as it was driven higher into the air by the hot air beneath it.

Minutes passed and a line of smoking, blackened stalks that sprouted from the bare ground for about six feet back from the firebreak formed as the fire devoured the vegetation. Emily caught a whiff of the pungent smoke as it floated across the distance to her. It reeked of a chemical causticity so unlike normal burning vegetation that Emily couldn't pinpoint exactly what the odor was. It reminded her of the smell of disinfectant that seemed to permeate every inch of any hospital she had ever spent time in. Whatever these plants used to draw their energy from the sun, it was not chlorophyll.

MacAlister was jogging back toward the gate, a wet cloth pressed to his mouth, his back to the fire now as it pushed away from him. His eyes caught Emily, Rhiannon, and Thor watching him, and he raised his right hand to give her a thumbs-up that turned into a wave.

Despite her best inner intentions, Emily found herself smiling and waving back. She glanced at Rhiannon and saw the little girl staring up at her, a huge grin on her face.

"What?" Emily demanded. Rhiannon said nothing, and turned to watch the show, giggling like a five-year-old.

"You're an evil munchkin," said Emily as she gave Rhiannon a gentle bump with her hip that sent the girl stumbling slightly, and brought more cackling laughter from her.

Emily and Rhiannon began walking toward MacAlister. The fire raged behind him, crackling flames dancing like dervishes against the gradually darkening sky, elongating Mac's shadow to three times its normal length.

Something fell out of the fire, about halfway along the break. At first, Emily though it was a burning tree trunk that had toppled to the ground. An ear-piercing screech shattered the evening air, removing all doubt that, whatever this was, it was alive, and it was truly pissed. The thing leaped and rolled in the dirt, trying to extinguish the hungry flames licking the majority of its huge body. It rolled and tumbled for a second more and then it began to run.

Straight at MacAlister's back.

In the few seconds before the burning creature reached MacAlister, Emily's mind registered several things: The creature was easily ten feet long, although it was hard to tell exactly as it writhed and rolled so violently. It had four muscular legs that drove it across the ground like a lizard, but the thick body—at least, the parts that were not already a blackened, burned goo—was covered in a red fur that extended from the base of the tail all along its body to the head. The head was long and narrow, like a crocodile's, but as the creature ran it let out another scream of pain, its jaws opening from right to left instead of up and down. There were teeth in that mouth, large, serrated teeth that Emily saw briefly before the jaws snapped together in agony. Its eyes were huge, raised on a broad skull and wide open, fixed on the back of MacAlister, who was still oblivious to the rapidly advancing creature as it pounded across the space between them.

Emily saw the sailors scattered around the edge of the fire line react as they spotted the creature, some dropped to a knee and raised their weapons to their shoulders, while others just began to fire from their standing position. The air was suddenly full of the sound of thunder as the weapons, set to fully automatic, unleashed a hail of bullets in the direction of the creature bearing down on MacAlister . . .

. . . who instinctively ducked and turned at the sound of the gunfire, just as the flaming thing barreled past him, its burning body sideswiping MacAlister and sending him flying toward the wall of flames. Emily saw him hit the ground hard, roll once as he tried to push himself to his feet before collapsing. The gunfire stopped momentarily when the creature careened into the Scotsman, and Emily felt her breath freeze in her chest; then it was gone, passing MacAlister's motionless body, more concerned with outrunning the fire that clung to its skin than the puny human that it could have undoubtedly devoured in a second if it had been so inclined.

"Shit!" she yelled, but in her mind she was yelling at MacAlister, *Get up! Get up, goddammit!*

It looks like a dragon, she thought as she watched one huge foot come down close to the unconscious man's head.

The gunfire began again as soon as the thing was clear of MacAlister and Emily saw chunks of skin pop from the creature as the sailors' weapons finally found their mark. The barrage of gunfire and the effects of the flames began to take their toll on the creature and it slowed to a virtual crawl. That gave the sailors time to readjust their position, advancing on the creature as it continued to drag itself, one huge clawed foot laboriously after the other, over the still-smoking ground.

It's heading to the ocean, Emily realized. The creature, undoubtedly mortally wounded now, was trying to extinguish the fire with water. It was intelligent then, clever enough to know what fire was and what water would do for its pain.

The advancing soldiers emptied clip after clip into the creature's heaving body, until, finally, it stopped, shuddered once along its entire body, and lay still.

The shooting died away.

Emily was running then. Sprinting toward the prostrate MacAlister. As she drew closer, she could see his jacket was smoldering slightly, a thin spiral of smoke also rose from a patch of singed hair. She skidded to a halt beside him and heaved him over onto his back. His eyes were closed and a trickle of blood ran from his nostrils down over his cheek. There was a nasty burn on the left side of his forehead where the flaming creature had struck him; the skin was already blistering there. She dropped her ear to his lips: He was breathing. Thank God!

Rhiannon reached them, Thor pulling her along like the sled dog he was, his leash stretched to its limit. The other sailors seemed to be more interested in ensuring the creature was dead, most of them were advancing on it, the barrels of their weapons not straying from the motionless body. A couple of other men seemed frozen in place, unsure of what they should be doing or what they had just seen.

"Grab his arm," Emily yelled at Rhiannon, struggling to be heard over the roar of the advancing flames, her eyes checking the fire line as it continued to rage and devour the jungle just twenty feet or so away. She could feel the heat beginning to singe the small hairs on her arms as she grabbed MacAlister's left wrist. Rhiannon did the same with his right hand and they tried to lift him but he was just too heavy.

"Pull, don't try to lift," Emily yelled.

The two women dug their heels into the soft ground and began to tug the unconscious soldier back toward the fence line. He weighed a freaking ton, but inch by precious inch they dragged him away from the flames of the fire.

A pair of arms seemed to appear from nowhere, reaching past her, grabbing MacAlister by the collar of his combat jacket. Another pair of hands reached over her own and grabbed the front of the jacket as another sailor ran past them and lifted MacAlister's legs off the ground.

Suddenly Emily was stumbling backward as Mac's weight was lifted from her. Then she was running alongside the sailors as they carried his unconscious body back to the safety of the encampment and the waiting medic.

She felt a childlike fear grip her, irrational and overwhelming. But wasn't that what fear was, at its essence? A direct conduit to the inner child, through all the armor and fortifications that we build as adults. Fear always managed to find that quivering child hiding in the center of every human, surrounded by darkness and cowering in the slowly dimming light of an exhausted candle.

As they ran for the gate they passed the smoldering body of the thing that had leapt from the fire. Flames still flickered along its flank. She could smell burning meat and the astringent reek of singed fur. It stank to high heavens and beyond. The creature lay on its side, its body twisted, huge jaws hanging wide open, a pink tongue, bleeding from where it had bitten itself in terror and agony, hanging from between razor teeth. One large round eye stared sightlessly toward the smoke-filled sky. The body was riddled with bullet holes.

They dragged MacAlister through the gates and straight to the waiting medic.

"Is he going to be alright?" Rhiannon asked, as she pushed herself close to Emily.

"Hard to tell at the moment," said Amar, as he ran his fingers around the cut on MacAlister's head, trying to gauge how deep the laceration was. He pressed harder and the soldier's eyes fluttered open, flicking first to Amar, then to Emily and Rhiannon, then back to the Amar.

"Do you make a habit of taking advantage of unconscious men?" MacAlister asked, his eyes on Emily again, his voice croaky, as though he had just woken up from a deep sleep. "Or is this what counts as a first date where you come from?" he added as he struggled to sit up.

"Why don't you just lay there a while so I can get a better look at you?" Amar insisted.

"Not going to happen. I'm fine."

With help from Emily and Rhiannon, MacAlister climbed to his feet. He wobbled for a second, leaning hard on Emily, and his arm slipped around her shoulder as his own hand found its way to her waist.

"You could have a concussion or a fractured skull for all I know," Amar continued, his exasperation obvious.

"I've taken worse knocks from your grandmother," MacAlister retorted. "Now, would someone like to tell me what the hell just happened?"

CHAPTER 13

She had miscalculated.

Both the captain and MacAlister insisted that they were as much to blame, but it had been Emily's idea to set the fire and she bore the responsibility completely for it getting out of hand. Her miscalculation had been in the ill-founded belief that the new plant life would react the same as the old; that if it wasn't dry, it would not burn. They had been wrong. *She* had been wrong.

The alien vegetation seemed particularly susceptible to fire, far more so than any Earth fauna that Emily had ever encountered before the red rain had come. What had started out as an attempt at a small controlled burn had escalated quickly into a ravaging conflagration as the fire MacAlister set ignited acre upon acre of the alien jungle around the camp. It devoured the vegetation like some ravenous monster. A huge tower of smoke rose from the fire, rolling into the air and blocking out the sun through the rest of the evening and into the next day.

The fire burned for almost twelve hours before it finally died away, stopped by a natural firebreak of rocky terrain that choked off the ravaging fire-beast's food.

Now, what should have been a bright morning was instead a dreary gray, smoke obscuring everything that was not within ten feet of the survivors as they looked out from behind the relative safety of Building One's windows.

"Everyone stays inside until the smoke clears," Captain Constantine ordered. "The last thing we want is any of you getting lost out there and overcome by the fumes."

So they sat and they waited.

Throughout the previous night a flickering orange wall of indistinct flames had been visible through the pall of smoke as the gluttonous fire ate its way through the jungle. But as Emily waited in the corridor with Rhiannon and several sailors, she could see nothing but smoke now. The fire was either out or it had moved far enough away that it was no longer a threat to the camp and its new occupants.

A sea breeze kicked up just before noon, wafting between the buildings of Camp Loma, probing the smoke and pushing it farther west, slowly emptying the courtyards as it spread the choking smoke away from the camp. The stench of burned vegetation mixed with the distinctive aroma of the sea remained though.

There had been a few touch-and-go moments during the night when embers carried by hot air from the fire gushed into the compound, but these had been ruthlessly tracked down by teams of sailors and, according to MacAlister, they had suffered nothing worse than a few singed roof tiles.

It was easy to spot those who had been outside on fire watch; their smoke-dirtied raccoon faces filed through the corridor as they returned to the building, eyes watering, coughing and hacking as their shipmates took them aside and led them to water stations.

Everywhere she looked, Emily saw nothing but zombies: bleary-eyed, sleep-deprived zombies. But as the hours ticked by the smoke thinned and eventually cleared and by mid-afternoon, the Point Loma survivors made their way cautiously outside again.

A thin layer of ash covered every exposed surface; it powdered beneath their feet as they stepped out into the courtyard in front of Building One.

"Good God," Emily said, standing in the gray shadow of the sun as it tried to force its way through the residual layer of smoke that still floated high in the afternoon sky. "We've only been here for a day and we're already back to our old ways."

"What do you mean?" Rhiannon asked.

"Nothing," she replied, but she couldn't shake the notion that the column of smoke rising into the atmosphere was a stark reminder of humanity's impact on the planet, a footprint, she supposed, of her civilization, of humanity's time spent at the top of the food chain. But by the same token, she delighted in seeing the blackened stalks and charred husks of the alien plant life that had spread across this land, or the iron ore–red soot that blew through the camp on the hot thermals of the fire. She felt a strange delight when she saw the burnt-down trunks of incinerated trees jutting from the still-smoking ground outside the fence like skeletal fingers.

There wasn't much left of the dragon—as everyone had now come to call the creature they had shot the previous day—left for them to examine. The out-of-control fire had caught up with it, roasting it to nothing more than a black lump of charcoal, save for the lower part of one leg and some skin on its underbelly.

"Is this the thing that grabbed Collins?" asked the captain, a handkerchief pressed to his mouth to keep out the residual smoke and the stink of burned flesh.

"No way to tell," said MacAlister. He had a bandage wrapped around the gash on his head, Vaseline spread over the burn—concessions to the medic who had finally persuaded the Scotsman to let him assess his wounds, with some encouragement from Emily and a liberal dose of chiding from Rhiannon—and had been deemed fit for duty.

"What we saw was nothing more than lights, this hardly seems to fit the description. But then, who can tell what this thing is exactly? I'd bet my last paycheck it wasn't roaming the woods before the rain came." He poked the carcass with a charred stick. The flesh cracked and flaked away.

"Yuck!" said Rhiannon, wrinkling her nose at the smell that flooded out of the gash.

"Well I guess this puts to rest any qualms we may have had about whether you were being entirely truthful with us, Emily," Captain Constantine said. "MacAlister, let's get a couple of men to drag this thing off. We don't want it stinking the place up; who knows what it might attract."

The fire had created an open stretch of blackened wasteland that stretched out in a horseshoe curve to at least a half mile of space around the compound. It looked like a scene from some catastrophe movie.

The ground was still too hot to examine closely, but where there had once been a jungle there was now nothing more than blackened skeletons jutting up from a carpet of powdery ash. Smoke still rose from the ground, like tiny genies searching across the bleak landscape. Oddly, there was still the occasional plant or bush left more or less untouched by the fire. Somehow they had survived with little more than a few singed branches or burned leaves.

It was an echo of Emily's own strange story of survival.

Given the circumstances of the past month or so, she had had little time to ponder the reasons as to just how or why she, amongst the billions on this planet, had somehow survived the red rain. But maybe she was alive for exactly the same reason these plants were still standing alone in this field of devastation—just blind luck. Right place at the wrong time.

"Well your idea certainly did the trick alright," said MacAlister, sidling up to her shoulder and gazing out over the devastated stretch of land that now surrounded the base.

"It wasn't exactly what I had in mind," she said.

"*Pfft!* It got the job done and we're all still here in one piece. That's a win in my book any day of the week."

"How are you feeling?" Emily asked without turning around, but she could sense the closeness of him, his breath brushing against her face as he spoke.

"I'm good. I'm good. Just this bump on my head and few bruises. Nothing a few days of light duty won't fix. Listen, I wanted to say thank you for what you did, pulling me away from the fire like that," he said, his voice a low whisper.

Emily turned to look at him, their faces just inches apart. "It was nothing," she said, her eyes fixed on his.

"No, it was definitely something, Emily. It was most definitely something. Look, I was thinking, wondering really, if—"

The sentence was broken by the sudden appearance of three sailors at their side. "Sergeant MacAlister. Captain Constantine told us to report to you for cleanup duty."

Emily smiled at MacAlister's obvious embarrassment. He smiled back when he saw her eyes still on him.

"Perfect timing as always, gentlemen," he scolded the sailor.

"Sir?" the sailor replied, oblivious to the connection he had just neatly severed.

"Don't call me 'Sir,' I work for a living. Oh, never mind. Emily, thank you again. Maybe we'll get a chance to chat later?"

"Maybe," Emily replied, then turned and walked back toward the camp.

■ ■ ■

The first anyone knew the power had finally been restored to the encampment was when the security lights around the perimeter fence crackled into life just before sunset. When the gantry lights mounted around the concrete concourse in front of Building One flickered on too, dusk was suddenly turned back into day. Light flooded the grounds and the still-smoldering area around the fence line. A loud cheer erupted from the sailors who were still working at clearing the vegetation from inside the fence line.

Somewhere, in one of the office buildings not too far from where Emily stood, an electric guitar began to play faintly, a ghostly yet unmistakable voice eventually joined the guitar, floating across the encampment. Even though she couldn't hear the words she recognized the voice and the song: the Rolling Stones's "Gimme Shelter." Kind of apt, in a freaky, déjà vu-ey kind of a way, she thought.

When Parsons walked out of the building housing the generator, wiping oil and grease from his hands with an equally dirty rag, he was greeted with more cheers and a round of applause from his gathered shipmates.

"Well done, Parsons," the captain told him, slapping the man on the back. "And perfect timing too."

"Thank you, sir," the engineer replied, a huge grin cracking his usually stern features. "We've taken stock of the camp's at-hand diesel supply, and I estimate we have a good four to five weeks left, if we're judicious with the demand we put on it. We could stretch it out another week *maybe*, if we only run the security lights for a few hours at night. We'll need to locate more diesel pronto though."

"Security is our main concern right now," the captain said. "I don't want to lose anyone else. So, no, the lights stay on all night, for now at least. Once we're dug in here a little more securely, we'll locate another supply at the earliest opportunity. There have to be other fuel dumps or civilian establishments we can commandeer more supplies from around here."

With the camp generator up and running again, Emily found herself once again donning her chef's apron. After raiding the sub's still adequately stocked cold-storage locker the smell of steak began to filter to the crew as their workday finally came to an end. The aroma of roasting meat was awfully close to the smell of the creature that had been caught in the fire, but Emily's stomach quickly overrode any objections her brain may have had, as she and Rhiannon joined the rest of the men of *HMS Vengeance* in the newly opened camp cafeteria.

Thor made the rounds from table to table, fixing each person who made the mistake of meeting his stare with starved puppy-dog eyes that would have surely gained him an Oscar, had he been human. Finally Emily had to order him to her side.

"I don't need you stinking the bedroom up all night," she scolded the dog, who settled on the floor between her and Rhiannon with a sigh, apparently content with his plunder.

The air around the room was lighthearted. Tired eyes brightened as several bottles of wine, found in one of the camp's officer's quarters during a scavenging mission by some of the men, were opened and dispensed, with the captain's permission. The sound of laughter and the hum of banter soon filled the room. The group, already tightknit, had grown even closer over the past few days of hard work clearing the weed from the compound, and Emily was glad to feel the warm glow of acceptance into the group.

Toward the end of the meal, Constantine stood and, as though he were presiding over a wedding ceremony, tapped the side of his wine glass until the room fell silent.

He cleared his throat then spoke. "We've come a long way, you and I. And we've lost some fine companions and shipmates along the way." He paused as he collected himself, gulping down a lump that had risen to his throat. "But we've also found new friends, and we have made a new start. So, I'd like you all to raise your glasses and toast with me our fallen comrades and our new friends. May God have mercy on us all."

The sound of scraping chairs rattled through the room as the group stood, echoing the captain's words with glasses raised high above their heads, before downing the remainder of their contents.

"To fallen comrades," Emily whispered, and tried to keep the ghosts of her life from her mind.

CHAPTER 14

The next morning, the fire-ravaged ground beyond the compound was still too hot to get too close to. While the majority of the smoke had been carried away by the Pacific breeze, the ground was still giving off thin plumes of gray smoke that stank to high heavens and stung the eyes of any at the camp unwary enough to venture outside the security fence.

Captain Constantine and MacAlister stalked the perimeter just clear of the choking smoke. The scowl on Constantine's face conveyed his annoyance. He'd planned for a small expeditionary group to reconnoiter the damage to the jungle and their surrounding area, but that was now going to have to wait until the ground cooled to a safe enough level. So the day was spent chopping and digging and sawing the remainder of the alien vegetation still growing between the buildings of the compound.

The stumps of the creeping vine that Emily had found so impossible to budge from the soil around Building One proved the hardest of all to clear. Less than twenty-four hours after Emily had chopped the clinging vine down, there were already signs of regrowth on the root bulb. Tiny feelers, three inches in length, were sprouting from it, inching their way up the wall of Building One.

When the first stump finally came free after several hours of hacking away at it with a pickax and shovels by three of the burlier sailors, it became clear as to why it had proved so difficult. The root system was almost as extensive as the sucking vines that had crawled up the exterior walls of the building. The thick, dark roots were lined with rows of barbs that clung to the soil like hooks, forcing each root to be dug out one by one to be sure it was completely gone.

Everything in this new world seemed tough, with an almost preternatural desire to live, expand, grow; desires that were matched by an innate ability to achieve those goals.

By the end of the day as the sun began to set, the compound and the space between the buildings was clear of all but a few of the more stubborn plants. Even with the leather gloves she had filched from one of the sailors, Emily's hands were blistered. But she did not mind; these past few days of physical exercise had reawakened something within her, and she found herself reveling in the purity of the simple task of manual labor. A definite sense of camaraderie had grown between the survivors, and Emily was happy to be a part of it.

Rhiannon, on the other hand, was not as enthusiastic about the brutal working conditions the California climate and salty air created. She had promoted herself to supplying the crews with water and food throughout the day, although she did stop by occasionally to check on Emily and carry a few of the branches and leaves she had cut down to one of the several growing piles of decaying vegetation that sat waiting for disposal near the exit of the camp.

"Emily!" a voice called to her, and she dropped her pickax to the ground, wiped the sweat from her forehead, and looked toward the source of whoever was calling her. It was Mac, standing in the open doorway of the main building and waving to her. "Come on in," he yelled again, "we have someone who wants to talk to you."

■ ■ ■

MacAlister escorted Emily inside the building and down the corridor to the makeshift radio room that had been set up on the ground floor of the building. The two of them squeezed in beside Jacob, Captain Constantine, and Parsons, making the room stuffy with their body heat.

Jacob sat at the desk, a pair of headphones over his ears, fine-tuning the portable radio. "Stand by, please, Commander," he spoke into the microphone, then switched the radio over to its loudspeaker mode. "Okay, you're good to go," he continued, placing the headphones on the desk next to the radio and grinning at Emily as he pushed his chair back from the desk.

Onboard the ISS, Commander Fiona Mulligan pulled the microphone from the wall of the observation module and switched on the speaker. Through the observation port she could see the coast of Chile creeping closer as the station followed its orbit northeast.

"Hello? Can you hear me?" she asked.

Miles below, in the confines of the small room, Mulligan's voice sounded extra loud and clear.

"We're receiving you perfectly, Commander," said Emily, finding it hard to keep the emotion she felt for her stranded friend out of her voice. "It's so very good to hear your voice again. We were a little concerned about you there for a while." She found herself returning Jacob's grin, in spite of herself.

The commander smiled although she knew no one could see

her. For a while, after their radio communications had gone down, both she and her crew had begun to wonder if maybe they might have lost contact permanently with the group of survivors from the Stockton Islands, or worse, maybe something had happened to them as they travelled to their new location. So it came as a relief when Jacob had finally managed to contact the station half an hour earlier. But it was especially good to hear Emily's voice again.

"Thank you for your concern, Emily, and sorry for the scare, but the inevitable breakdown we were worried about now seems to be taking place. We lost several of the relay satellites we use to communicate when we're out of normal radio range while you were travelling to your new home, and the red storm seems to have created some kind of residual electrical interference too. So, I'm afraid our contact with you is going to be a little unpredictable from this point onward. The sat-phone networks all seem to be down now, so we'll be using our amateur radio rig from here on out and that will mean we will only be in range a few hours each day from this point onward, I'm afraid."

"May I?" the captain asked Emily, nodding to the microphone.

"Sure," she said, "go ahead."

"Commander, this is Captain Constantine. It's a pleasure to speak with you again. I want to thank you personally for everything you have done for me and my crew."

"Likewise, and you are more than welcome, Captain," came the static-riddled reply from the station.

"I know Jacob has filled you in on some of the events that have transpired since we arrived here at Point Loma, but I believe we have everything under control now. So I think it's time we turn the focus on you and your crew: Can you give us any information relevant to your reentry and how best we should go about the recovery efforts once you join us back here on Earth?"

The commander and the captain exchanged information about location, trajectories, and possible emergency scenarios over the next thirty minutes.

Parsons stood elbow to elbow with Emily, taking copious notes on a steno pad. Emily found herself tuning out their voices as the conversation turned technical, but her attention snapped back to the cramped room when a sudden rattling burst of static drowned out the commander's voice.

". . . tain. Is there's anything . . . eed to . . . bout. Hello? Can you . . . me?"

"I'm sorry, Commander. Please repeat all again. Can you hear me?"

". . . eed to talk wi . . . Do you . . ."

As Commander Mulligan's garbled words faded away they were replaced with a low, constant hiss of static from the speaker. Jacob reached across and flicked the radio's off switch, silencing the machine.

"Damn! When do you think they'll be in range again?" the captain asked Jacob.

"Their amateur radio rig is going to give them significantly less range and power," Jacob explained, closing his eyes as he did some quick math in his head. "I'd estimate sometime between twelve and eighteen hours until we can establish a clear contact again, but I really don't know for certain."

"Okay, well I'll position a man to monitor the radio overnight and let you get some sleep," Constantine said. "On the off-chance that we hear back from the commander sooner than expected, he'll have orders to wake either you or Emily, okay?"

Emily and Jacob nodded their agreement.

"Now," the captain said. "I think it's time we all got a good night's rest."

CHAPTER 15

Emily repositioned the backpack to a less awkward position against her shoulders. It felt almost comforting to have it on her back again, although it was not the same pack she had used on her travels—that one had finally been retired. This one was smaller, just large enough to carry some water, a first-aid kit, and a day's worth of rations. After all, this was just a quick foray to survey the area around the base. The Mossberg was slung over her shoulder, and extra shells rattled in the pockets of the light windbreaker jacket she wore. A machete hung from a loop on her belt, slapping against her thigh as she walked.

By their fourth day at the base, the stretch of land they had put to the torch was finally cool enough it would no longer melt the soles of the shoes of the first scouting party to leave the base. There were still hot spots scattered across the desolate field of pink ash, silently smoldering, but the smoke rising up from them was an easy indicator of where the group should steer clear of.

Rhiannon, after much complaining, had agreed to stay behind.

Thor, however, trotted by Emily's side, as she, MacAlister, and two sailors headed out through the security gate just after sunrise. Thor seemed as happy as Emily to be out of the encampment again. He had put on weight since the arrival of the submarine crew; a combination of lack of exercise and overfeeding by the crew, who had all seemed to take a very protective attitude over what could be the last of his species. Though, after everything Emily and he had been through, the last few weeks must have seemed like doggy heaven for him.

The small group followed the main road out of the camp north along the peninsula. The fire had consumed almost everything in its path for about a mile in each direction, but eventually, as the fire's fuel had been depleted or natural firebreaks had impeded its progress, the jungle of red again began to assert its hold over the land. A quarter mile farther on and the road was so choked with growth that they could no longer push ahead, and had to zig east until they located a smaller path to continue along.

The few buildings on the side of the road were all but covered in the same latticework of creepers that had given her and the rest of the crew such trouble back at the base. The buildings were only recognizable as being man-made by the vague outline of their shape beneath the plants. It wasn't hard to imagine, given another month or two, as the vegetation grew up through the spaces between the offices and apartments, that there would be little identifiable proof of humanity's existence left to see here.

Some of the homes and offices that were still visible suffered from very obvious storm damage. Walls had been toppled or ripped away, roofs perforated by flying debris, windows shattered, and retaining walls crumbled to little more than boulders of concrete. One entire building had apparently been ripped from its foundation, leaving nothing but the bare concrete slab, broken rebar, and, most curiously, a single staircase that rose into the air, climbing past floors that no longer existed.

The travelers cut across the surface of the exposed pad, stepping over the vines and creepers that laced it like a carpet. Something glittered in the early morning sun, flashing baubles of light into Emily's eyes like pieces of broken glass.

"What *is* that?" she asked MacAlister, pointing to the side of a nearby building where the scintillation originated from. MacAlister looked in the direction she was pointing and caught the same twinkling light.

"I have no idea," he said as he diverted the team toward the source, a two-story building just a few yards away.

"What on earth . . . ?" he exclaimed as they approached the wall. It was covered in a sapphire-like crust that spread out for about eight feet along the side of the wall and another four or five up toward the second floor. Bathed in the light of the slowly ascending sun, whatever this growth was made of reflected the sunlight beautifully, refracting it into scintillating colors that lit the surrounding area.

"It's beautiful! Like mother-of-pearl," one of the sailors said, reaching out a hand to touch the thin membrane of jewel-like growth. The kid let out a sudden yelp of pain as MacAlister slapped his hand before he could touch it.

"Jesus, kid. Didn't your mother ever teach you to look and not touch?" He gave the chastened sailor a hard stare. "You have no idea what that is, so keep your hands in your pockets from now on, okay?"

Emily gave the sailor a sympathetic smile. "Best to take that advice to heart," she said. "We have no clue what's dangerous out here and what's not. It's better to assume everything is going to try to kill you, until we know for certain." Then added, "Because, it probably is."

"Yes, Miss," the sailor said, his face still flushed red with embarrassment.

"Oh please, please, please, stop calling me 'Miss.' You're making me feel like I'm an eighty-year-old schoolmarm. My name is Emily."

"Yes . . . Emily," the kid said, some of the embarrassment forgotten.

"Come on you lot," MacAlister insisted as he continued to watch the growth. "Time's a-wastin' and we need to get out of here."

■ ■ ■

They found a road that was almost entirely clear of growth and followed it as it curved slowly downhill toward the bay. Until now, the only sound had been the crunch of the group's feet as they walked and Thor's panting breath, but now the roar of the surf crashing against the shore filled Emily's mind with scenes from her childhood of trips with her parents to the seaside. The only thing missing was the screech of seagulls and the smell of cotton candy and funnel cake . . . and the background noise of humanity at play, of course.

"Bloody Hell!" The exclamation came from one of the young sailors—his name was James but his shipmates called him Rusty, due to his red hair. As they rounded the bend in the road the vegetation on either side of them finally fell away, giving the group an unhindered view out over San Diego Bay out past Coronado Island. The fog that had covered the horizon since their arrival at Point Loma had finally burned off, revealing a clear view into the distance and what should have been the city of San Diego, three miles or so across the bay.

Instead of the city all they could see was red jungle stretching out along the curve of the distant coast. The red vegetation obscured everything. It was as though the mainland had been somehow transported back in time to the Jurassic period, all trace of humanity's influence in the area was gone, covered under a blanket of red and purple.

Well, *almost* all signs.

The only clue that there had once been a major city located just across the water was the prow of a sunken ship—maybe an oil tanker or maybe it had been a naval vessel—that jutted out from the water near the shore. Its deck dripped with red fronds.

MacAlister took a pair of binoculars from his pack and raised them to his eyes. He scanned back and forth along the distant shore then offered them to Emily.

"Tell me what you see."

Coronado Island sat a half mile or so offshore of San Diego, parallel with Point Loma, giving the bay between them a distinct horseshoe shape. Point Loma was an extension of the mainland, a long spit of land that looped down toward the southwest tip of Coronado Island. Of course, it wasn't *really* an island, just a pork-chop-shaped landmass with a skinny sandbar that extended off its southern tip until it reconnected with the mainland again. She swept the binoculars over the island past the airport and several aircraft, including a couple of military helicopters that still sat on the relatively unmolested runway, then across the water to the mainland beyond. There was nothing but a wall of tangled red vines and alien trees. The trees were huge, but nowhere near as large as the ones she had seen during her journey north. These ones seemed more organic; in fact, if it wasn't for their dark-red hue and jutting branches they could easily have originated from some distant corner here on Earth.

With the aid of the powerful binoculars Emily could make out several almost intact jetties still visible along the San Diego coastline, but, other than the wreck in the bay, there was no sign of any of the yachts, boats, or ships that would have surely been moored there. They must have been washed away by the huge storms that had swept over almost every mile of the planet. Several huge buildings, hotels or office blocks she assumed, it was impossible to say now, rose up above the trees. They too were wrapped in the ubiquitous red vines, but Emily could see the occasional glint of sunlight reflecting off windows buried deep within the alien vegetation that draped every side.

She moved the binoculars first left then right along the coast, then up and beyond where the city should have been, focusing the binoculars to their highest magnification. She could see no roads, no buildings, nothing! All had succumbed to the creeping, insidious plant life that had taken root.

"It's gone," she said, finally answering MacAlister's question. "It's all gone." San Diego had been completely swallowed up beneath the sea of red.

Emily pulled the binoculars' focus back to the shoreline and moved north again, but as she passed the red monoliths of hidden hotels she stopped, her eye caught by blurred movement. Several indistinct blobs of light had risen up from what would have been the roof of one of the shrouded tall buildings and now swirled in the air above it.

She adjusted the focus until the blobs became sharper, more distinct. Whatever they were, they moved fast and Emily had to move the binoculars around for a few seconds until she found the darting shapes once more.

Birds?

She followed one shape as it sped directly upward before swooping down toward one of the towering trees. Pulling up at the last second, it settled onto an outstretched branch near the top of the foliage. It was too far away, too indistinct to make out, so Emily zoomed in on the creature.

"What is that?" she said, as the blurry image finally swam into view.

It was beautiful. It was massive. It was *no* bird.

It was also difficult to make out exact details at this distance but she could see a slender body, covered not in feathers but what might have been short fur. A curving neck, like that of a swan, terminated in a small head with two forward-facing eyes and a narrow mouth that was more of a snout than a beak. It had binocular vision! That was something new. Everything she had seen created by the rain and dust had been very different from anything that had come from Earth, monstrous in appearance. This new creature flew using huge whisper-thin wings, four of them: two large petal-shaped wings that sat close to where its shoulders would be, then two smaller ones budding out from the rear of its abdomen. The creature sat upright, its two lower limbs grasping onto the upper branches of the tree, while it occasionally reached into the foliage surrounding it and plucked something from it with a pair of long, dainty arms. It pulled whatever it had found to its mouth and began to chew.

Occasionally, one of the creature's wings would beat, blurring into invisibility as it stabilized itself on its perch. As she watched, the first creature was joined by a second that landed next to it. The first looked up, seemingly unperturbed by the new arrival. It dipped its head toward it in a sinuous up-down motion. The second creature did the same and then it too began plucking food from the tree. It almost seemed like some kind of greeting. Maybe they were a pair? Mates, perhaps?

"Beautiful," Emily said aloud.

"What do you see?" asked Rusty.

"Here, take a look for your—"

She was about to hand the binoculars back to MacAlister when there was a disturbance in the trees close to the creatures she was watching. One of the giant birds sprang into the air, fluttering away to safety, but the other was not so lucky.

A huge tentacle, at least eighty or more feet long with rose-thorn-shaped barbs running along each edge of it, appeared from somewhere deep within the jungle. It arched backward until it resembled the top half of a question mark, then whipped forward and up.

It caught the startled creature around the midsection and immediately flicked backward with such force that it snapped the fragile body in half. Although the scene was playing out close to two miles away, Emily grimaced as her mind imagined the snapping sound the creature's body must have made as it folded in on itself. The tentacle rewound down into the trees, dragging the creature with it until it disappeared within.

A single torn wing fluttered down into the trees like an autumn leaf.

"Come on," Emily said as she handed the binoculars back to MacAlister. "Get me the hell out of here."

■ ■ ■

Emily and her companions continued their trek for another half mile before stopping again, confronted by yet another barrier of vegetation that had overgrown the path almost all the way down to the bay. It effectively blocked any further movement north, except along a narrow strip of beach at the waterfront.

As they walked, Emily told the others what she had seen earlier, how the flying creature had been plucked from the tree in the blink of an eye by the tentacle that must have belonged to some far larger creature, hidden within the depths of jungle that had overtaken San Diego.

"We keep a healthy distance from the edge of the jungle from now on," MacAlister ordered. "At least twenty meters."

Unwilling to risk moving forward so close to the jungle's edge, the group reversed direction and retraced their path back toward Point Loma, but when they reached the edge of the fire-cleared area they cut diagonally across the ash-covered ground, heading toward the western side of the peninsula. They were stopped again by another wall of jungle left untouched by the fire. They switched directions again, heading south, following the line of the jungle at a healthy distance until, eventually, after several miles of walking, the jungle slowly began to thin before it finally faded to nothing more than a few small bushes and saplings.

Ahead of them Emily saw a hill and they climbed the hundred feet or so to the top. From its summit the group had an unhindered view of everything south of their position all the way to land's end. Off to the east, across the plain of ash, Emily could see Point Loma, and beyond that, anchored in the bay, was the black silhouette of the *HMS Vengeance*. But south of the base, apart from the ubiquitous coating of red lichen that covered every inch of the ground around them that had not been consumed by the fire, there was little incursion of the larger alien plant life. Sure, they could see sporadic clumps of red vegetation sprouting seemingly at random from the landscape, or the occasional small cluster of half-grown reeds reaching skyward, but for the most part, the southern end of the island remained clear.

"If we keep this area free of that alien crap, we have a nice defensible section of land. We should be able to see any of those *things* that got Collins before they get anywhere near us," said MacAlister as he traced the outline of the clear land with an outstretched hand. "Of course it means we're going to be doing most of our traveling by boat and foot. But it's a start. We got lucky."

Emily took the opportunity to take a long swig from her water bottle and pour some into a plastic bowl she had brought with her for Thor. "Just so long as there's nothing nasty in the ocean either," she said.

"Always the optimist, I see," said MacAlister, giving her a sardonic raised-eyebrow smirk.

Emily smiled too. "Better a living, breathing pessimist than a dead optimist."

"You do have a point. Ready?"

They followed the coastline south for a few more miles but as their hilltop reconnoiter had predicted, there were few signs of the jungle expanding any farther. By the time they reached the nub of land where it met the ocean, Emily could feel the ache in her underused calves and she gave a silent cheer when MacAlister cut back inland and began the trek back to the camp. By the time the group stepped through the security gate and into the compound, Emily's feet and thighs had begun to complain too.

■ ■ ■

Commander Mulligan watched the world spin by beneath her. The ISS was over land now. South America, maybe Bolivia, she guessed. It was hard to be really certain anymore. In the week or so since the storm had ended, every mark of man on the planet had been overrun by the red vegetation as it rapidly spread out in thick clumps from all of the major population areas, much as the storms had done. Now there were few visible signs left, other than the occasional stretch of highway or coastal town, to even hint that this planet had once been home to almost seven billion people and cultures that had existed and molded the planet to their will for thousands of years.

"I'm sure I don't have to tell you that the planet has changed on a radical scale but what I thought you might appreciate is some good news for a change," Mulligan said.

"We're all ears," said a new voice. The commander smiled again when she recognized her friend's voice.

"Emily. It's good to hear your voice."

"Same here," said Emily.

"So, in the time we've been incommunicado we have been busy monitoring the weather patterns since the storm and you'll be happy to know that, as far as we can tell, everything seems to be pretty much returning to how it was, before—"

Emily finished the sentence for her, "—everything went to hell in a handbasket?"

"Precisely. So the good news is, the weather patterns appear to have only marginally shifted away from what the typical trend was pre–red rain, and the consensus up here is that we think you will probably see a return to 'normal,' whatever that might be, over the next few weeks to months. The good news is, that means we'll be able to attempt the Soyuz reentry within the next couple days to a week; we just need to be one-hundred-percent sure of the weather conditions before we leave."

"Well that's certainly good to know," said Emily, smiling. She was looking forward to finally putting a face to the angel that had helped guide her to safety.

"Unfortunately, there's bad news too," said the commander, "but it's news I think you already are aware of. The spread of the red vegetation, it seems to have encroached on almost every continent and island, other than the poles. It's as though . . ."

Mulligan's words trailed off suddenly as a hint of movement on the edge of her peripheral vision caught her attention out beyond the observation port of the ISS. She repositioned herself just in time to catch a bright flash of light against the blackness of space.

"Stand by a second, Emily. There's something—"

Another brilliant flash appeared in the distance, close to the curve of the Earth's horizon. It was followed in rapid succession by two more blinding bursts as, one after another, dazzlingly bright globes of white light punctured the blackness of space. They materialized just outside the Earth's atmosphere, bloomed momentarily, and then streaked down toward the surface. In the space of a few seconds, Commander Mulligan counted five . . . no . . . seven blindingly bright flares.

"My God," said Mulligan, the intensity of the light so great her eyes reflexively shut as she turned her head away from the window. "Emily, there's something happening outside the station," she said urgently. "I can see objects, huge spheres of incredibly bright white light; they're appearing outside the planet's atmosphere and streaking toward the earth." The commander opened her eyes fully again, the afterimage of the lights still flaring in her vision. She could see the tails of the orbs as they dropped through the atmosphere toward Earth.

"There are multiple objects," Mulligan continued, breathless with excitement. "Each one appears to be heading to a different continent, I could be wrong though. They're spread out so widely I—"

"Commander? Are you alright?" Emily interrupted. The other

occupants of the makeshift radio room had seemed to freeze in place as they listened to Mulligan repeat what she was seeing through the observation window.

"Yes, I'm fine. Emily, I think I know what these are, Emily. My God, they are so incredibly beautiful. It's as though—"

Commander Mulligan's words were cut short as another of the immense orbs, dwarfing the space station and burning with an intensity that blotted out the sun, materialized just several hundred feet off the station's dark side.

"Oh no," said Commander Mulligan and closed her eyes.

■ ■ ■

Far below, on the narrow outcropping of land they had claimed for their own, Emily and the others waited for the radio signal to reestablish with the ISS.

"Commander? Can you hear me?" Emily asked for the third time in as many minutes. Her reply was a static hiss. Through the window she could see that night had finally chased the sun from the sky, and darkness now cloaked everything that lay beyond the illumination of the camp's security lights.

"They probably just moved out of radio range," said Parsons.

"They only just got *in* range," MacAlister reminded him.

Emily felt a pang of nervousness tingling in the pit of her stomach as her mind ran back over the final words of the conversation before the connection was severed so abruptly. "She said something about seeing some kind of objects, spheres of light?"

"Aurora Borealis, perhaps?" suggested Captain Constantine.

"Maybe," said Emily without conviction. "Surely they would have seen the northern lights on an almost daily basis? I doubt that would have stopped her mid-conversation."

"Maybe it's just a coincidence," Parsons added.

The headphones Jacob had placed on top of the table next to the radio moved slightly, and for a second, Emily thought that the sound had simply switched back to them, but a low-frequency, throbbing vibration passed through the soles of her feet as she started to pick them up, and she stopped mid-reach. The vibration was faint at first, like the gentle purr of an engine, but the sound grew increasingly louder. The headphones rattled away from her reaching fingers and then rolled off the edge of the table, tumbling to the floor. The glass panes of the window thrummed and vibrated, rattling in their fixtures . . . then the entire room began to vibrate like the cone of a huge speaker.

"Earthquake!" someone yelled.

"Christ!"

Emily looked at the other confused and frightened faces staring back at her as she grabbed the table for support. From elsewhere in the building she could hear yells and curses as the thrumming grew toward a bone-rattling crescendo.

A pane shattered in the window, spraying the room with shards of broken glass, and suddenly the sound became even louder.

This was no earthquake.

"Outside," Emily yelled as the whole building began to shake. She bolted for the door as Thor raced ahead of her, closely followed by the men. But instead of running for the exit, Emily sprinted for the stairwell, pounded up the stairs, and rushed out onto the roof.

She didn't know whether it was the cold California night air or the strange mix of fear and excitement that raised the gooseflesh over her skin, she was more concerned with the deep rumbling filling the air, like approaching thunder, bouncing from one side of the night-black hemisphere to the other.

"What the hell is it?" MacAlister yelled, struggling to be heard over the deafening roar.

"It's no earthquake, that's for sure," Parsons yelled back, twisting on his toes as he tried to identify the source of the sound.

The night was suddenly rent open by a bright flash of light that appeared to the southwest, far out to sea and high up in the atmosphere. It was a bright white ball of light, already half the size of the moon and growing rapidly as it sped toward them.

Instinctively, everyone threw themselves down flat onto the roof as it roared over their heads, their eyes drawn to the sky in pure fascination, even as their instincts told them they were all about to die.

The fiery orb streaked across the sky, a bright tail of flashing embers that flamed momentarily then disappeared trailing behind it. The object began to grow smaller and smaller as it thundered north, then dipped suddenly, its trajectory no longer a natural parabolic curve but a definitive course alteration, as though it had been suddenly swatted from the air by some unseen hand. It plunged rapidly toward some distant point far north of Point Loma and then hit the ground with a bright flash that almost instantly dissipated into the blackness.

There was no sound, no thunderous crash of impact or massive explosion. No pressure wave or fireball. Just the ghostly afterimage of the object burnt onto Emily's disbelieving eyes.

They lay unmoving for what seemed like an eternity, so still that only the sound of their breathing proved they were all still alive.

Minutes passed, then a faint but audible rumble found its way to them; nothing like the one that had heralded the arrival of whatever that thing had been but almost certainly the residual shockwave of its fall to Earth.

Emily was the first to raise herself to her feet. She looked back in the direction of the piece of sky where the object had appeared. In the inky blackness, tumbling and falling in a slow arc and chased by its own blazing tail of burning debris, Emily could see something else falling toward the Earth.

When she was a child, she had witnessed the destruction of the *Columbia* that fateful day that damaged heat shielding had caused the space shuttle to disintegrate on reentry.

"Oh no," she said, her hand flying to her mouth as she immediately made the connection with what she was seeing now; she was witnessing the fiery death of the ISS as it and its crew made their final return to Earth.

CHAPTER 16

At daybreak the following morning, the glowing remains of the ISS could still be seen scorching slowly through the atmosphere as, piece by piece, it was inexorably drawn back to the planet it had originated from, tiny pieces of man's last foothold in the stars burning brightly in the upper atmosphere like meteors.

And not just metal and plastic, Emily thought, as she watched another flare of light burn up in the atmosphere above Point Loma. Her neck was beginning to ache from staring at such an acute angle for so long. She let out a long sigh, cracked her neck left and then right, and began making her way toward the dining area where everyone else was already gathered waiting for news.

While the majority of the crew of the *Vengeance* had not even heard the voice of Commander Mulligan, let alone spoken with her, they all *knew* of her. Her loss, along with the destruction of the space station, was a major blow to the morale of the survivors. And, judging by the sullen and disconsolate looks on the faces of the sailors as they gathered for their morning meal, the news had hit home extremely hard. While the station had circled overhead, there had been a sense of safety, of almost God-like protection afforded by their constant vigilance. Now, with the survivors' vision forever tethered to the ground, there was a distinct sense of loneliness within the group.

"Do you think it might not be them?" Rhiannon said, picking at her food, her eyes still red from the tears she had shed when told that the commander had most likely perished. "Maybe it's something else, one of the satellites . . . maybe?"

Parsons squeezed the girl's shoulder, "Maybe, *cariad*," he said. "Who knows, eh?" But even Parsons's attention could not lift Rhiannon's spirits from this latest tragedy.

"We have to figure out what we are going to do about the new arrival," said Emily, switching the conversation to the phenomenon that they had all seen in the previous night's sky. "Commander Mulligan said that she saw multiple objects outside the atmosphere, but we only saw the one. That means whatever they are, they were heading to different locations, and they were dispersed far enough apart that we only saw the one."

MacAlister looked up from his breakfast of scrambled eggs (powdered, but not bad considering). "We checked the sub's tracking radar this morning. The telemetry data we pulled gives us a good estimate of where that thing came down last night."

Emily continued to chew her own food, and raised her eyebrows in lieu of the obvious question.

"It came down in Nevada, right around Las Vegas. Give or take fifty miles."

"Always wanted to go to Vegas. Anybody up for some blackjack?" Parsons quipped.

Emily swallowed her food. "Do we even know what the hell that thing was? I mean it looked like a meteor but then it altered course so obviously . . ." She left the sentence unfinished, testing the response of the others.

"From what I saw of it," said Jacob, "and from what everyone else described, as well as Commander Mulligan's initial response, I think it's patently obvious what that thing was, don't you?"

Parsons decided to fill in the blanks. "You're going to tell us that it was some kind of spaceship? Right? That there are little green men onboard that thing that have come to suck our brains out through our noses? Am I close?" Parsons's words were dripping with sarcasm, but beneath the disdain, Emily could sense the rough rope of fear intertwined with every word.

"No," said Jacob slowly and emphatically. "Not little green men." He continued to speak quietly, refusing to rise to the bait, an honestly jovial smile creasing the corner of his lips. "But it most definitely signifies the arrival of something new. From what Commander Mulligan managed to tell us before the station was destroyed, it sounds as if my theory was correct: What she saw, what we all saw in the sky last night, was maybe a scouting party for the intelligence that created the red rain. Perhaps they are even the colonists themselves."

Rhiannon looked aghast.

"It's alright," said Parsons, giving Jacob a hard stare that the scientist did not seem to notice.

Jacob appeared to have recovered a lot of the patience Emily had become familiar with during her trip across the United States, because now he used the same voice, the same quiet tone of knowledge and assuredness that she had heard when she had only been able to speak to him via her sat-phone.

Jacob continued, "My personal belief is that this is a vanguard. It would make sense that they would send a small force ahead to ensure the transformation of the planet has gone according to plan.

That is, of course, assuming that these were even ships and not something entirely different. That would be my initial assessment."

"Couldn't this just be a coincidence?" MacAlister asked. "Commander Mulligan would have been under an enormous amount of stress, what with her predicament and all. Couldn't she have made a simple mistake and misidentified a meteor shower? I mean it's possible, right?"

"We can speculate about what it *might* be forever, but the only way to be absolutely certain is to go and take a look at the ship, meteor, whatever," said Emily. She was surprised by the look of acceptance to her suggestion that she received. She had expected a straight-up no-way-José response; instead she was met with a steady gaze from each of those sitting next to her.

"I'd like a crack at these bastards," said MacAlister. "At the very least, I want to see what kind of a being is able to bring an entire planet to its knees in a day."

"So, let me get this straight: You're suggesting that we travel to Nevada, track down where this thing landed, and try and make contact with them?" said Parsons.

"Pretty much," said Emily.

"Okay, well, count me in."

MacAlister glanced across the table at Captain Constantine, who had remained out of the conversation.

"It's your call, skipper."

"If Jacob is correct, and what we witnessed last night *is* some kind of an alien craft, then we need to know how much of a danger they pose," Constantine said after a few moments' thought. "We need to assess their capabilities and whether they pose any imminent threat to our safety here. If they do, then we will have to reassess our decision to stay here and find someplace else, somewhere safer to settle as far away from them as possible. I think it's worth the risk to send a reconnaissance party out there and see what we're facing. Mr. Parsons, do we still have that drone onboard?"

"Yes, sir," said Parsons. "She's stowed away and ready to roll out."

"Drone?" asked Emily.

"We have a short-range aerial drone that we use for observation and reconnaissance work. It's basically a big radio-controlled aircraft with a camera attachment that can relay live images back to a remote video unit," the captain explained. "So, as long as you can get within three miles of the landing site, you can send the drone in and stay at a safe distance. If we decide to do this, I don't want to unnecessarily risk lives. We have no idea what kind of a wasp's nest we might be sticking our fist into."

"How we get there is the next question," MacAlister said. "From what we saw on our little walkabout yesterday, there's no way we're going to make the trip overland, there's just too much growth. We could skirt back north along the coast, maybe see if there's any kind of break in the jungle. It's going to be a hell of a trek, though. Probably looking at weeks' worth of walking, maybe longer if we don't have a clear shot to Vegas and have to lug the drone along too."

"Can anyone fly a helicopter?" Emily asked, half-jokingly. "I think I saw two across the bay."

The crew all turned their heads to look at MacAlister.

"I may have some experience in that department," he said, smiling. "Actually, I have about two hundred hours of flight time. So . . ."

Emily smiled back at him. "Well, you're just a jack-of-all-trades, aren't you?"

MacAlister's smile grew into a broad grin. "Oh, I've been called worse . . . much, much worse."

CHAPTER 17

Emily climbed into the dinghy and settled down onto the wooden seat next to MacAlister. There were five more onboard with her, including the boat's pilot who stood at the raised steering column toward the back of the boat. Emily recognized Rusty from their first exploratory trip into the wasteland created by the fire. She smiled warmly at the young sailor.

"Morning, Miss," he said. "Thor not with you today?"

What Emily wanted to say was: "Call me 'Miss' again and I'll knock you on your ass." *God! She was barely ten years older than him.* She had not had the best night's sleep, and it was showing in her mood. What she actually said was: "No, no Thor today." She had left the dog with Rhiannon. She was going to be travelling with a bunch of edgy armed men, and she did not want to take the risk that her dog would be shot by some nervous, trigger-happy sailor.

With everyone fastened in, the boat accelerated quickly away from land and headed out toward Coronado Island, east of Point Loma.

The trip across the inlet was rough, the water choppy with rolling swells that rocked the boat up and down. Emily felt her stomach roll with every unexpected rise and fall of the boat, and after a few minutes she began to feel a little queasy.

The rough water didn't seem to bother the sailors who all seemed relaxed, almost nonchalant.

"Just fix your eyes on one of the rivets," MacAlister said, his voice struggling to be heard over the roar of the engine and whoosh of spray as the boat cut through the waves. "It'll help with the nausea."

She took his advice, fixing her gaze on the head of a rivet bolted into the bottom of the boat. By the time she realized it was just a clever distraction to take her mind off the trip, the boat was only a few hundred yards off the beach of Coronado Island.

MacAlister gave a quick raise of his eyebrows and smiled as she looked up from the floor.

"Clever," she said. "Thanks."

"I aim to please."

Emily wasn't sure whether that was just an innocent reply or whether he was flirting with her . . . again.

The boat's pilot began to ease off the throttle as they approached the shale beach. As the nose of the dinghy cut through the pebbles and the boat came to a shuddering halt, the sailors leaped to the shore, their weapons at the ready but not raised. For some unknown reason, the alien vegetation had not managed to take as strong a hold on this extreme western side of the island, the ground and expanse of concrete and asphalt that stretched out in all directions was free from all but the occasional plant. In the distance, Emily could see a large building, its curved roof and huge doors made it instantly recognizable as an aircraft hangar. Several other smaller buildings—offices, perhaps?—were in stationary orbit around it. The hangar was the only building that appeared to have made it through the storm more or less undamaged. But beyond the cluster of buildings was an all too familiar wall of red, bisecting the island across the middle.

Several fighter planes, or what was left of them, at least, lay broken and twisted on the concrete parkway in front of the hangar. They looked as if some cruel child had reached down and snapped their backs. The two helicopters Emily had spotted when she first landed looked as though they were still in one piece. One was obviously canted to the right, though, the left side of its bottom fuselage resting against the runway. But the other helo was still upright, riding on three wheels, its four rotor blades hanging limply like wet black hair.

MacAlister raised his binoculars to his eyes and glassed the buildings then tracked across to the helos. "That's where we need to be, lads," he said. "Let's get a move on." At his command the group began to jog cautiously toward the hangar, their weapons raised to their shoulders and sweeping the scenery as they approached the building.

The team reached the nearest building and proceeded along the western edge in single file, Emily in the middle, the sailors covering angles with their weapons.

This close Emily could see the damage to the buildings was mostly cosmetic: Large chunks of stucco had been ripped from the fascia and windows had been blown out, the broken glass crunching under their booted feet. Sheets of paper, the contents of some filing cabinet, blew through the space between the buildings before collecting like snow in a drift against the wall of the hangar.

When they came to the farthest corner of the building, MacAlister flicked a quick hand signal and the two leading sailors sprinted across the open space between buildings. "Let's go," he whispered when the men had reached the cover of the next building and the rest of the team sprinted to join them. They continued the same leapfrogging maneuver from building to building until they were as close to the two helicopters as they could get.

Emily watched MacAlister closely, his eyes scanning the buildings and the aircraft, looking for any movement, anything out of the ordinary. When he caught her watching him, he smiled, "Ready?"

She nodded.

"Let's go," he said. They dashed across the concrete to the two helos, coming to a standstill next to the fuselage of the first helicopter. It was huge, far bigger than Emily had thought it would be, but then the closest she'd ever been to a helicopter was on TV.

"It's a Black Hawk," MacAlister said, running the flat of his hand over the machine's nose. "Haven't flown one of these since Iraq."

The machine was badly damaged; a support strut for one of the two front landing wheels had snapped, tipping the Black Hawk to the ground. Two of the blades of the tail rotor, the one that would stabilize the craft in flight, had been bent, as though something heavy had hit them. The side door of the helicopter must have either been left open or blown open by the storm, because the interior was a wreck of debris and rain damage. It was useless.

"Well, I don't think this is going to be much use to us," Parsons said, patting the side of the machine like it was a dead horse. "Let's take a look at the other one."

They walked around the front of the damaged aircraft and over to the second helicopter. This one looked to be in much better condition; it was upright, the door hatches for both the passenger area and pilot's cabin were closed, and as far as Emily could tell, everything that was supposed to be there was where it should be.

"This looks promising," said Parsons as a rare smile bordering almost on adoration lit up his face. He skirted around the edge of the helicopter, checked underneath it, and then moved his attention to the twin General Electric T700 turboshaft engines sitting just below the main rotor on the roof of the Black Hawk. The smile faded from his face.

"Bastard!" he spat. "The damn things are full of that red shit. 'Scuse my French."

Emily followed the others around to the front of the helicopter to get a better look. Sure enough, the air intakes of the engines were spilling over with bunches of red veins, reed-thin stalks that had grown or were blown throughout the engine housing, clogging the intake.

"What do you need?" asked MacAlister.

"I need a metric fucking ton of weed killer, is what I need. Spray these bastards all the fucking way back to where they fucking came from." The Welshman was red in the face. "Sorry. 'Scuse my language again, Miss."

"No fucking problem," said Emily, which brought a sudden and incongruous burst of laughter from everyone on the asphalt.

Parsons reached for the handle of the hatch to the passenger area of the helo. He pulled hard and the door popped out and slid backward along the fuselage, revealing a spotless interior.

"I have to give it to you Yanks," Parsons said as he climbed first onto the lip of the bulkhead, then eased himself up into a standing position, his body inside the helo and his head outside. "You certainly know how to build a flying machine." With one hand holding the upper lip of the frame for support, he reached up with his free hand and began to rip out clumps of the red vegetation. The severed ends oozed red goo that dripped onto Parsons's chest and down the front of his tunic.

Emily felt an automatic revulsion at the sight of the red fluid, memories of the red rain flooding back into her mind. She didn't think whatever was running through the plants was anywhere near as deadly as that first fall of red rain, but still, she wouldn't want any of that stuff on her. It either didn't cross Parsons's mind or he could not have cared any less; he dug in and continued to pull handfuls of the weeds out and toss them on the ground beneath the helicopter.

"Alrighty tighty," he said after a few more clumps of red splattered on the ground. "Maybe it's not as bad as I thought it would be. It's still going to take me a couple of hours to clean this bugger out before we can even think about giving her a test drive. I'll be able to give you a better idea of where we are then."

"Anything we can do to help?" Emily asked.

"Unless you feel like keeping me company, you can make yourself scarce for a while."

Emily turned to MacAlister. "How about we check out the buildings over there? See if there's anything worth scavenging?"

"Sounds like an idea. Better than standing here and working on our suntans, at least. Rusty! You're with us. Come on lad."

The young sailor had settled himself against one of the helicopter's landing wheels. He pulled himself to his feet, grabbed his rifle, and joined MacAlister and Emily.

"Just scream if you need us," said MacAlister as they walked off toward the nearest group of buildings.

Emily saw a hand rise from behind the cowling, a single index finger extended.

Jesus, Emily thought good-heartedly, these guys should have their own damn comedy show.

■ ■ ■

The buildings near the hangar rose three stories high and looked as though they had probably been used for administrative purposes. The parking lot at the front of the building was still filled with cars, a clear indication that most of the base staff had apparently remained at their posts when the rain hit. That fact made Emily oddly proud and afraid at the same time.

The approaching jungle had not yet managed to completely consume the buildings, but it lay just a matter of a few feet away, and leafy runners had already extended out in front of the main wall of vegetation, creeping over the concrete pavements.

The entrance of the nearest building was covered in the same ropelike vines Emily had spent the first few days clearing from the buildings on Point Loma. MacAlister pulled enough of the vines away from the door to clear an entrance, then pushed the door carefully open.

"Wait here, please, Emily," he said. He was no longer the wisecracking sailor she had begun to grow so infuriatingly attached to; now he was all soldier, his rifle pulled to his shoulder as he edged his way inside the building. He swept the muzzle from left to right, checking corners and nooks and crannies, the flashlight on the barrel of his weapon illuminating even the darkest spaces. Then he disappeared around a corner and Emily felt a sudden sense of nervousness as she lost sight of him.

A few minutes later, he reappeared and walked back to the door.

"Welcome to my humble abode," he said, holding the door open and gesturing Emily and Rusty inside with a dramatic sweep of his hand. "Let's go see what we can steal."

■ ■ ■

Emily spotted large patches of the same creeping red lichen that seemed to have covered most open ground growing on the walls and floors of the building they now stood in. It wasn't as prevalent inside, but the ubiquitous red carpet seemed to be independent of the larger body of jungle vegetation that grew just feet away.

Emily had been right about the place being offices. They were standing in a reception area with a set of stairs that climbed up to the second floor, and corridors running north and south.

They moved silently through the lower corridors of the building, checking room after room. The majority of the office's windows had survived the storm intact, apart from the occasional crack or missing pane. Oddly though, the offices looked to have been picked over already. Desk drawers hung open, their contents spilled on the floor, security lockers too. The glass front of a vending machine at the end of the corridor they stood on had been smashed and emptied of its contents.

At the sight of the broken vending machine, MacAlister put a finger to his lips and then beckoned Emily and Rusty to him. "I think we may have stumbled on some survivors here," he said in a hushed voice.

"Couldn't this have happened before the storm, during the panic after the red rain?" Emily asked, her own voice barely a whisper.

MacAlister shook his head. "I don't think so. This is all too methodical. Either way, it's best if we continue with caution, okay?"

"We should get out of here," said Rusty, his voice hushed, nervous.

Emily shook her head. "No, if there's someone else alive in here we need to find them and help them. We're going to need all the warm bodies we can get." MacAlister nodded his agreement. Rusty did not seem happy with the decision but he was outranked and outvoted.

They took the stairs up to the next floor. MacAlister led the way, his weapon raised and covering the landing, Rusty followed at the rear covering their six, and Emily stayed in the center, her Mossberg in hand. On the second floor landing, they moved down the left corridor, MacAlister quietly sweeping each room as they went, while Emily and the young sailor monitored the corridor.

When they reached the third room, MacAlister hissed quietly to Emily to come and join him. She glanced in the room. The desk that had occupied it was gone and the filing cabinets and other furniture had been pushed to one end of the room to make way for three adult-size sleeping bags. An assortment of military clothing, mostly fatigues, hung from a makeshift clothes rack in one corner, and a propane stove sat on a table beneath the window. Under the table were several boxes of MREs, Meals Ready to Eat. There was also an assortment of candy, probably from the ransacked machine on the first floor.

"Looks like we definitely have company," said MacAlister.

They left the room as it was and continued moving farther down the corridor. MacAlister's flashlight played over the wall.

Something on the wall ahead of them reflected the light back at them; it glinted and scintillated like cat's eyes on a highway. MacAlister moved the light back over the wall again and Emily recognized the same beautiful sapphire-like glow of the substance she had seen when they first explored Point Loma after the fire. They had found it on the walls of one of the buildings near the harbor. While the lichen and jungle flora seemed to be almost everywhere, this oddly reflective substance seemed to prefer flat surfaces like walls. The refracted light from the beam of Mac's flashlight made a beautiful, oily mixture of color over the floor.

"Move your light over the far wall," Emily asked MacAlister.

The opposite wall was covered in the same sapphire-like crust too, and as he ran the light along the walls, they could see it extended about ten feet farther down along each surface of the wall and up onto the ceiling too. It looked almost like a cave entrance, or a grotto.

"What is it?" asked Rusty.

"I have no idea," whispered Emily, "but we saw it on some of the buildings when we were reconnoitering the day after we arrived, remember? It looks too hard to be a plant." She remembered how the alien dust had eventually become inert, turning to crystal once its job had been completed back in her apartment in Manhattan. "Maybe it's just some kind of residue left over from the storm?" she offered.

Rusty reached out a hand to touch the crust.

"Will you never learn?" MacAlister slapped his hand away before he could touch it. Rusty was living up to his name doubly so now, his face flushed almost as red as his hair. "Come on," said MacAlister, "let's check the last stretch of the rooms, then we're out of here."

They doubled back to the landing then crossed to the second corridor. The first room was clear, but in the second they found more of the sapphire growth. It was plastered over one wall and all around the window, completely covering the sill and one pane of glass. In the natural sunlight it was even more beautiful. The blue rays sparkled and painted the room like a laser show.

In the third room they found the survivors.

Emily gave a gasp of surprise and horror as she peeked her head into the room. There were three bodies lying on the floor. Actually, not bodies, they were little more than brown-stained skeletons, the flesh stripped from the bone.

The room looked like a medical-student prank, as though the three skeletons had been purposefully placed there for maximum effect. The skeletons were fully clothed, two in Marine fatigues and the third in a skirt and blouse. The white cotton of the blouse was stained with blood. A pistol and a submachine gun lay near the two deceased Marines.

MacAlister said nothing, his eyes taking in the scene with the dispassionate professionalism of a soldier who knew he was looking at something he had not been trained for.

"Fuck me!" Rusty exclaimed as he stepped into the room. "Would you look at that?" He stepped closer to the bodies, peering with morbid curiosity at the remains.

Emily noticed more of the sapphire growth on the wall around the window. The growth extended out across the floor to the foot of one of the dead Marines.

"What do you think killed them?" said Rusty as he took another step closer, dropping to one knee to get a closer look at the skeleton of the deceased woman.

A shimmer passed over the surface of the sapphire growth on the wall.

At first Emily thought it was maybe the light from MacAlister's flashlight that he had forgotten to switch off, but in the split second it took for her to process the thought she knew that she was wrong, and she knew that it was already too late.

"Rusty! Get back!" she yelled.

The sailor started to turn in her direction, a look of confusion on his face that instantly turned to horror as the sapphire growth on the wall began to break apart and cascade down the wall and flow across the floor toward him.

Beetles. Hundreds of tiny beetles, their hexagon-shaped shells, glittering like cascading jewels, swept across the floor and onto Rusty's boot then swarmed up the legs of his combat fatigues.

There was just enough time for Emily to register a multitude of tiny black feet beneath the shell of each beetle—*like a centipede*, she thought—before Rusty realized something was terribly wrong.

He looked down at his leg and screamed, a high-pitched yelp of horror, girlish in its shrillness. He swatted furiously at the bodies of the creatures as they swarmed up the material of his trousers, knocking a few off while he backpedaled away from the stream of iridescent creatures, but not nearly enough to change the direction of his fate.

They were on him in a heartbeat, skittering over his chest, climbing over his face and hands as he tried to bat them away. The beetles instantly headed toward the soft parts of the sailor's body. He managed another brief scream but that was choked off to a wet gurgle as the beetles flooded into his mouth and began burrowing down his throat and through his cheeks.

Instinctively Emily started forward to help the sailor, but she felt herself grabbed roughly around the waist and hoisted into the air as MacAlister set her down in the corridor.

"Run!" he yelled as she caught a final glimpse of Rusty, one arm outstretched, reaching toward her, his body already invisible beneath the cloud of beetles as he fell forward, knocking some of the creatures off only for them to bounce to a stop and scuttle back to their dinner.

"Run!" MacAlister yelled again, but this time Emily was already moving.

Emily and MacAlister sprinted down the corridor toward the landing, just as a second stream of the beetles flooded from the door of the room they had passed earlier. They spread like spilled water across the floor, wall, and ceiling. Emily ducked her head and leaped over them, racing toward the stairway.

"Fuck!" The sound of MacAlister's curse brought her to a skidding stop and she turned. "Don't fucking stop, run," he yelled as he swiped at several of the beetles that had managed to land on his shoulder and were now rushing toward his neck. He knocked them away and ran past her, grabbing at Emily's hand and missing.

On his back she could see more of the beetles, at least five, as they scrambled over the cloth of his combat jacket and headed toward his head. She flashed a look back over her own shoulder, the main wave of the beetles were still rushing in their direction, the sound of their tiny feet against the wall and ceiling like crushed dry leaves.

Shit!

MacAlister skidded to a stop and turned toward her. "Emily, come—" The words turned into a yell of pain as one of the beetles made it to his ear and began to chew on the lobe. His hand smacked it away, sending a spray of blood with it, as he started again in the direction of the staircase and their only chance of escape.

More scuttled over his shoulder, biting at his face and neck. He yelled in pain, cursing at the things, spinning and wheeling as he tried to fight them off and keep ahead of the others.

Emily chanced another look back just in time to skip ahead of the overflowing frontline of beetles as they gushed across the landing floor. She sprinted to catch up with MacAlister then stopped and grabbed something from the wall just as MacAlister reached the stairs, his hands covering his head as he tried to protect his eyes and throat from the tiny nipping jaws. She could see beetles on his hands, burrowing into the flesh, sending thick streams of blood over his wrists. God, if one of those managed to get to an artery, could she even hope to stem the flow?

Then MacAlister slipped, his foot missing the second step. He stumbled forward, flinging a hand out to try to steady himself, sending the bugs on his hand flying away and over the stair's handrail. He fell, tumbling and rolling down to the middle landing of the stairs where his head hit one of the metal upright supports of the handrail. He lay still.

Emily yanked the pin from the red fire extinguisher she had just pulled from the wall, and in one swift movement depressed the handle and swung around, aiming the nozzle at the beetles hell-bent on making her their next meal. It was a risk, she knew, quite possibly a stupid one, but she also knew that if she didn't slow the rush of these things there would be no way she would be able to reach MacAlister and get them both out of here alive. And there was no way on God's good green earth . . . actually, scratch *that* thought, but the sentiment remained the same: There was no fucking way she was leaving without MacAlister.

A cloud of white powder gushed from the cone of the fire extinguisher, smothering the frontline of onrushing creatures three feet deep. Whether they reacted to the fire retardant, the propellant, or some pheromone-communicated threat alert, Emily didn't know, but the effect was instantaneous. A concavity appeared in the ocean of onrushing beetles as they sprang back or tried to move around the spray.

Emily moved the nozzle back and forth across the creatures while she continued to backpedal toward the stairs, filling the corridor with the white mist of the extinguisher, pushing the beetles back the way they had come like tiny vampires facing a cross-waving Jesuit. A couple of the beetles made it through the fog and she viciously ground her heel down on each of them in turn. They made a satisfying pop as she crushed them beneath her boot.

The wave stalled, the beetles milling and climbing over each other in a confused mass of glimmering carapaces, flashes of black underbelly and furiously jiggling legs waving beneath each carapace. She had managed to buy herself and MacAlister a few precious seconds. Now she needed to make the most of it before the little bastards changed their collective hive-mind. Emily threw the almost-empty extinguisher at the disorderly mass of bugs and ran to the stairs, bouncing quickly down the steps.

When she reached MacAlister he was conscious at least and sluggishly trying to dislodge the remaining bugs crawling on his chest. He plucked them one after the other from his tunic, and smashed their twitching bodies into a gooey pulp on the step beneath his clenched fist. His face was covered in blood, but his eyes met hers as she took the steps two-by-two down to the landing. Emily leaped the final few steps and grabbed one of the bugs the soldier had missed.

"Ouch!" The thing sank its teeth into the soft flesh of her palm. "You little fuck!" She smashed her hand down onto the handrail, crushing the creature into extinction. She rubbed the goo that was left onto her pants.

"You look like shit," she said to the soldier. This elicited a burst of grumbling laughter from MacAlister. "Can you walk?" she continued, not waiting for an answer, as she slipped her hand under his armpits and helped him to his feet. He was still disoriented, swaying as his hand searched for the guardrail. She moved an arm around his back and he wordlessly threw his arm around her shoulder, allowing her to support some of his weight.

"I think I might have broken my ankle," he said matter-of-factly.

"Come on, we need to get moving," she said. The sound of a hundred thousand tiny legs, like sandpaper on wood, had begun again. She had mere moments before those things would figure out where they were and be on them.

Emily and MacAlister limped together down the last section of stairs to the ground floor, just as the beetles cascaded over the top step of the staircase and flowed toward them in a tumbling waterfall of shimmering hues of blue, and quickly began to close the gap between them.

"Shit!" she murmured under her breath and hauled MacAlister toward the exit, his injured foot dragging behind him.

Emily started screaming for help as soon as they hit the exit doors. She could see Parsons and the other sailor look up from their work on the Black Hawk's engine, their heads swiveling back and forth like disturbed prairie dogs as they tried to locate the source of her cry. She yelled again and this time she saw Parsons point in their direction, then he was down off the copter and running toward them.

"Bloody hell, girl, what happened? Where's Rusty?" he asked, panting for breath.

"Dead," she said, as Parsons and the other sailor slipped MacAlister's arm from around her and over their own shoulders. They carried the dazed soldier double-time to the cover of the helicopter. Emily kept checking behind them, watching for the beetles to suddenly appear in the doorway, but there was no sign of them. Territorial, she thought, like spiders, who preferred to hunt in very localized areas.

"What happened?" Parsons demanded.

"Later," she said, as a wave of exhaustion overtook her. "We need to get him back to the base."

By the time they reached the boat, MacAlister was fully conscious again but still unable to walk without the help of the others.

"Are you okay?" he asked Emily through dry lips.

"It's just a scratch," she said, probing the chunk of flesh that had been bitten from her palm.

The damage from the beetle's bite was not as serious as it could have been, probably because they hunted as a pack. Just as a single bee sting would not have killed the average human, a single bite from one of the creatures was not going to prove fatal. They relied on their sheer overwhelming numbers to take down their prey. *Unless the bite also conveyed some kind of toxin or poison*, her mind added. Unless it was a slow-acting one, then that seemed unlikely. Still, the thought lingered.

MacAlister let out a hiss of pain as his companions hefted him into the boat.

"I'll get his boot off," Emily said as the other sailor moved to the boat's controls and started the engine. She unlaced the boot and began to gently ease it off his foot. MacAlister's clenched teeth were enough to tell her it was painful.

"Sorry," she said, wincing as she pulled the boot away with a final tug. She stripped off the thick sock. Beneath it she could see his ankle was swollen and there was some bruising around the joint. Gently, she ran a finger over the swelling, expecting MacAlister to cry out in pain, but he didn't even wince. "No pain?" she asked.

"Just a little," he replied. "Not too bad."

"What the hell happened back there?" said Parsons.

Emily began to explain, but MacAlister interrupted when she stumbled over her words describing the fate of Rusty. "She saved my life is what she did. If it hadn't been for Emily, those little bastards would have been chowing down on the both of us, as well as Rusty."

"The little ginger bastard didn't deserve that," Parsons said somberly. "I hope he gives the fuckers food poisoning."

■ ■ ■

"I don't think the ankle is sprained, but without an X-ray, I can't be sure. There's some mild swelling, but your boot probably saved you from a severe sprain or a broken ankle," said Amar. They were in a room on the ground floor of Building One that had been designated as a makeshift medical center. Amar had been using it to treat the inevitable cuts and scrapes that the crew had incurred since landing. The majority of the *HMS Vengeance's* sick bay had been destroyed in the sub fire, so Amar had resorted to some painful probing of MacAlister's ankle. "I've given you a tetanus shot for the bite and stitched the ear and other bites. You will live . . . probably, but you'll need to keep off your feet for a few days at least. We'll keep an eye on the swelling and assess accordingly."

Emily had also received a tetanus shot for the injury to her hand. She scratched absentmindedly at the puncture wound on her butt from the injection. It itched worse than the bite.

"Will I still retain my dashing good looks and cutting wit?" MacAlister asked good-humoredly.

"Unfortunately, you will remain just as bloody ugly as you've always been, there's no cure for that. As to the cutting wit, that's been dead for far too long," Amar fired back, then added, "Rest, understood?"

MacAlister nodded. He lay on a cot, his injured foot elevated on a pile of manuals they had liberated from an unused room, an icepack wrapped around his ankle to help relieve the swelling.

"How long before he's able to walk?" Captain Constantine asked.

"He needs to keep off it for a couple of days, just to be sure. Like I said, he was lucky."

"Captain, it's nothing. I'm okay, really."

The captain gave MacAlister a long appraising stare. "I know you, Jimmy. So I'm giving you a direct order: Stay off your feet for the next few days. You'll be no good to us if you make that injury worse, do you hear me?"

Emily could see the reluctance in MacAlister's face as he nodded his acquiescence.

"Rhiannon and I will keep you company," said Emily. "You
won't be bored."

"I found some new books," said Rhiannon from the opposite
side of the cot.

MacAlister threw up both hands in mock surrender. "Alright,
I give in. I'll stay put."

"Great," said Rhiannon, "what would you like me to read to
you first?"

■ ■ ■

Jimmy MacAlister had always known he had wanted to go
to sea.

When he was growing up in Rosyth, he told Emily, he would
spend every free hour wandering around the navy yards and dock-
lands, watching the ships come and go, listening to the different
accents and languages of the sailors as they disembarked, wondering where they were coming from and where they were bound.

At nineteen, he'd joined the Royal Marines, the elite amphibi-
ous infantry branch of Britain's Royal Navy. He was a natural soldier, not because he was good at killing, but because he was good
at not getting himself or the men who inevitably fell under his
command killed. Moving up to the Special Boat Service, the Royal
Navy's Special Forces, was the next logical step in his career. He'd
failed on his first attempt, but a few years later, he tried again and
was accepted. He'd been with them ever since.

"My dad left when I was just a wee lad, I don't even remember
him," he told Emily on the second day. "And my ma died when I
was twenty-two. No brothers or sisters, so there was never any-

thing to tie me to my hometown. The place was a shithole, anyway. So, the navy became my family."

Emily was surprised at how at ease she felt around MacAlister. So much so that she found herself sharing her own past with him. Perhaps it was because he was such a willing listener (or a captive audience, she wasn't quite sure which). He was never judgmental of any of the decisions she had been forced to make. Which was why, on the third day of his recuperation, she told him about what she had done to Rhiannon's little brother, Benjamin. How he had slowly transformed. How she had taken the pillow and suffocated the boy.

Emily found herself crying at the memory. Her shoulders heaving as she sobbed quietly into her hands.

MacAlister reached out and eased her hands away from her face. "There's no shame in doing what you have to do to survive," he told her. "You chose the only option that made sense under the circumstances. You made the right choice to ensure you and Rhiannon survived."

"But he was just a boy," she whimpered.

"We've all done things we regret, Emily. We try to make the best decision we can when we're faced with a shitty choice. I would have done the same thing in your situation. This world is going to be nothing but hard choices from now on. Most people would not be able to make them, they would not be able to do what you did. *They* would die. You, you're a *survivor*, Emily. Survivors are always the ones that make the hardest choices."

Emily wiped away the tears from her eyes with the back of her hand, leaned in, and kissed MacAlister on the cheek. She began to pull back but stopped and moved in closer, kissing him lightly on the lips.

"Thank you," she said.

"Am I intruding?" came a voice from over Emily's shoulder. It was Amar, the medic.

"No," she said and forced a smile to her lips as she pulled away. "Come on in."

■ ■ ■

"Does it hurt at all?" Amar asked as MacAlister took a few tentative steps with his injured ankle, Emily on one side of him, Amar on the other, lending support.

"I'm not going to be playing soccer anytime soon, but, no, there's not too much pain."

Amar bent to check the elasticated support sock he had slipped over MacAlister's ankle. "Lift your leg up," Amar ordered. "Good, now move your foot from left to right." MacAlister did as he was ordered. "Okay, now up and down . . . good, good. Let's see if we can get the foot into your boots."

MacAlister sat down and Emily helped to ease his boots on. "Feels good, doc," he said as he cautiously stood up, shifting his weight slowly from his good foot to the injured one.

Amar looked pleased with the results. "Good," he said. "Now for God's sake, try to be more careful from now on, will you?"

CHAPTER 18

The Black Hawk looked like a huge black bug sitting on the pad, Emily thought as they walked over to it, the early morning sun already beating against her exposed skin. Today was going to be a scorcher.

While the rest of them gathered in a small cluster near the front of the helo, MacAlister walked around the outside, occasionally bending to check some protrusion or pull on some part of the fuselage. When he was satisfied, he made his way to the pilot's side of the cockpit and pulled the door open, then climbed in.

Emily could see him systematically checking gauges, flipping switches, and pushing on levers on the Black Hawk's console. Several minutes passed before he turned his attention back to the group waiting patiently outside. The gesture he made through the cockpit window was clear: Move back.

As one the group automatically backed away until they judged they were at a safe distance, well away from the rotors. MacAlister flipped a few more switches and Emily was pretty sure she saw him suck in a deep breath.

A high-pitched whine grew steadily in volume and pitch as the twin engines kicked into life. A few seconds later both the main and tail rotors began to spin, slowly at first, then faster and faster as MacAlister fed power to them, until they quickly became just a ghostly blur. A wave of hot air and dust rushed over the crowd of onlookers, kicked up by the downdraft, and Emily covered her eyes to avoid getting peppered with dirt. When she looked again, the helicopter was twenty feet off the ground and climbing. It banked to the left as its nose dipped slightly and the helo looped out over the water. It roared out across the bay, gaining height as it went, then banked left again and flew directly over Point Loma, before circling around and heading back toward Emily and the others. MacAlister circled the helo overhead one final time, then set the Black Hawk down almost exactly where it had taken off.

From the pilot's seat MacAlister turned to face Emily and the others, gave them a thumbs-up accompanied by his trademark grin.

The rotors of the Black Hawk gradually became motionless and the world grew silent again, but not before a huge cheer from the gathered onlookers ripped over the island like a thunderclap on a clear day.

■ ■ ■

MacAlister's flyby had apparently got the Point Loma survivors' attention. He had to run a gauntlet of backslaps from the rest of the crew who had assembled on the beach to welcome him back.

"Alright, alright," he called out, raising one hand in mock acceptance of the praise being heaped on him. "Don't you lot have somewhere else you should be?"

Emily found his embarrassment terribly amusing. She stifled a laugh as she followed him up the beach path, the cavalcade of congratulations being heaped on the SBS soldier showing no sign of subsiding.

"Jesus," Mac said eventually, "all I did was fly a bloody helicopter. It's not like I walked my way back here over the bloody water."

As the hoopla began to die down, Emily added a couple more *whoops* of her own for good measure, only to trigger another round of backslaps and cheers.

"Oh, thank you *very* much," Mac said, but turning to give her a fuck-you-very-much look that brought tears of laughter to her eyes.

"You . . . Are . . . Welcome . . ." she stuttered between guffaws.

Before the boat ride back to Point Loma, MacAlister had spoken with Parsons and his team. "Good work. She runs like a dream," he told them. "Fuel her up, give her another once-over and get her ready to fly again. I want to be out of here again this time tomorrow morning. That doable?"

Parsons had nodded and motioned his helpers to get to work. "You heard Sergeant MacAlister. Do you need me to hold your hands? Get to work."

As MacAlister and Emily walked back to the camp she pulled him aside.

"Mac, listen, I've been meaning to ask you something. I want to come with you when you go to Las Vegas."

"No way," he said without hesitation. "This is just an observation mission. We're getting in and getting back out again. And, no offense, Emily, but I can't risk having you along."

She tried not to take offense, to keep her tone level, but it was hard not to feel a little hurt. "Listen, I'm the only one that has any real experience with the aliens. You think those bugs were bad? Wait until you meet up with one of the things that got to Rhiannon's dad and brother. Besides, you said yourself, it's just an observation mission. I've got camera experience, I can help."

"I'm sorry Emily, really I am, but I can't." MacAlister began to walk off.

Emily reached out and grabbed his hand, pulling him to face her. "Mac. Don't you get it? I have to go, I have to see these things for myself. I'm the only living survivor of the red rain; I have to know why."

MacAlister stared back, not breaking eye contact. "It's not up to me, Emily. The skipper is the one with the final say." He paused. "I'll see what I can do," he said finally, his voice softening. He squeezed her hand and walked away.

Emily watched the rest of the crew file past her back to the base. MacAlister's impromptu flyby had obviously lifted their spirits, judging by the smiles on their faces and the lighthearted banter she caught snippets of. But she was not sure any of them really appreciated the depth of their predicament. She was convinced that what she had seen on her sojourn across the country was just the tip of the proverbial iceberg, a prelude of the world that now lay out there.

And there was no way in hell she was going to miss out on discovering it.

CHAPTER 19

Jacob intercepted Emily as she walked through the compound back toward Building One. The squeak of his wheelchair's tires on the concrete gave away his approach before she even saw him. She kept on walking, hoping it wasn't her he was looking for.

"Emily. Got a second?"

She gave a deep sigh, put on the best smile she could muster, and turned to greet him.

With the pathways between buildings cleared he now had more or less full access to all ground-level areas. In all fairness, the freedom seemed to have done him a world of good, his mood and attitude seemed to have returned, his usual sullenness replaced by an almost permanent smile. He was even starting to get a bit of a farmer's tan, thanks to the California climate.

Still, she really wasn't in the mood to talk to him right now.

But the Jacob she faced when she turned around looked as unhappy as he always had. A frown creased his forehead, pulling the skin around his eyes up until he looked like he was squinting at her.

"You saw the helicopter?" she said by way of introduction.

"Hard not to, it damn near broke every window in the compound when he flew overhead."

Emily shrugged. "Boys and their toys."

"So they are still intent on going ahead with their plan?"

"They seem to think it's a good idea. I have to agree. We need to know what we're dealing with, don't we?"

Jacob shook his head no. "Just think about it for a moment, will you? We are talking about an intelligence that can manipulate matter, turn it to its own needs. And whether that's a ship that landed or not, have you given any thought to what it means if it is?"

Emily's expression conveyed her answer. Now it was Jacob's turn to let out a long sigh of exasperation when he saw she had no idea what he was talking about.

"Not only can they manipulate matter, they can also send objects over inconceivable amounts of space. I can guarantee whatever that thing was the other night, there's no way it came from anywhere near our neck of the universe. And yet, if Commander Mulligan's observations were accurate, they appeared out of nowhere, materialized just a few miles outside of Earth's orbit. Do you have any idea how incredible that is? The kind of technology and math and intelligence it would take to send something as massive as just *one* of those things potentially over millions of light-years and have it pop out right next to a planet? Hell, don't even get me started on how they managed to gather the energy to send it."

"Of course I understand. Well, sort of. But so what? All the Brits are planning on doing is getting close enough to take a few pictures; we'll be in and out before they even know we're there."

Jacob shook his head again. "My point is," he continued, "whatever made these things, whatever intelligence sent them here, *you* are not going to creep up on them. They *are* going to know you are coming before you even do. And if they are so inclined, they will knock you out of the air with as much impunity as we swat a fly."

"I think you're worrying about this way too much. MacAlister's a careful man, he's not going to put his men at risk if he can help it," she explained, then echoed MacAlister's own words, "It's just a reconnaissance mission, anyway."

"Do you *really* want to risk disturbing that hornet's nest, Emily? Right now, we're not even on their radar." He struggled to come up with a suitable metaphor. "Look, you own an old house; you know you have bugs, spiders, roaches, right? But if they stay in the walls, out of sight, you don't think about them, you don't worry. But all it takes is one of them in your kitchen or on your bed and you're on the phone to the first pest-control company you can find."

"You're saying we're bugs?"

"I'm saying that if we stay here, keep our heads down, and don't piss them off, maybe they'll leave us alone. But if we start sending our people to them, they *are* going to notice us, and if we are an annoyance to them, they might just come here and finish what they started. I have to talk them out of this madness."

Before Emily could say another word, Jacob swiveled his chair and rolled past her toward the administrative building. The concrete path sloped at an angle and he accelerated quickly, the chair rattling every time its wheels rolled over an expansion joint in the concrete.

"Jacob, wait a second," she called after him but he ignored her, intent on achieving his goal.

A cloud moved in front of the sun, its shadow darkening the path between Emily and Jacob as he raced away from her. When the cloud passed, the light bounced off a nearby window, dazzling her eyes. In that momentary disorientation she heard the first fear-tinged yell of warning from somewhere behind her. The shooting started a second after the first cry had died. Emily instinctively ducked to the floor and turned in the direction she thought the firing was coming from. In her peripheral vision, she saw Jacob wobble in surprise, his wheelchair almost overturning as he spun it around to face the same direction she was looking.

Two *HMS Vengeance* crewmen, one a lookout perched on a rooftop, the other taking cover along the side of a wall, had their guns pointed at her and Jacob, their faces contorted in fear.

No! The gun's muzzles weren't aimed *at* her or Jacob, just in their direction. The men were yelling at her to *run, just fucking run!* But instead her eyes followed the trajectory the sailors were aiming, back over her shoulder and into the air and . . . "Oh, fuck!" she blurted out and dived to the ground just as a huge pair of talons closed around the space she had just occupied, the razor-sharp claws giving a resounding *click*, like the sound of a tripped mousetrap as they snapped around empty air.

The impression of something huge, something with diaphanous wings that hummed as they vibrated with a thrum like a million bees, cut through the air with razor-like sharpness. An oily, rainbow-stained tail flittered behind it like a cape, and Emily felt the rush of disturbed air as the creature flew not three feet over her head and soared into the sky. She rolled over on to her belly and watched as it climbed higher into the air. It reminded her of how a stunt plane at an airshow might fly; it was as big as a plane too.

It reached its zenith, and like her imaginary plane, stalled and flipped onto its back, its four wings flicking backward to form a delta shape . . . then it dived.

It rocketed toward the sailor perched on the roof. He held his position, his fully-automatic weapon flaring as he fired an entire magazine at the creature in a few short seconds, then he dived into the safety of the nearby doorway. Emily was sure the creature would slam into the concrete roof but instead, its target unreachable, its wings popped out from its side and it came to an abrupt, impossible stop that would have broken the neck of a human. Its wings became a blur as it hovered thirty feet above the roof, its long neck moving back and forth as it hung in the air, searching for another target.

It was only for a second, but when its eyes locked on hers, Emily felt the most fear she had ever experienced. There was an undeniable intelligence behind those orbs that skewered her in place, reaching some primal part of her brain and readying her for extinction.

And then the creature arrowed down toward her, streaking through the sky, chased by a hail of bullets that either missed or it was impervious to. As it neared her, the two taloned feet that had missed her the first time flicked open, readying to sink into her flesh.

Her legs would not move. She was ice, frozen to the spot.

The creature grew larger, filling her vision, then it swept over her, gone except for a rush of air from its passing that dragged her hair after it.

From behind her she heard the creature give a mighty cry that resonated around the camp. She spun around and watched as it again soared into the air before shrinking into the distance, vanishing into the jungle.

Something was clamped between its claws, she realized, something that still moved.

Emily pushed herself to her feet, brushing away gravel that had lodged in a bloody graze on her left hand. People were still yelling, their voices mingling together in confusion as others who had been inside the buildings came out and demanded to know what had just happened, the event over before most had even managed to make it to a window.

Something squeaked and rattled behind her.

Emily turned to see Jacob's wheelchair rolling slowly down the path, its rubber-coated wheels jostling and bumping over the uneven concrete before it tipped over the lip and fell on its side, exposing a bright slash of blood splashed across the wheelchair's foam seat.

And Jacob was nowhere to be seen.

■ ■ ■

There was little doubt of Jacob's fate. One of the sentries who had opened fire on the flying creature confirmed he had seen it pluck Jacob from his chair and fly off. Neither Emily nor the second sentry—he had still been hiding in the doorway when the creature struck, he said—had witnessed it happen, but Emily confirmed that she had seen the creature flying away with *something* clutched in its talons.

The logical conclusion, given the blood and Jacob's reliance on his wheelchair, was that it had taken him. The man could not have simply gotten up and walked off, after all. No one else was missing and a search of the area revealed no trace of a body, just a small amount of blood ten feet from Jacob's empty chair.

"We should organize a search party," Emily said, still stunned at how swiftly death could arrive in this new world. *But he wasn't dead, was he?* she reminded herself. She had clearly seen his arms waving as the thing had carried him away. *And that beak, just imagine what it must have done to him.*

Stop it! Her inner voice yelled at her. *Just stop it.*

"I'm sorry, Emily," Captain Constantine said. He placed a hand on her shoulder. "I just cannot risk any more men for a search party. I know he was your friend, and God knows we owe him a debt of gratitude, but the risk outweighs the probability of finding him alive. I'm sorry."

Emily stared at the hand on her arm for a moment, then nodded silently and walked back to her room.

CHAPTER 20

They postponed the Nevada sortie until the following day. No one was going anywhere until they were sure the creature that had snatched Jacob from his wheelchair wasn't coming back for seconds, MacAlister said later that day as he, Captain Constantine, and Emily met for an update to the plan.

"Sorry, Emily," MacAlister said, realizing his comment may have sounded insensitive. "I know Jacob was your friend."

That was the second time someone had called Jacob her friend today. *Jesus!* Why did it stir up such a mass of confusion inside her? Either the man had deceived her into travelling to the back-end of nowhere to save his ass, *or* he had been astute enough to figure out what was coming after the red rain, and saved *her* ass. She still did not know which of those was the truth. Maybe both? Either way, she was never going to get an answer now that Jacob was dead, but she *was* surprised at the pain she felt at his death. It was a sharp quandary of a pain that lodged itself somewhere in the space between her heart and the bottom of her throat. She may well have harbored a grudge against him, but they all undoubtedly owed him their lives to some extent. Truth was, there were so very few of them left here that losing a single person was a blow they could ill afford, and Jacob's technical expertise was going to be sorely missed in the coming days.

Her thoughts trailed away as she realized that everyone was expectantly watching her, including MacAlister, waiting for a reply.

"Ummm . . . thank you?" she eventually said.

Emily barely remembered anything else about the meeting. Something about effective ranges and combat readiness preparedness.

■ ■ ■

That night, she barely slept. It wasn't like she was restless, there was no tossing and turning, instead she just lay on her cot, her eyes wide open, staring at the ceiling through the darkness as Rhiannon and Thor slept peacefully.

Now, as she stood on the shore waiting for the boat, the early morning fog rolling in from the bay, she found herself nervously fingering the harness of her backpack. Here she was again, setting off on another journey into the unknown, but this time, it would be without the guiding voice of the man who had effectively been her compass, her lodestone. While his voice had reached out over the miles to her she had always felt as though there was someone with her, someone watching over her. Even with MacAlister and his team standing just feet from her as they checked their gear for the third or fourth time, she felt more alone than she had ever in her life.

"Shit!" she said.

"Are you okay, Miss Baxter?" the captain said from behind her. She had not heard his approach across the shale beach.

"I'm fine," she said, forcing a smile to her lips. She turned her head to face the sea and caught MacAlister looking at her. His eyes watched her with an intensiveness that was almost as unnerving, although in a pleasantly opposite way, as the nervous flutter she felt facing the unknown again.

"You know, you're in the best hands. MacAlister is one of the finest men I've ever served with. You have nothing to worry about."

"I know. I'm fine," she said again, this time more to reassure herself. "Where's the boat?"

As if her words had summoned it, the dinghy appeared from the direction of the dock and skittered across the waves toward them.

As soon as it beached, the sailors and Emily threw their kit onboard and climbed in.

"Good luck and keep your heads down, understand?" the captain said from the shoreline, the fast approaching high tide lapping around his shoes.

The sailors each snapped off a smart salute and then the boat was off again, scudding out across the bay toward the waiting helicopter on Coronado Island.

CHAPTER 21

Emily squeezed herself into the Black Hawk's copilot seat, pulled the safety harness over her shoulders, and fastened it into place.

"Thor, lay down," she ordered over her shoulder. The dog obeyed, settling down between the back of her chair and the passenger compartment behind it. While Thor had seemed at ease in every vehicle they had used during their journey to Alaska, Emily wasn't sure how he was going to react to a helicopter ride. Truth be told, she wasn't exactly sure how *she* was going to react. She had never flown in a helicopter before. That her first flight would be in a military one seemed pretty much par for the course when it came to her experience of "firsts" these days.

MacAlister appeared at her door and climbed up, his head ducked down to avoid the low ceiling. He visually checked her safety harness then gave it a sharp tug.

"Looks good," he said, smiling at her, a pair of aviator sunglasses he had found in the helo's cockpit covering his eyes but not his smile as he gave the harness a second yank. "Here, put these on," he said, reaching for a pair of headphones that hung from a cord dangling from the ceiling. When she had placed them on her head, MacAlister pulled a microphone down from the side of the headphone and positioned it just in front of her mouth.

He said something that she couldn't hear. "What did you say?" she said, lifting one headphone from her ear.

"I said they look very becoming on you. They'll allow us to communicate during the flight. Just say what you need to say and the microphone will engage automatically."

She nodded and let the headphone snap back against her ear.

MacAlister checked on the two sailors who had fastened themselves into the seats in the passenger compartment, making sure they were all secure and that everything that could move was either stowed away or tied down securely. He gave Thor a pat on the head and fired a thumbs-up at Emily as he climbed back into the cockpit, settling into the pilot's seat. He began methodically working through the engine startup routine, his hands moving over a console that looked like something out of a sci-fi movie: so many dials and levers and switches.

Mac's voice crackled over the intercom: "Okay, let's get this thing turning and burning."

A low rumble began to vibrate through Emily's seat and up her spine. The wall of the cabin began to tremble. She looked out through the side window at the collection of sailors who had accompanied them across the bay, their hands already raised to protect themselves from the whirlwind they knew was coming. The four rotor blades of the Black Hawk cast shadows against the concrete of the landing pad and she saw them slowly begin to move. Then, as the vibration began to increase to a bone-shaking rattle, the ground began to drop away and she felt her stomach lurch as the helicopter lifted from the ground and rapidly ascended. She looked down at Thor. The damn dog was asleep already, totally unfazed.

Emily swallowed rapidly as her fingers searched and found the chair's seat, curling around the metal frame. Her ears popped but gradually the weird feeling of falling up began to fade as their ascent slowed. Then the engines began to thrum faster and louder as the Black Hawk picked up speed, the nose dipped down slightly, and the helo swung around in a wide, lazy arc until it faced northeast toward their destination, Las Vegas.

Emily started as MacAlister's voice suddenly filled her head. "Lady and gentlemen, this is your captain speaking. Please remain seated for the duration of the flight. Our expected flight time is two hours and we do hope you enjoy your flight. Unfortunately, the only inflight entertainment will be my rendition of 'Danny Boy,' please do try to refrain from leaping from the aircraft while we are still airborne. Thank you for flying MacAlister Airlines."

Through the window Emily watched the concrete of the airfield slip away into the distance only to be replaced by water as they left Coronado Island and crossed the channel to the mainland. By this time the Black Hawk had already climbed to several thousand feet, and their bird's-eye view gave Emily a unique, unobscured perspective of the world beneath her. It was a world that she could no longer recognize.

Jacob had explained to her that the red storm had acted as some kind of incubator, creating just the right environment to catalyze the substances released by the trees. She understood that, for the most part, at least, but good God, the scale of it all from up here was just overwhelming.

During the time it had enclosed the world within its deadly embrace, the storm had changed *everything*. There was no green left now, it was all reds and purples and browns. Here and there were gaps in the canopy that might have been fields before the rain, but were now tangles of smaller red plants. Beyond them was the jungle, a huge alien mix of trees and vegetation and vines. Giant fronds and branches reached out to each other, tangling and intertwining together to form a cratered landscape of twisted foliage.

It was only from up here that she could truly appreciate the total and absolute finality of the planet's overthrow. While she had still been on the ground Emily could always imagine that beyond that great barrier of red there was still *somewhere* that remained normal, somewhere that was still Earth. But now, as she looked out over the uninterrupted landscape of red spreading from one horizon to the next, all hope that there was anywhere left evaporated.

"It's devastatingly beautiful, isn't it?" MacAlister's voice whispered in her ear.

"Terrifying," she said back. "It's terrifying."

"Look at that," said MacAlister. "To the west, do you see that?"

Emily adjusted her position so she could get a better view through the window. In the distance, reaching up through the jungle she could see a collection of tall buildings; at least, she could just make out the top floors of the skyscrapers. While the majority of the upper parts of the skyscrapers were clear of the invasive red plants, thick ropes of red had climbed up from the jungle below and wound their way around the walls, entwining the buildings. To Emily it looked like the skyscrapers were slowly being pulled down into the jungle below. Nothing would escape the slow, inexorable takeover. She had no doubt that, given enough time, even these last few examples of man's fragile dominion over the planet would crumble and fall beneath the weight of alien life. More of the huge birds that she had come to think of as phoenix circled and swooped around the top of the building.

"They want it entirely for themselves, don't they?" Emily said. "Not a trace of the old world, our world, left."

MacAlister nodded silently, his eyes fixed on the northern horizon.

"Why?" Emily asked, voicing a question that had bugged her since her first inkling of what was going on. "Why would anyone, any *thing*, go to such great trouble to wipe out an entire planet's life and replace it with another?"

"We'll know that in a couple of hours," said MacAlister.

Let's hope it's an answer we can all live with, Emily thought as she watched the towers disappear into the distance behind them.

■ ■ ■

The unearthly jungle rolled by beneath them as the Black Hawk thundered onward toward their destination. Occasionally, Emily would see a break in the canopy of red that exposed open ground and she would catch a glimpse of houses or buildings, their gardens overrun, their roofs punctured by the limbs of the trees and plants that grew around them.

Eventually, as they drew closer to what had once been the border between California and southern Nevada, the deep waves of lush vegetation began to fall away, replaced by waist-high reedlike plants that swayed and billowed like corn in the summer, caressed by a brisk wind.

"According to my map, that used to be the Mojave Desert down there," said MacAlister, the noise of the rotors bullying his voice over the headphones.

"Doesn't look like much of a desert now," Emily replied. Whatever it had looked like before, now it was a plain of lush, red plant life spreading out toward a quickly approaching mountain range to the north. The plants extended halfway up the sides of the mountain before petering out as they drew closer to the snowcapped peaks.

MacAlister had spotted it too. "Looks as though this new plant life has as much of an aversion to the cold as your creepy-crawlies do," he said over the intercom. They flew what seemed to Emily to be perilously close to the mountains, before turning a few degrees to the east.

"Look," said Emily. "On the right. There's a road."

A strip of six-lane highway, a few miles long, had appeared as it climbed over the mountain before dipping down again and vanishing into the waves of red as the road dropped down toward the plain below.

MacAlister said, "That should be the Fifteen down there. Means we're on the right track. Vegas shouldn't be too far away now. I hope you all remembered to bring your suntan lotion and swimsuits."

No one said anything, so MacAlister kept flying.

CHAPTER 22

Las Vegas, or, at least, what was left of the city of sin, appeared out of the morning haze like an oasis.

The miles of undulating plants that had turned the desert into a lush, red sea were again replaced by the towering trees and twisted vines of the jungle that had sprung up to claim the city. MacAlister adjusted the flight path so they would approach from the southwest, skirting around the edge of the town.

"I'm going to do a little reconnoiter," he said, "just to see what we're dealing with."

Just as they had seen over San Diego and every town they had flown past since leaving Point Loma, the alien jungle was well on its way to having claimed Las Vegas as its own. Creepers and tendrils clung to every wall, streetlight, sign, and walkway in the town, obscuring all but the uppermost parts of the tallest casinos and hotels.

The thrum of the Black Hawk's powerful rotors echoed back to the occupants of the helo, bouncing off the buildings as it cruised slowly around the westernmost edge of the Las Vegas Strip. The hotels and casinos that had made the desert town so famous had mostly disappeared beneath a cloak of scarlet. The roads and side-walks were choked with plant life, obscuring all but the occasional street sign or stoplight. Only the taller casinos and landmarks still pushed their way through the canopy of the red jungle.

It was a dead town. A city of ghosts.

Emily saw a glint of sunlight bouncing off an odd angle. It was the Luxor casino, the giant glass pyramid jutting out of the jungle like the ancient wonder it was modeled after. Farther on she spotted a huge arm thrust into the air, the forever-extinguished torch it held aloft in what seemed to Emily to be a final desperate gesture of defiance was all that was still visible of the New York–New York Statue of Liberty, drowned beneath the sea of red leaves and branches.

The Black Hawk descended and Emily felt the safety harness hold her in place as it swung sharply east. MacAlister guided the helo between two nameless hotels and headed in the direction of where the main drag would have been visible if it was not concealed beneath the fifty-foot-high wall of vegetation. He slowed their forward momentum until the Black Hawk was hovering at roof level with the nearby buildings, then slowly began to rotate the aircraft 360 degrees, as he and his passengers took in the full effect of what lay just beyond the safety of their cabin.

There was some kind of visible damage to almost every building still left standing, either as a result of the red storm or from the panic and aftermath of the first fall of red rain, Emily assumed. She could see the remains of what had once been Bally's jutting up like a broken tooth. The hotel wing of the casino had suffered some kind of traumatic accident, half of the building was missing, sheared off as if the missing part of the structure had simply slid away, lost in the jungle below. Emily could see into rooms opened up to the elements. Curtains and blankets hung from broken timbers and shattered windows, blowing crazily in the downdraft of the helicopter's rotor wash. As MacAlister continued their slow rotation, she saw an exposed wall wobble, then topple in slow motion, falling silently into the jungle canopy below. Beyond the remains of Bally's, unidentifiable because of the amount of damage it had sustained, a burned-out shell of what must have been another landmark hotel was silhouetted starkly against the blue sky, scorched beams and fire-blackened buttresses the only indication that a building had once stood at that spot. Alien trees already sprouted from the gutted skeleton of the building, twisting their vines around the remnants as they claimed the decaying remains for their own.

"Jesus! Look at that," MacAlister said in a hushed tone as he surveyed the damage. "It looks like a war zone."

"Yeah, but it looks like a war that was fought fifty years ago," Burris said from the passenger cabin.

He was right too, Emily thought. The town had a sense of abandonment to it, as though something terrible had happened, but long ago. It was as though they had stumbled across an ancient abandoned city lost to the red jungle and to time, a Machu Picchu, or perhaps, more aptly, El Dorado.

"Look on my works, ye mighty, and despair!" Emily quoted beneath her breath quietly. It was as fitting an epitaph for this town as any.

MacAlister allowed the Black Hawk to hover for a few more seconds, then dipped its nose and guided the helo along what had once been Las Vegas Boulevard.

■ ■ ■

"McCarran Airport—no relation to yours truly, to the best of my knowledge—is northeast of here," MacAlister said over the intercom as he powered the engines up enough to allow the helicopter to climb above the debris-strewn roof of a towering nearby casino. Emily found herself staring into the building's windows as the Black Hawk climbed higher, the neatly cut, almost-perfect circular holes she saw in many of the rooms' still-intact windows told her everything she needed to know about what had happened to the majority of the town's vacationing tourists and staff. "I'm going to circle us around toward the airport," MacAlister continued, "and see if we can . . . *holy shit!*" The last two words were a hiss, like gas escaping from the Scotsman's mouth, and his head spun around to face Emily as his hand jerked the joystick, wobbling the Black Hawk away from whatever it was that had taken him by surprise.

In the distance, running along the base of the sweep of a mountain range, a huge chunk of earth had seemingly been scooped out of the ground, leaving a ragged, black crater where whatever had fallen from the sky had finally come to rest. A scar, at least two miles long, extended out from behind the impact site like a dirty tail, delineating where the object had hit the ground, careening through a housing development before finally coming to rest close to the base of the mountains. All the alien vegetation along the edge of the crater had either been burned away by the approach or intentionally removed in the days since it had "landed." Whatever the reason, a swath of desert, unsullied by the red vegetation, now lay on either side of the crater and along the trench that stretched for what looked like miles out behind it.

Whatever this thing was, it had come in nose first and it had come in hard and fast. A huge wave of dirt had been pushed up on either side of the crater, demolishing houses and roads and whatever else was unlucky enough to have been in the way. The debris had formed a berm of dirt and debris around the depression's perimeter. But there was no other sign of damage to the immediate area surrounding the crash.

The thing that had passed overhead less than a week earlier had been massive and travelling at a tremendous rate of speed, and the destruction they were now looking at just did not jive with what any of them had expected to see.

Emily had read an article once on the Barringer Crater in Arizona; it was massive, around four thousand feet in diameter, and almost six hundred deep, if she remembered correctly. It had been created by a meteorite that was pretty small, around a couple of hundred feet. She would have expected to see massive devastation for miles around the crash site if what had crashed here had been a meteorite. The shock wave alone should have flattened most of the vegetation in the area, but aside from the damage along its approach and around the actual crater, the surroundings looked to be untouched, as though there had been a degree of control exerted on the landing.

Still, the crater was huge. Easily a quarter mile across and maybe a mile long. At its center, Emily could see a vague shape, something rounded, with jagged points jutting out at odd angles. It was impossible to see clearly from this distance, even with their bird's-eye view of the area.

"We need to get closer," Emily said finally.

MacAlister nodded, his eyes already scanning left and right as he maneuvered the Black Hawk higher. The ground between their location and the downed craft might just as well have been an ocean, there was no place for them to set down safely.

"What about the open ground around the crater?" Emily suggested.

"Too close," MacAlister said, shaking his head. "Besides, we don't know what's in the crater. If Jacob was right, and we have some unwelcome visitors, it stands to reason that they will have a weapon system. And I don't think it's a good idea to announce our presence just yet. We're going to have to find somewhere safe to land this thing and then we'll use the drone to get a better peek at what's in that crater."

"Don't some of these casinos have landing pads?" Emily said.

"That's what I was thinking. Let's take a look," said MacAlister as he fed power to the engines and Emily felt the helicopter begin to rise quickly until they had a better view of the roofs of the remaining still-intact structures on either side of the Vegas Strip.

The roofs of everything Emily could see either had no landing area or if there was one, it was either storm-damaged or covered in debris.

"Nothing on my side, either," said MacAlister. "Let's head downtown a wee bit." The Black Hawk banked left and started heading toward the opposite, older end of the Strip.

"Try over there," Emily said, pointing to an ugly square of a building, its architecture tasteless enough it might as well have screamed it was built during the 1970s. THE TACOMA read a faded sign running around the top of the building. The sides of the casino were covered in red creepers that had spread like engorged veins across the walls and windows, but as the helicopter flew closer, Emily spotted a raised circular dais with a large *H* printed on it in red. It looked intact and free of plant life. She tapped MacAlister on the shoulder and pointed in the pad's direction.

"Let's give it a once-over," said MacAlister, gently maneuvering the helo in the direction of the landing pad. He flew twice around the roof, inspecting the pad, looking for any obvious structural damage. "Wouldn't want to land on it and have the damn thing collapse beneath us, would we?" he informed his passengers.

He must have been satisfied because the next words out of his mouth were, "Okay, here we go," and the helo abruptly dipped toward the landing pad.

Emily found herself once again searching for something to hold on to as the Black Hawk swooped down toward the Tacoma and her stomach tried to claw its way up her throat.

"Shit! Shit! Shit!" she mumbled. She thought she heard MacAlister give a cackle of glee at her discomfort.

And then with a bump and bone-rattling shudder they were down and Emily felt her fingers slowly begin to unfasten from the chair.

"Welcome to Las Vegas, lady and gentlemen," said MacAlister, smirking beneath the mirrored lenses of his aviators. "Just stay in your seats until I tell you, please." And with that, he began flipping switches on the console to their off position.

Emily punched MacAlister hard on the arm. "Bastard," she said, with a half smile.

■ ■ ■

MacAlister cut the engines, grabbed his rifle, and leaped out onto the roof of the Tacoma, quickly followed by Reilly and Burris, their rifles raised and at the ready.

A set of rickety-looking steps led down from the landing pad onto a flat roof surrounded by a raised wall along its edges. Air vents protruded seemingly at random from the rooftop cover, their aluminum skins dully reflecting the sun. Access to the roof from the hotel was via a wardrobe-size stucco box with a large door that stood off toward the eastern side of the roof. At the center of the oblong-shaped roof sat two massive cages containing what Emily assumed must have been industrial-strength air-conditioning units or pumps of some kind. The three sailors methodically fanned out across the top of the building, checking every possible location as they maneuvered between the air vents, scrutinizing the opposite side of the roof access, the blind corners, and shadowed access passage between the two cages.

"Clear!" MacAlister yelled after he completed the scouting run across his section of rooftop.

"Clear!" the two sailors echoed back within seconds of each other, lowering their weapons, even as their eyes continued to move, checking the sky and every shadow for any sign of movement.

Emily opened her door and was immediately hit by a wave of desert heat that sucked the moisture from her throat.

"Good God, it's hot," she said to Thor as she slid open the passenger compartment door and enticed the malamute down onto the pad. They both stretched, and then quickly joined the three men in the shadow of one of the huge air-conditioning units.

"Alright," MacAlister said, "let's get this show on the road. Reilly, unload the UAV. Burris, lend a hand." Both sailors nodded and moved back to the helicopter and began to unload the case carrying the drone. They hefted it out and moved it onto the landing pad next to the helo and quickly began pulling pieces of the disassembled drone from the foam-protected interior.

"Excuse me for a minute while I make sure those two clowns don't bugger it up," MacAlister said and joined his comrades.

Emily moved to the edge of the roof. A brick security wall that came up to just above her midriff ran around the circumference of the Tacoma. She leaned over and looked down almost fifteen stories to where the pavement should have been. Below, she could see nothing but a red sea of creeping vegetation. It filled the space between the Tacoma and every other building. The alien plants had found easy purchase on the white filigree panel decoration fixed below each set of room windows on every floor. The rising tide of jungle had managed to make it to the eighth floor of the Tacoma, obscuring every level below that with its red vines and branches; skinny shoots had already begun their ascent toward the next floor.

A heat shimmer lay over the red canopy of the jungle, the light refraction giving the reaching shoots and vines on the side of the building a disconcerting illusion of movement; at least, Emily *thought* it was an illusion.

The town smelled . . . dank, wet. It was how she imagined the Amazon rainforest might smell: pungent with humidity and strange, unknown life. All that was missing to complete the picture were the wild screams of monkeys as they flung themselves from branch to branch or the shrill mating calls of birds echoing from deep within the foliage. But there was no sound other than the rustle of leaves and branches as the hot Mojave winds blew between the buildings. That and the occasional cuss word from the men on the pad as they tried to follow the instructions for assembling the UAV.

Emily was already sweating—it must be at least ninety degrees thanks to a cloudless sky and a merciless sun—but the humidity made the air feel thick and slow and Emily found herself sucking in rapid, deep breaths of the hot air. Thor was panting loudly, drool falling from his open jaws, droplets hitting the hot roof around his paws and evaporating before they could form a pool. He had positioned himself in the limited shade offered by the shadow of the security wall. This was not the kind of weather a thick-coated mutt like him was designed for and she made a mental note to make sure she gave him plenty of water while they were here.

A few minutes later MacAlister rejoined Emily at the ledge. He was wearing his combat jacket and trousers, a scrim-net scarf tied around his neck, and a camo baseball cap perched on his head. He cradled his rifle in one arm like a child; in his other hand he held a canteen of water, which he offered to her.

"No thanks," she said, tapping her own water bottle on her hip.

Mac took a long swallow of the water then wiped his lips with the back of his hand. "Well, apparently they actually do know what they're doing. The UAV should be ready to launch in a couple of minutes. Care to join us on the veranda?" He made a sweeping gesture toward the helipad.

"I'm sure I'd love to," Emily replied in her best Southern belle accent. She was rewarded by one of Mac's wry smiles as they walked back to join the two seamen.

CHAPTER 23

The UAV did not look like anything Emily had been expecting. She had thought it would resemble a model airplane or maybe a miniature version of the Black Hawk. Instead it was circular, about three feet in diameter, with four electric motor-driven propellers positioned toward the outer edge, supported by an x-frame with a larger central section that housed the battery and the essential electrical systems. It stood on three stubby legs that raised it just over a foot off the bitumen-covered rooftop. Positioned between the legs of the aircraft, fastened by a cradle fixed to the underside of the fuselage, hung a digital video camera.

"It's a quadcopter," Reilly said, as if he could sense her confusion. "Much more agile than a plane or a helicopter, more versatile too. And because the motors are electric rather than internal combustion, it's quiet as fu—. It's just really quiet. I can sneak this little bugger right up next to 'em and they won't even know it's there. The camera's fully adjustable, zooms up to times-twenty magnification. Takes video and stills and feeds it all back to this laptop controller."

Reilly tapped the cover of a modified laptop computer sitting next to the UAV. Most of the keys on the computer were the same as would be found on any regular laptop you could buy from a big-box electronics store, but to the right, where you would usually find a numeric pad, was a small joystick and a set of sliders.

"I control it with the joystick and we can see what it sees on the screen here," Reilly continued. He ran his hands over the surface of the quadcopter like it was a pet. "Beautiful," he said.

"Alright Gollum," said MacAlister, raising his eyebrows. "Why don't we get your precious up into the wild blue yonder, eh? Think you can do that? I'd like to get home as soon as possible; I could murder a cuppa."

"Yes, sir," Reilly replied, picking up the UAV. He leaped from the landing pad and positioned it on an open piece of roof. He made a few adjustments to the machine and jogged back to the laptop. He pressed a key on the laptop and Emily heard the soft purr of the UAV's engines as they sprang to life. On the screen a fish-eye view of the roof appeared from the machine's perspective.

"Alright, here we go," Reilly mumbled, his attention focused entirely on the screen and keyboard as he grasped the joystick between thumb and forefinger and gently eased it back.

The view on the screen changed in unison with the UAV as it leaped upward. It ascended about thirty feet into the air and then darted around the roof with, Emily had to admit, impressive adroitness. The image on the screen changed to an overhead view of the four humans gathered around the laptop, then changed to a blur of red as the machine sped off in the direction of the crash site.

"Batteries are good for forty minutes of flight," Reilly informed them. "Should be more than enough time to get there and back." They watched as he guided the drone back up Las Vegas Boulevard, flying just feet above the canopy. On either side the vague outlines of what had maybe once been stores were momentarily visible as the UAV sped past, behind them the rising tide of red edged up the side of the larger casinos and hotels, the high watermark increasing on a daily basis.

"It looks like we've been gone a hundred years," said Burris, his voice echoing the melancholy Emily thought they probably all had felt at some time. She was glad that she was not the only one who had noticed the aged, dilapidated look the town had taken on in such a short period of time. The parts of buildings she could see flashing by on the computer screen looked weatherworn, their fascias dulled and pitted. Bright signs that had once called out to the thousands of visitors who made their way to this Mecca of self-indulgence and excess now hung dirty and dull from their fixtures, extinguished forever, or had vanished altogether.

The scenery changed again as Reilly banked the drone a sharp left and headed out over McCarran Airport, the control tower and tailfins of landed jets poking through the canopy the only way anyone would recognize that an airport had ever been there.

Generations from now, Emily wondered, should their tiny group of humanity manage to survive and thrive and begin to explore this world again, how would this place look to them? This strange new world would be their new normal; her world, the old world that had existed for thousands of years only to disappear in the space of eight hours, would be the alien one to them. A place of legends. It would be a distant racial memory of greatness, passed down from generation to generation, pieces of reality disappearing with every new voice that carried the story onward. She, and the other survivors, would become fable.

"Look," said MacAlister, pointing a finger at the screen and simultaneously dragging Emily's thoughts back to the present. "There it is."

Sure enough, in the distance, a pixelated black form had appeared against the sea of red. The crash site, stark against the backdrop of the mountains rising up behind it.

"Can you make the approach from the south?" MacAlister asked. "I want to follow the path it took."

"Can do," Reilly said and banked the drone hard right, heading toward the trench the object had dug out of the ground when it landed/crashed.

The UAV skimmed over the canopy top. It was surprisingly uniform in appearance, as though the plants that formed the jungle grew at a constant set rate. Reilly only had to make the occasional small adjustment to the craft's flight, dodging to the left or right to avoid the occasional protruding limb or particularly large branch that rose above the canopy cover.

Gradually, the vague line of black pixels coalesced into a berm of debris, dirt, and dead plants that started just a few feet high at its southern end then gradually grew taller as the heavenly body had finally hit the earth, furrowing a *V*-shaped scar in its wake. On either side of the channel her earlier suspicions about the level of damage to the surrounding area were confirmed: Little seemed to have been affected. The housing estate it had first landed in—overrun with the alien vegetation and only discernable by the box-like shapes hidden beneath the vegetation—still stood for the most part. Some of the flora had been blackened by heat and hung limply from scorched trunks, but there really was surprisingly little in the way of heat damage considering whatever the object was had burned with such an intense ferocity, Emily noted.

"Hold it there," MacAlister ordered suddenly as the quadcopter maneuvered over the start of the channel. The picture wobbled as the UAV pulled up then stabilized again as it hovered in place. "Okay, now rotate it around through three-hundred-and-sixty degrees." The image on the screen showed an almost untouched landscape beyond the debris field kicked up by the furrow; it was barely a few feet deep at the tail end, but quickly deepened to a good thirty or so feet, by MacAlister's estimation.

"Alright, let's go see what we can find at the end of this thing. Take us up there, slow and steady."

The image on the screen began moving again as the quadcopter advanced along the gully. It was almost perfectly straight, and Emily could begin to make out a shape forming at the distant far end of the trench. It was still nothing more than a dark blob of gray-and-black pixels from this distance, but there was definitely *something* in the crater.

"It's like *Star Wars*," said Burris, watching the screen as his compatriot piloted the drone expertly between the canyon walls of debris and shifted earth.

MacAlister stared hard at the kid, an expression of bewilderment on his face. "How the hell did I wind up with such a bunch of bloody nerds on my crew?" he asked, before turning his attention away from the red-faced sailor and back to the screen.

"Slow it down," MacAlister said as the distant blob began to form into an indistinct shape. "Can you zoom in?" he asked.

"Not without stopping. I'll lose orientation really fast," Reilly answered.

"Do it," Mac said.

The quadcopter slowed to a standstill again, hovering close to the peak of the west side of the berm. Small particles of dust and debris kicked up by the four motors flew past the lens of the camera like bugs. Reilly rotated the camera using the keyboard's arrow keys until it was centered on the crater at the far end of the canyon, then pressed and held another key. The image blew up to twice then three times its size as the camera zoomed in, but the image remained just a blurry mass of black-and-gray blobs, obscured for the most part by the natural curve of the trench.

"Can't you make it any clearer?" Emily asked.

"Sorry, this is the best I can do from here. Let me take it up a bit higher." The screen wobbled and tilted like a ship in a storm as Reilly commanded the UAV to climb higher into the crystal-blue sky. The screen swayed first left then right as the drone was buffeted by a gust of wind that rustled over the sheet of red below it, then leveled again as its gyros automatically corrected for the pitch and yaw.

This new vantage point wasn't much better, the resolution of the camera simply was not high enough to capture a clear image at this range, but Emily was confident she could see *some* kind of structure in the shadows cast into the pit. Of course, it *could* just be her mind trying to make sense out of unrecognized shapes, but she didn't think so, she had a distinct sense of complexity, of mass within the blackness.

"Is that some kind of tower?" MacAlister said, pointing with a gloved finger at a dark line that rose out of the main body of black on the screen.

"Impossible to tell. It could just be an artifact of the software," Reilly said. "Sorry, sir. We have to get closer if we're going to know for certain."

MacAlister sighed, thought about it for a second, then said, "Go ahead. But only close enough that we can positively ID whatever is in that crater."

The camera zoomed out as the UAV began moving forward again, the distant image gradually becoming clearer but still remaining frustratingly indistinguishable.

"Does that look like—*Woah!*" Reilly exclaimed as something zoomed in front of the UAV, filling the lens for a moment, buffeting it enough that the image jerked violently up and to the right. "What the fuck was that?" He placed the aerial vehicle in hover mode and panned the camera first right then left, searching the surrounding area for whatever had just dived by the aircraft. Nothing but red ground and blue sky filled the screen.

"Maybe it's above it?" Emily said.

Reilly panned the camera up toward the twelve-o'clock position.

"Ahh, fuck!" said Reilly. Something was falling toward the UAV, a silhouette dropping out of the sky, using the sun to hide its approach like a World War I fighter plane.

"Move it!" yelled MacAlister, but Reilly was already ahead of him and had shifted the quadcopter to the right into a shallow dive that tilted the distant horizon until it was almost at ninety degrees to the perpendicular. Then the video feed was spinning crazily as the shape collided with the UAV. A set of jaws and a single red eye appeared briefly, the mouth lined with two rows of serrated teeth. It appeared on the screen for a second before disappearing in the twirling blur of images as the machine continued its tumble toward the ground. The final image was of a large, red branch rushing toward them, then the screen went black. Two words appeared in flashing white on the screen: SIGNAL LOST.

"Well shit!" said Mac as he stood from his crouch, picked up his rifle, and slung it across his shoulder. "Looks like we're walking from here, gentlemen."

■ ■ ■

"No way, Emily. You are staying put, right here where I know you're safe," MacAlister insisted for the umpteenth time since the drone had been knocked out of the sky.

Emily continued to ignore him as she collected her own gear.

"I can always detain you, you know?" he said. "I can have Burris here keep you under close arrest."

"Thor!" Emily commanded. The big dog was at her side in an instant, his ears up and his eyes on the three men, the tone of his mistress's voice communicating the rising tension he already sensed. "And I could always have Thor here argue the point with him." She nodded toward Burris. As if on cue, Thor's long pink tongue slipped from between his jaws and ran over the length of his muzzle as he licked his chops, a long strand of drool dripping to the floor. Emily thought she saw Burris swallow hard. He *did* throw a nervous glance in Reilly and MacAlister's direction.

"I'm going with or without your 'permission,'" she continued. "I have to know what that thing is, what kind of threat it poses to us. Jesus! It's not about my safety, or my pigheadedness. This is about our survival, the future of our species, of which there are very fucking few of us left. If we're going to be able to fight these invaders, then I *have* to know everything!"

MacAlister continued to insist Emily was going nowhere. She wasn't sure whether to be angry or flattered at MacAlister's determination that she remain behind, but it didn't really matter either way, she *was* going, he just did not realize it yet.

"Look," Emily continued, taking some of the edge and attitude out of her voice, "I've survived a trek across this country that would make Lewis and Clark think twice. I've already proved myself. You *need* me, not the other way around."

MacAlister regarded her with those cool green eyes, his face betraying nothing. "Okay," he said eventually, "but you have to keep up. We won't slow down our pace for you. We're out of here in five minutes. Be ready or stay here."

MacAlister pulled a compass from the breast pocket of his combat jacket and took a bearing on their position. "We're going to head for the trench south of the crater. That's a good five-mile hike as the crow flies, but it should get us close enough to the crater that we can get some optics on it and see what's what. Normally, I could travel five miles in an hour or so, but we have no idea what it's going to be like on the ground down there, but if Emily's prior experiences hold true for Las Vegas, then it's going to be a bit of a slog, so we'll pace ourselves, but I want to get to our rendezvous point by early afternoon. That'll give us enough time to assess the situation and still have enough of the day left for us to make it back here again. I do not want to spend a night out there. Burris! You'll be staying with the helo. Drop anything that sticks its head up here that isn't us. Am I understood?"

"Yes, sir," the young sailor replied, obviously nervous about being left alone.

"You sure you don't want to stay here?" MacAlister asked Emily as they waited at the roof access while Reilly collected his gear.

She turned to face him. "I'm sure," she said, trying to keep the offense she still felt from her voice. "Besides, if I'm not with you, who's going to rescue your Scottish ass the next time you get into trouble?"

MacAlister let out a deep guffaw of laughter. "You are so right. One question though: Who the hell are Lewis and Clark?"

She couldn't help herself and smiled back. Something passed between them right there on the roof of the hotel. She felt the energy flow between them like water, warm and comfortable. Now the only question was whether they would stay alive long enough to act on those feelings.

CHAPTER 24

Emily felt a disquieting sense of déjà vu shiver through her as she stood in the dim stairwell of the casino. Memories of her flight through her apartment complex in the first days of the end flashed through her mind. They disappeared as the beam from MacAlister's high-intensity flashlight illuminated the cramped landing as though it were day.

"Something wrong?" MacAlister asked when he saw her hesitate on the first step as Reilly handed him his backpack and he slipped it over his shoulders.

"Just some memories I'd rather forget. Nothing I can't handle," she said and shrugged her own backpack of supplies, including a digital camera rig MacAlister had supplied her, onto her shoulders. She checked her shotgun, then double-checked she still had the extra ammo she had stashed in the pockets of the light jacket she was wearing. She had more than enough to ruin any *thing's* day. Still, the echoing clang of the door to the roof swinging shut made her heart skip a beat as it echoed down the empty stairwell like the first toll of a funeral bell.

Nothing to worry about, she told herself, and took a deep breath. She had Thor, MacAlister, and Reilly with her. They should be more than capable of handling anything that tried to screw with them. And she had been through much worse all on her own, so she would be damned if she was going to lose it here. But still a vague shadow of unease hovered over her heart.

The first two levels of the stairwell were bare, unpainted concrete, the floor number of each new level stenciled in large, bright fluorescent spray-paint over the doorway leading off the stairs. It was a fair bet that no hotel guest or tourist was ever supposed to see these areas, they were probably just for the maintenance and hotel staff, hence the lack of even a coat of paint. Their boots scuffed the uncarpeted steps as they made their way cautiously downward.

A second security door, easily opened by a crash bar on their side, marked the transition from utilitarian to Vegas kitsch, the naked gray concrete walls and floors suddenly replaced with a nice, if slightly worn, carpet and peach-painted walls.

"Hold the door open," MacAlister told Reilly as he shined his flashlight through the doorway toward the opposite end of the corridor. A table with a vase full of fake flowers rested against the wall on the next landing down. MacAlister grabbed it, tipped out the plastic roses, and placed it between the doorjamb and the door to keep it open.

Even with the thick layer of carpet beneath their feet, their footfalls still echoed ominously through the stairwell as they descended through floor after floor.

The lower they got, the more cloying the air became and Emily found herself intermittently having to wipe a combination of perspiration and humidity from her forehead with the arm of her jacket before it dripped into her eyes. She could feel the slick dampness of sweat under each arm and along the small of her back.

"Where the hell is all this moisture coming from?" she whispered.

"It's like a tropical rainforest out there," said MacAlister after they had descended past the eighth floor. "Most of the moisture must be coming from . . . *hold it!*" His arm shot out to block Emily's progress.

Ahead of them, the stairwell had disappeared, leaving only a ragged lip of ripped carpet and empty black space.

"Careful," said MacAlister as Emily moved closer to the edge, shining her own puny flashlight down into the darkness. It barely penetrated.

"Let me borrow your light," she said to the Scotsman. MacAlister's more powerful flashlight illuminated a gaping hole that dropped down the remaining eight levels to the ground floor of the casino. She could see a pile of concrete, debris, and the glint of scattered and crushed slot machines far below. Thick red vines and creepers twisted through the rubble.

"What the hell would cause that kind of a collapse?" Reilly asked.

Emily swung the flashlight down to one ruined floor then the next. The concrete-and-steel rebar that jutted out from each shattered level looked odd to her. There were none of the sharp edges or points Emily would have expected to see if the collapse had been caused by stress, instead, the edges of the exposed floors below her looked worn, rounded even, as though it had been eroded away by water or friction over a significant period of time. She shined the light up the walls; there was no sign of any water damage on the walls or staining on the carpets.

"Look at that," Emily said to MacAlister, pointing to the exposed face of the level beneath them as he stepped in close to her, his hand holding onto the metal banister attached to the wall for support. "That doesn't look right to me."

MacAlister took the flashlight from Emily's hand and focused it on the next level down, slowly running the beam along the broken concrete edge of the floor and then up the supporting wall to their level. The wall was pockmarked with tiny dimples. Each dimple had some kind of powdery residue in it.

"It looks pitted," he said finally. "Almost as though it's been worn away by rain or some kind of attrition. Maybe it's a result of the storm? Internal stresses? There could have been a water pipe running along this floor that burst, maybe?"

"Maybe, but there's no sign of water damage," said Emily. "And I doubt that even if a water pipe had broken above us that it could have done this kind of damage this quickly, could it?"

MacAlister moved the light over to illuminate the wall next to where they stood. It too was dimpled and pitted. The holes were roughly circular, less than a half inch wide and about the same depth. They reminded Emily of bullet holes.

MacAlister probed one of them with a gloved finger, disturbing a fine powder the same gray color as the concrete. The wall flaked away under the pressure of his probing fingers, crumbling to dust. He pressed harder and a ragged slab of the wall a foot high and two feet wide slipped away and fell to the carpet, disintegrating and scattering like sugar across his boots when it hit the floor.

"Shit!" MacAlister spat. All three of them took an involuntary step away from the edge of the precipice. "It's like it's just crumbling away." There was nothing left of the slab of wall that had fallen other than the powder.

"Could just be a bad concrete mix," Reilly suggested. "I doubt there were many building codes when they built this place back in the sixties or seventies. Could just be cheap material."

"Whatever the reason," MacAlister continued, wiping his hand on his trousers, "there's no way we're getting across that hole. We'll have to find another way down."

The trio doubled back up to the landing on the ninth floor and slipped through the door into the main hallway. A corridor of rooms, some with the telltale sign that their occupants had transformed and escaped through the locked doors, extended out in front of them.

MacAlister shined his light down the corridor, illuminating an EXIT sign at the far end.

"Let's give that one a try," said Mac.

They began walking toward the other stairwell, their shadows leaping and dancing along the walls like gibbering demons.

"Well this brings back memories," said Emily quietly.

"Of what?" asked MacAlister.

"I'll tell you about it sometime."

"Over dinner?"

Emily laughed, "God, you're persistent. Sure, over dinner."

"So, it's a date then?"

"Don't push your lu—" Emily felt the floor move beneath her feet. For a second she thought she was okay, that it was just something loose, but then she felt the floor shift and crumble, and she fell into darkness.

■ ■ ■

Emily's head was filled with darkness and noise.

She heard Thor's panicked bark and MacAlister yell a curse. She saw his hands reaching for her as the floor beneath her crumbled beneath her weight. Her hands flailed for MacAlister's outstretched hand but all she found was empty air as she dropped through the floor and into the blackness below. She exhaled a shocked half yell of surprise, half scream as she fell, her arms and legs windmilling in a vain but gallant attempt to fly.

She landed with a jarring thump on the level below, her legs crumpling to the floor, quickly followed by her ass as she inelegantly flopped to the ground with a gusty *oomph*, the air knocked from her lungs.

For a moment, she lay there, stunned, disoriented, and shaken, spitting dust and bits of concrete from her mouth, but thankful she was still alive. She had only fallen about ten feet through the ceiling and onto the next level, her descent slowed enough by the crumbling floor to not have gained too much momentum.

Carefully, she began to feel her way around, her hands automatically moving in the darkness to where she sensed the wall should be. She felt the warmth of the wall beneath her fingers . . . then it too crumbled under the pressure of her hand and she felt the wall disintegrate. Disoriented in the darkness, she fell sideways, following her hand as it pushed through the plasterboard of the wall like it was wet paper and, she guessed, into the room that must lie beyond it. She coughed twice in rapid succession as she inhaled the dust, then hacked it up and spat onto the floor.

A pool of light from above appeared like a spotlight on the floor near her, quickly moving to illuminate her and the surroundings.

"Em, can you hear me? Are you hurt?" MacAlister yelled.

"No, I'm okay, I think," she spluttered as she spat more of the dust from her mouth and brushed remnants of the ceiling from her chest and shoulder. It had been a short, abrupt fall that could have been much, much worse. If she had dropped awkwardly or the ceiling-slash-floor had not slowed her fall, she could have easily broken an ankle or an arm, and then she would have been screwed. They would have had no other option than to return her to the helicopter and go on without her, or even abandoned the mission completely.

Slowly, she withdrew her arm from the hole it had made in the wall. In the light of Mac's flashlight she could see the same pockmarks scattered across it. Her arm brushed gently against the hole as she extracted herself, sending a cascade of fine gray dust to the floor. The drywall was completely desiccated.

Her arm now free, Emily tried to stand up, carefully monitoring herself for any injury that might be lurking beneath the rush of adrenaline that still had her heart beating like a drumline.

The floor shifted beneath her again and she froze.

"Shit!" she murmured as she felt the carpet sag. "This whole fucking place is crumbling around us," she yelled to MacAlister. His face was faintly visible next to the white flare of his flashlight, peering through the ragged hole in the ceiling. "I don't think I can move without risking another collapse." As she spoke the floor dropped another inch and she let out a squeak of fear.

"Hold on," MacAlister called down, his voice calm enough to worry her.

"Not like I can go anywhere, is it?"

MacAlister's face disappeared from the hole; it came back a few seconds later and Emily could just make out something in his hands through the dazzling light. "Here," he called out, "I'm lowering a rope down to you."

The floor shifted again beneath her as Emily reached out to take the length of Paracord as it dropped down from above. MacAlister had tied the end into a large loop with a slipknot. She was going to have to sit up to get it over her head and shoulders, and as she carefully repositioned herself, the floor buckled beneath her butt again, and Emily felt something give. Part of the floor to her right dropped away, tumbling to the level below. Emily glanced down through the newly formed hole. Illuminated by Mac's light she could see that the next floor down was also gone and maybe even the one below that. It was as though the building was dissolving, from the ground on up. If she fell now it would be at least a three-story fall . . . and that would be it. Game over.

Slowly she slipped one arm through the loop of rope, then her second arm. Only then did she let out a sigh of relief.

"Okay, I'm—" The floor beneath her gave a loud crack and she felt herself falling again. Her scream became an *Oomph!* as the loop of Paracord pulled taut around her chest and jerked her to a halt, leaving her dangling over the three-story drop. Above her she heard Thor's frantic barks echoing down to her, mixed with grunts of exertion from Mac and Reilly as they strained to hold her.

"Hold on, Em," Mac yelled, his voice echoing through the empty corridors and floors below her. "We've got you."

Emily concentrated on controlling her breathing as she swung like a plumb bob at the end of its line. *Just breathe*, she told herself. *Slow, deep breaths.* Her eyes searched the exposed space around her, looking for anything she could use to hold her weight, to give the two men above her some help.

She had come to a stop just below the ceiling that had, moments before, been the floor that had broken her fall. She saw that the floor of this corridor was almost completely disintegrated, collapsed along with thirty feet or so of wall, exposing the rooms beyond and the ones below that. A lichen-like mold covered most of the remaining walls and the ceiling above her. The mold was a dark-brownish color, covered in small tubular fronds, similar to those of a sea anemone. The fronds undulated back and forth, swaying as though driven by a breeze, and as the creaking rope swung her back and forth, she saw a piece of the remaining wall crumble and fall in a cascade of mortar and red.

"Oh, shit!" she exhaled as what she had thought was lichen suddenly and inexplicably began to inch its way in the direction of the newly exposed wound in the wall.

As the men two floors above her began to slowly raise her back up to safety, a single thought occupied Emily's mind: The destruction to the building wasn't because of bad workmanship or poor material, it was being slowly but surely being devoured by the plant life that was growing around it.

MacAlister grabbed Emily under the arms and heaved her over the lip, dragging her away from the crevasse. When he let her go they were both lying next to each other on the carpet, panting hard, almost face to face, and she peered into his eyes for a second, analyzing the emotion she saw in them.

Thor's wet tongue on her cheek broke the moment.

"I love you too," she said, then quickly added, "Thor."

MacAlister stood and held out his hand to her, hefting her to her feet.

"That's one less 'I owe you,'" he said. "But don't think this means you're getting out of dinner with me."

■ ■ ■

They edged their way carefully along the corridor toward the stairs, their backs against the wall with enough distance between them that if one fell, the others would at least have a chance to react. They might just as well have been walking across a glacier, at any time a crevasse could open up and swallow one of them . . . or all of them. But they reached the landing of the stairwell with little more than a few worrying moments brought on by sagging floors and the occasional loud crack beneath their feet. Feeling secure in the shelter of the stairwell Emily began to explain what she had seen while she was dangling so precariously from the rope.

"It makes no sense," said Reilly when she was done telling them about the strange building-eating mold she had seen while she was, quite literally this time, at the end of her rope.

"The one thing I know for certain about these aliens is that they are super-efficient, they waste *nothing*. If the lichen I saw really was eating the concrete and the drywall, then I would say it's a safe bet that it was *designed* to do just that."

They had already passed beyond the level that had been blocked on the opposite side of the building. The rest of this stairwell seemed to be intact, but as they dropped level after level they began to see pockmarks in the wall again where the lichen had begun to eat its way through.

"Well, at least it only seems interested in devouring the building rather than us. That's a refreshing change," said MacAlister. He pushed open a door onto the corridor with the barrel of his rifle and stuck his head through to check out the damage for himself.

"Jesus, that's a hell of a mess. This place isn't going to be standing for very much longer. If that shit keeps eating through the walls, it won't be long before it hits a support wall. All it's going to take is for one of those to give way and the whole thing is going to come down like a house of cards. We need to get this job done and get the hell out of here."

The stairs terminated at the ground-floor casino level next to a bank of closed elevators. Row upon row of slot machines lined the floor of the room beyond, deactivated robots standing sentry over gold that no one was ever coming back for. The only light other than their flashlights came from a set of smoked-glass doors at the opposite end of the huge gaming room and they threaded their way through the dead machines toward it.

"Would you look at that?" MacAlister said, his voice filled with awe as they approached the exit. Through the doors the group could see the red-covered floor of the alien jungle. Before them lay a primal spectrum of red hues laid bare by bright shafts of light that had managed to cut their way through the thick foliage of the forest's canopy far overhead. Everything else was blanketed by deep shadows and ominous-looking silhouettes of what Emily imagined were the huge trunks of trees. The result was a surreal palette of color that was completely disorienting to their eyes, as though they found themselves at the bottom of an ocean.

"Where's the fucking Mad Hatter?" said Reilly.

Thick roots and branches had pushed open or shattered several of the glass exits, allowing runners and vines to creep inside the entrance of the casino, across the floor, and along the walls.

"You're not kidding," said MacAlister, "but we're not here to sightsee. Are you both ready?"

Emily nodded and repositioned the shotgun.

MacAlister and Reilly readied their weapons and stepped closer to the exit, covering each other as they advanced. Emily unslung her Mossberg from her shoulder.

"Everyone remember where we parked," MacAlister quipped and gave the door handle a tug. It rattled open far enough for him to kick away the creepers winding up the pane and through the door handle and slip through, followed quickly by Reilly and Emily.

CHAPTER 25

"Jesus, why is it so quiet?" Reilly asked, his voice so low you would have thought he was in a library instead of standing on the edge of a sprawling alien world.

He was right, though; it was eerily quiet out here. What sound there was came from the rustle of the canopy a hundred or more feet above their heads and the scrape of stiff vines against the side of the Tacoma as the vibration travelled down their stems.

Emily was glad it wasn't just her that found the silence of the jungle more disturbing than the actual presence of the alien plants themselves. It was as though the three humans had walked out onto a movie set or a theatre stage, the actors and audience not yet arrived. *Or maybe we are the actors in this particular movie?* Emily thought.

The air was thick and wet, and Emily felt her lungs complain as she sucked the heavy air in. The exterior walls of the Tacoma, those that she could see through the thick tangle of vegetation that clung to its walls, were dimpled with huge pits, the bigger brothers of the holes they had seen inside. It looked as though direct exposure to the exterior environment either sped up the process of deterioration or there was a more potent agent at work out here.

The forest in Valhalla she had travelled through on her way to Alaska had been something to behold, and she had barely managed to make it out of there with her life, but it paled into insignificance compared to the space she now stood within.

Looking up, she could see the boughs of giant trees intermingling in the canopy, twisting into tight bundles and knots, then exploding outward to form a latticework of chaotic branches that blocked all but the smallest amount of light from reaching the ground. It looked so different from below than when they had flown over it in the Black Hawk. From down here, she could see the same mesh of broad, overlapping leaves that gave the roof of this forest an almost skin-like texture, but below it the intricate tangle of branches, ropelike vines, and hanging creepers ran across the surface like veins, fastened to the main lattice of thicker branches. Below that was level upon level of twisted limbs running from one corkscrew tree trunk to the next. The floor was littered with the twisted roots of trees and a thick, red carpet of lichen as well as an ever-growing layer of detritus falling from the limbs above that carpeted what had once been road and sidewalk.

Down here, it smelled even more dank, musty, and moldy, like a laundry basket full of soiled clothing.

MacAlister pulled his compass from his pocket and took another bearing. "Our target came down just on the other side of McCarran Airport. We're going to get as close as we safely can to the landing point and lay up there while we recon the area and see what we can see. Once we've got an idea of what we're dealing with, we are out of here. So, consider this a friendly reminder that this little excursion is *strictly* a recon trip. Once we get the intel back to

Point Loma we'll figure out what we intend to do next. No heroics. Am I understood?" As he spoke he adjusted the backpack he carried to a more comfortable position on his shoulders.

Emily nodded. Reilly just shrugged.

"It's a five-mile hike through this jungle. We don't know what might be waiting for us, and I don't know about you, but I sure as hell don't want to end up as lunch for some beastie. So, we keep it tight and we keep it quiet. If you see anything, I want to know about it. Do *not* engage unless I give you the go ahead. You both understand?"

They did.

"Alright, let's get a move on then. Time's a-wastin'."

MacAlister positioned himself at the front of the group and took a final bearing from his compass. Reilly dropped back behind Emily and Thor.

Then they were off, moving in the same direction the UAV had taken along the Strip.

■ ■ ■

Unlike the majority of the towns Emily had travelled through on her way to Alaska, it looked as though very few people had actually made it out of Las Vegas. The main drag was choked with vehicles, tail-to-nose lines of car after car, with the occasional truck or Metro bus thrown in for good measure. It was a total state of disarray; carnage might describe it best if it wasn't for the absence of bodies.

It was a snapshot of a moment in time, frozen along this street for eternity. It marked the end of humanity, a final chapter to a story that was now lost forever to time. Each vehicle they passed was both a tomb and a metal monument, a eulogy written in plastic and chrome and aluminum, with no one left to observe or mourn the occupants' passing.

It stood to reason, when Emily thought about it, that there would be so many cars clogging the streets considering how most of the town's residents would have been temporary, vacationers trapped here in the middle of the desert with no way to get home, the only way out by vehicle or through the airport. This city's final moments would have been of panic and absolute terror. She shuddered to think what it must have been like in the casinos as desperate vacationers sought some way to escape the catastrophe falling toward them like a tidal wave. It must have been terrible. Truly, truly terrible.

What happens in Vegas, stays in Vegas, Emily thought as she passed a light-green Ford, three perfectly round holes drilled through the windshield and side windows. Well that slogan sure as hell turned out to be truer than most people ever expected it would.

Sidewalks were all but impassable, between the vehicles that had careened into storefronts and the thick knots of roots forcing their way through splintered and cracked concrete. Add to that the accumulation of fallen debris from crumbling buildings littering the street, and the ever-present danger that part of the hotels and casinos lining either side of them might collapse on top of the travelers at any moment, and it was safer to simply walk in the road.

And anywhere there was still an exposed stretch of road or shop façade or section of sidewalk that had not yet succumbed to the creeping red invader, the same pockmarked deterioration devouring the innards of the Tacoma could be seen. The town was dissolving bit by bit around them, being picked apart like a turkey carcass dropped near a nest of ants.

Almost two miles later and Emily began to feel the effects of the almost constant up and down and over as they negotiated their way around the labyrinth of abandoned vehicles. It was like climbing rather than walking, that and the fact that she was soaked

EXTINCTION POINT: REVELATIONS

through with perspiration from the humidity. She had to resist constantly reaching to pull her clammy shirt from her chest, the jacket was already off and tied around her waist. And God! Her underarms itched like a mother too.

No conversation passed among the group. Only the occasional grunt of exertion as they negotiated yet another obstacle broke the monotonous silence.

Ahead of them, a large swath of the forest had been swept aside, crushed and broken by the collapse of an entire hotel, its name lost forever in the rubble, as it had swept down into the street like an avalanche. Emily wanted to climb over it, but MacAlister diverted them around instead.

"Can't risk the chance that there might be hidden pockets that might collapse under our feet," he said.

The deeper they moved into this jungle, the more Emily had the feeling that they were walking through a living, breathing organism rather than a simple collection of plants and trees. To her there was an almost physical sense that the twists and knots of vines and branches, and the seemingly never-ending rows of triple-trunked trees, were aware of them all as they sweated their way forward. It was a spooky yet strangely unthreatening sense of trespassing.

Eventually, MacAlister stopped ahead. "Let's take a twenty-minute breather," he said, his face wet with perspiration, his jacket, underarms, and back stained a deep black.

Reilly didn't need to be told twice; he dropped his backpack and sat down, his eyes almost instantly closed, and, if Emily wasn't mistaken, he was asleep in almost a minute.

"Does he suffer from narcolepsy or something?" Emily said, nodding at Reilly, as she joined the two men against the side of a Buick that had found its final resting place buried engine-deep into the driver's side of a Toyota Land Cruiser.

Mac gave a good-hearted laugh. "No, in the navy you learn pretty quickly to grab as much sleep as you can whenever the opportunity presents itself."

Emily emptied water into a bowl she took from her backpack and held it while Thor lapped thirstily from it, then swallowed down a couple of gulps of the lukewarm water from the canteen herself.

"This place is creepy as hell," she said when she was done, wiping away the excess water from her lips.

"Oh, I don't know," MacAlister replied. "I've seen worse. At least nobody's shooting at us."

"You've seen a lot of action?"

"I've seen my share, more than my share, maybe."

"Have you ever shot anyone?" She mentally kicked herself as soon as the words had left her lips.

MacAlister looked up at Emily. "That's kind of a personal question for someone you barely know, don't you think?"

"Sorry, can't help it, I'm a journalist. Okay, how about, has anyone ever shot you?"

MacAlister laughed, more from exasperation than mirth. "No," he said, adjusting his backpack so he could lean back against it comfortably. "But I was blown up once."

"Really?" Emily said, her voice incredulous.

"Yup, I'll tell you about it sometime. In fact, not only was I blown up, I was also technically dead for a whole eight minutes."

"No way? You're shitting me, right?"

"I am most certainly not. I saw the whole white light and everything."

Emily said nothing this time, but her expression said go on.

Mac gave another long sigh of exasperation but the smile on his face spoke otherwise. "I was involved in an operation in . . . well, let's just say, overseas. It went pear-shaped at one point and we were engaged by a much larger enemy force. While we were waiting for the helo at the extraction point, the vehicle I was taking cover behind was hit by an RPG, and I was blown up with the truck. *Boom!*" He used his hands to illustrate the blast.

When he started talking again his voice became quiet, almost wistful.

"I don't remember anything about the explosion, but I do remember standing in a very long tunnel with a white light at the opposite end. I couldn't walk but I kind of floated toward the light, there were figures in the light that I know I recognized, knew exactly who they were, but now there's just a faint memory of recognition and I have no idea who I think I saw. Anyway, while all this was going on, my mates grabbed me and brought me back. They kept me alive long enough for the helo to pick us up and get me to a field hospital in Germany. Next thing I remember, I was back home and laid up in hospital. Since then, I've tried to keep an open mind about death and what comes next."

"I would imagine that kind of an experience could change your outlook on life pretty quickly," she said gently.

"There are more things in heaven and earth, Horatio, than are dreamt of in your philosophy," MacAlister recited.

"Now you're quoting Shakespeare? There's a lot more to you than meets the eye, Mr. MacAlister."

"My guys chose not to leave me behind that day. I left them all behind the day the red rain came. I'm really not sure how I'm supposed to handle that."

A sudden wave of snoring rattled from Reilly's slack-jawed mouth, interrupting them.

"Get some rest, we'll be out of here again before you know it," MacAlister said, and closed his eyes.

CHAPTER 26

An hour's walk brought them to the edge of the destruction.

The lush red jungle stopped abruptly, and Emily and her companions found themselves standing in the devastated area near the initial impact site of the object. The tall trees and sweeping branches were suddenly replaced by a carpet of severed trunks, their ends cauterized by the intense heat of the object from space. Everything else in the area was incinerated to a gray dust that lay all around them, creating tiny smoke signals beneath Emily's feet as she and the others maneuvered through the gravestone-high stumps.

One after the other, MacAlister, Emily and Thor, then Reilly picked their way out of the forest's demarcation line and onto the scar of furrowed ground the object had created as it burned through the atmosphere and crashed into the Nevada desert. Each instinctively raised their hands to shade their eyes against the sudden transition from the gloomy interior of the red jungle to the bright luminescence of the Nevada afternoon, brutally reminded again that this was a desert.

Emily fumbled for her sunglasses, her sweat-drenched clothing already beginning to dry under the pounding sun, rubbing uncomfortably against her chafed skin.

"Damn that's bright," said MacAlister, reaching for his own sunglasses and sliding them over his eyes.

Reilly stepped up beside MacAlister and Emily, a baseball cap had magically appeared on his head along with his own sunglasses. "Jesus! Would you look at that," he said.

The images the UAV had relayed back to the computer screen on the roof of the Tacoma had not done the destruction the justice it deserved. It looked to Emily as though a giant hand had reached out of the sky and scooped out a furrow through the desert landscape, leaving a huge tidal wave of dirt and detritus frozen in the second before it crashed ashore. On this side of the trench, the berm was perhaps thirty-plus feet high, tall enough that it would be impossible to see the other side without climbing up the steep bank of debris and poof dirt. Random pieces of the old world poked out of the wall of dirt: Broken shingles lay everywhere; a sheet of plasterboard waved in the breeze halfway up the wall of dirt; a power socket, the electrical wires still trailing from it and its broken serrated edges an indicator of the violence with which it had been ripped from the home that had surrounded it.

A crushed and crumpled minivan, its door hanging limply from a single hinge, lay at the base of the dirt wall, the breeze pushing the driver's side door back and forth with an unsettling metallic squeak. Dead alien trees and plants were strewn throughout, their stems and limbs already desiccated to a mummified-skin brown by the dry heat of the desert. A street sign, ripped free of its pole and bent almost into the shape of a boomerang, lay at Emily's feet. She kicked it over and scraped off the dirt with the tip of her shoe, it read: HUMMINGBIRD.

From the fish-eye aerial view of the UAV the trench had looked to be plumb-bob straight, but standing this close to it, Emily could see there was a very slight curve to it. The deforested edge of the jungle mirrored the curve until the trench wall and forest seemed to merge into one at the horizon.

But the new jungle, insidious and indefatigable in its growth, had already started to reclaim the ground lost to the huge cut that had been slashed through it. Tufts of new growth had begun to appear like spots of blood between the remains of the first wave of dead plants, tiny red shoots pushing their bulbous heads through the gray dust. As Emily's eyes finally acclimated to the glare she spotted the pinpricks of red all over the wall of the trench, completing the image of a blood-splattered murder scene. Which was ironic really, Emily thought, as the whole planet was the largest murder scene in the universe.

"Come on," Emily said, a narrow but sharp anger at the seemingly unstoppable growth of the alien plants that had materialized from nowhere clutching at her chest. She kicked at one of the tiny shoots, splitting the bulb from the rest of the plant with a satisfying splat and gush of liquid that brought a smile to her face. She crushed the remaining shoot under the heel of her shoe.

As the two men looked on, Emily began to climb the embankment toward the summit, Thor scrambling up alongside her while MacAlister and Reilly looked wordlessly at each other, then began to climb too.

■ ■ ■

Emily used a branch protruding from the dirt wall to pull herself up the final few feet to the crest of the ridge, her breath relegated to short panting gasps of the hot, dusty air. She stopped mid-inhalation when she gazed down into the valley of the gouged-out ravine she now stood above. While the wave of dirt thrown up from the impact was all of thirty feet high on the side she had just climbed up, the drop down to the apex of the *V*-shaped ravine below was closer to one hundred or more. The brown clay strata lay bare and turned light pink by the unfaltering attention of the sun, a knife wound sliced deep into the flesh of the earth.

"Jesus!" said MacAlister as he pulled himself up next to Emily and looked over the devastated landscape. Up here the breeze, which had been barely noticeable on the ground, had turned into a gusty, hot wind that periodically pulled splattered dirt and dust over the three humans as they stood on the thin curve of ground looking down into the trench. Emily found herself spitting the crap from her tongue every time she opened her mouth to speak.

MacAlister's navigation had successfully directed them to just north of the midpoint of the trench. It stretched out toward the northwest and the hills where the object had finally come to rest, and to the southeast where the trench eventually tapered away to nothing, disappearing into the welcoming red foliage of the jungle as though it had never existed.

On the other side of the pit from where they stood, the remains of the housing division teetered precariously, the bank of dirt thrown up high enough to bury a lot of the houses on the estate, but here and there, the fleshless skeletons of homes appeared from within the dirt wall like ancient Egyptian tombs.

"While I enjoy a bit of sightseeing as much as the next man, we better get going if we intend to make it back to the chopper before dark," MacAlister said after a minute of staring at the devastation. The wind was kicking up foot-high tornados of dust that skittered across the surface of the cut, the only movement on this barren, lifeless ridge. There was barely enough room at the top of the berm for one person to walk safely, so they resumed their Indian-file line as they moved out northeast in the direction of the mountains and whatever it was that lay in the crater.

It was only a matter of minutes before Emily found herself wishing she was back in the jungle; the sun was pitiless. It had to be one hundred degrees and the exposed parts of her body were already beginning to tingle and flush pink. She undid the jacket she had tied around her waist and threw it on. It would give her some protection, at least. This was no place for an East Coast girl who spent the majority of her time under cloudy skies and in darkened rooms where the most UV exposure she would get would be from the glow of her computer laptop's display.

"We'll lose too much time picking our way along the base of this thing," MacAlister said, as if reading her thoughts. He had pulled the scrim-net scarf he wore around his neck up to cover his mouth from the dust kicked up by the wind. "But we shouldn't have to go too much farther to get a decent view of the target with these." He tapped the binocular case hanging over one shoulder.

"God, I hope not," said Reilly. "This sun is frying me from the outside in."

"Quit moaning," MacAlister shot back over his shoulder, his attention already focused on carefully picking his way along the debris-strewn peak.

Although a fall down either side of the berm would not spell certain death—the slope down to both the valley and the jungle was just too gradual for that—there was more than enough chance of hitting something that could break a bone or cave in a skull on the way down. *It's not the fall that kills you*, Emily thought, remembering one of her father's favorite aphorisms, *it's the sudden stop at the end.* Or in this case, the snapped branches, huge boulders, and millions of other pieces of detritus that lay scattered over the slow curve of the trench on either side of them. They continued on in silence, the narrow shoulder at the top of the berm more or less free of the debris. The earth that had been pushed up here had dried to form an almost natural pathway.

The ghosts of the homes that had haunted their every step finally faded away, exorcised as they reached the edge of the development, obscured somewhere on the opposite side of the furrow in the surrounding red jungle.

The farther along they walked, the deeper the gulley to their right grew, a result, Emily assumed, of the object finally colliding with the earth and dissipating the energy it carried with it out into the surrounding ground. The deeper the ravine became the more nervous Emily became that a sudden gust of wind would knock them from their precarious path and send one, or all of them, tumbling down the litter-strewn sides.

She was so focused on placing one foot carefully in front of the other while keeping a tight hold of Thor's leash that she only realized MacAlister had stopped when she walked head first into his back. MacAlister didn't seem to notice. His broad shoulders obscured the way ahead but Reilly spotted what MacAlister had seen and he deftly sidestepped around Emily and then in front of MacAlister. He dropped to one knee and unslung his rifle from his shoulder in a single motion, training the barrel ahead of them.

Emily took a step sideways and looked past MacAlister's right shoulder.

About a mile distant of their position, the opposite wall of the ravine sloped suddenly away, dropping down to ground level then curving sharply to the right before it rose skyward for two or maybe even three hundred feet.

It was the crater. They had found it.

From this angle, only a slice of the enormous depression was visible, but it was more than enough for them to know they were now just a stone's throw from their target.

MacAlister pulled the binoculars from the case and glassed the distant sliver.

"What do you see?" Reilly asked. His voice had a nervous edge to it.

"Hard to tell. There's an awful lot of shadow from the mountain and the lip of the crater." MacAlister continued to scan the area, then replaced the binoculars into their case. "We're not going to see anything from here. The angle is too tight," he said, never taking his eyes off the distant crater.

"So we have to get closer?"

"No, not closer, that's too risky," said Emily to Reilly. She had already guessed MacAlister's plan. "We need to cross over the culvert and get up to the mountain next to the crater. It's the only way we're going to be able to see down into the pit without getting any closer."

MacAlister nodded. "If we continue this way, we'll be close enough to kiss whatever is in there. No way can we take that chance. Emily's right, the only way we're going to be able to get a clear idea of what's in there is if we get above it. Getting up the side of that mountain is our best option."

Reilly did not look convinced. "Can't we just go back and climb in the helo and get some pictures from the air?"

"Can't risk it. You saw what happened to the UAV. This is the safest choice. You two can stay right here; I can do this on my own."

"No," said Emily. "We're coming with you."

"Jesus!" said Reilly with a huff, knowing he had no choice in the matter. "I thought I joined the navy, not the infantry." He swung his pack over his shoulder and started to climb down the slope toward the valley floor.

MacAlister smiled and raised his eyebrows questioningly at Emily: You sure about this?

"Come on, let's get this over with." She peeked over the edge and picked what looked like the safest route down to the wide rugged bottom of the valley floor. Then she and Thor followed Reilly down the side of the wall, MacAlister close behind.

■ ■ ■

The scramble down to the valley floor wasn't as difficult as Emily imagined it was going to be. The clay kicked out by the object's entry was dense enough to support their weight, and it had formed a number of almost sedimentary levels, creating a natural set of steps that at least allowed for some confident footholds on the way down. The hard part was the exhausting climb back up the opposite side.

Emily winced when Thor yelped in pain as she tried to encourage him to climb up the sun-scorched side. Hours of exposure to the heat of the day had baked the ground to the point that it was just too hot to touch, and the pads of Thor's paws were as tender as a human's bare feet on the scorching clay.

"I'm not leaving him," said Emily as she shaded the dog the best she could with her body.

"I wouldn't ask you to," said MacAlister as he knelt down beside the panting dog. "But if we don't get him out of this sun as quickly as possible he's going to get heatstroke. Thor, come here, mate."

The dog obediently trotted the couple of steps to MacAlister's side, tail and head down, ribbons of drool dropping from the soft lips of his muzzle.

MacAlister stripped off his own backpack and laid it on the floor, quickly retrieving his water canteen, rifle, and binoculars and slinging them over his shoulder. "I'll grab the pack on our way back," he said, as he reached down and picked up the dog with both arms as if he weighed nothing.

Emily wasn't quite sure who was more surprised, herself or Thor, as MacAlister began climbing up the wall toward the top of the embankment. MacAlister positioned the dog against his chest and slipped one arm securely under his furry butt while he used his free hand to pull himself up the slope of the trench. Thor, his head perched over the soldier's right shoulder, regarded Emily wide-eyed and unblinking.

"Don't look at me," Emily mumbled to the dog, "you wanted to come along." Then she grabbed a handful of roots jutting out from the valley wall and began to pull herself up after them.

■ ■ ■

Emily heaved herself over the lip of the embankment and rolled over onto her back, her heart pounding in her chest, utterly exhausted. Her hands felt raw and her shoulder muscles throbbed, stiff from the climb. Her legs were the only thing that didn't ache, and she again thanked her years of biking for providing her with a good strong pair of pins. She fumbled her canteen and unscrewed the top, spilling some of the water over her face to wash the stinging sweat from her eyes. Sitting up she took two long pulls on the water that was now just a degree or two short of being reclassified as hot.

"You okay?" MacAlister's voice sounded as though he had just taken a light stroll rather than pulled himself and a dog weighing close to one hundred pounds up a two-hundred-foot embankment. Thor padded over to her, sniffed her once in greeting, and proceeded to clean himself as if being carried around was the most natural thing in the world for him.

"I'm fine," said Emily as she climbed to her feet and offered her hand to Reilly, whose head had just appeared above the edge of the chasm. He took it and allowed Emily to help pull him over the lip. *He looks how I feel*, she thought.

This side of the chasm had suffered a similar fate to the one they had just hiked over from: half-incinerated with shattered, spikey remnants of the alien flora stuck up from the ash-covered ground like Punji stakes, waiting to impale them. The red jungle started up again just a few hundred feet away. But beyond it, rising above the canopy as though it had been Photoshopped into place, Emily could see the mountain range they needed to reach, just a few miles away it looked like. Its west face was covered to the midpoint by alien plants, but from there on up, only sporadic clots of red ran along the mountain.

"Catch your breath," said MacAlister as he swallowed water from his canteen, sloshing some over his face.

Minutes passed and Emily pulled herself to her feet as they set off again. They picked up the pace, moving at a fast walk as they headed out, and Emily welcomed the shade of the giant leaves of the canopy as they once again stepped into the jungle and pushed on toward the mountain.

The gradient of the ground beneath their feet began to increase the farther in they walked. Emily could tell when they hit the foothills of the mountain range because ahead of them; she could see the black-and-purple roots of trees rising above the ones they still had to climb over. They moved quickly now, with a definite sense of purpose.

"Let's get to the top ridgeline of the jungle. We'll stay under cover to avoid detection and then move closer about a half mile or so; that should give us enough elevation to get a clear view of the crater," MacAlister ordered.

Emily could feel the muscles in her calves complaining as the gradient increased sharply. They climbed higher and higher. The canopy overhead began to thin out as the alien trees and plants grew less and less abundant. The ground lost its almost carpet-like softness of fallen leaves and lichen, replaced by rocks about the size of apples that threatened a twisted ankle or a sudden landslide with every step they took.

A quarter mile of walking later and MacAlister signaled for them to stop.

"This should do," he said, hunkering down in the bowl of a nearby tree's roots. He pulled the binoculars from the case again, and Emily took that as a sign to pull out the digital camera he had supplied her with when they'd landed. She fit the telephoto lens onto the camera body and turned it on, sighting through the viewfinder to check it worked.

"Reilly, you're providing cover. Let's keep as low to the ground as we can, follow my lead, and then we can all get the hell out of here. This place gives me the bloody creeps."

That was the first time Emily had heard MacAlister give any kind of admission of nervousness. The light-hearted delivery did not match the frown lines crinkling his forehead.

"Okay. Ready?" asked MacAlister. Emily and Reilly both nodded. "Let's go." He headed directly up the slope of the hill at a jog, crouched low, past the final line of trees toward an outcropping of rock he had spotted about seventy yards farther up the side of the mountain. Emily followed his lead, avoiding the occasional rock that bounced past her, dislodged by MacAlister's combat boots. She found herself denying the temptation to stop and look back, to just take a quick peek at what was in the damn hole.

All three made their way to the outcrop, using the enormous chunk of stone that jutted out from the mountainside to block any view of their presence from below. They leaned against the cold rock, panting for breath in its shadow.

The outcropping was a wedge-shaped protuberance of limestone and granite, the top rough but comparatively flat considering it was on the side of a mountain. It formed a perfect ledge to observe the crater from. MacAlister led them up the blind side before dropping down onto his belly as he began to slither across the ledge toward the lip that overlooked the crater, less than a mile away.

"Sit and stay," Emily told Thor, making sure the dog understood he was to stay in the shadowed coolness of the high leeward edge of the outcrop. She followed MacAlister, sliding herself across the rough surface of the outcropping on her belly, holding the camera off the ground in front of her with one hand as she crawled forward. Pieces of gravel dug into her knees and chest, but she barely felt the discomfort, her eyes fixed on the ledge and MacAlister, who was propped up on his elbows, his binoculars already to his eyes. Emily slowly edged herself elbow-by-elbow next to MacAlister. When she finally slipped in beside him she had an unobstructed line of sight down into the crater.

"Holy . . . shit!" she whispered.

Even without the aid of the telephoto lens or Mac's binoculars, Emily could see that what was hidden in the shadowed crater could not possibly be from this planet. As the ship—and there was now no doubt whatsoever in her mind that this thing in the crater *was* a starship, a spaceship, whatever you wanted to call it—had slid along the ground creating the ravine they had just travelled along. It had also pushed a huge bank of debris and dirt ahead of it and off to the sides. Part of that wall had collapsed over the front of the ship or its momentum had buried it into the ground. Either way, only the rear portion of the craft was visible.

It was a dull metallic gray. A bulbous abdomen, pitted with circular concavities, jutted out from the ground at a forty-five-degree angle into the air. What looked like giant, articulated mechanical legs sprouted from a thick tubular body, the ends of each leg had punched deep into the ground, stabilizing the craft. Emily counted ten of the legs thrust into the surrounding walls of the crater.

If there was more of the ship than that, it was below ground, buried in the wall of the crater.

Emily raised the digital camera to her eye and instinctively started taking photographs of the machine. Although she wasn't sure "machine" was the right classification for what she was looking at. It looked almost alive, like it was some kind of massive creature, yet, it was obviously manufactured. She pulled back the focus and got several wide-angle shots, then zoomed in to get more detailed photos.

"A fucking spaceship," she heard MacAlister whisper in disbelief, his eyes locked onto the binoculars. "Who would have believed it?"

What looked like either smoke or steam rose in thin streams from outlets periodically dotted along the length of each leg, rising into the air before dissipating quickly. And there was an odd glow around the edge of the craft, a halo of sorts; it shimmered like a heat haze distorting the view as though it was an image cast on the surface of a lake. A dull, low throbbing reverberated through the ground like a heart beating deep in the bedrock. Even at this distance, Emily could feel the throb transmitted through the stone of the outcrop she lay against and into her chest cavity.

While they watched, Emily became aware of another sound. It was a high-pitched quavering, growing quickly in volume and sharpness.

"You hear that?" MacAlister said.

"Hard not to," Emily whispered back as she continued pressing the fire button on the camera.

The high-frequency trill suddenly transformed into a sharp metallic screech . . . as, unbelievably, one of the machine's massive legs began to pull itself free from the surrounding wall of the crater, along with chunks of earth that tumbled in an avalanche of rock and dirt to the crater floor. The leg rose up into the air, extended forward, and then came down again with a resounding thump and geyser of shattered rock as the barbed tip of the machine's mechanical leg sank itself back into the ground, this time above the lip of the crater.

"Oh, that's just bloody priceless. The thing can walk?" said MacAlister.

A second, then a third leg followed the first, pulling free and repositioning itself on the outer edge of the crater. The throbbing pulse resonating through the rock began to beat faster and faster until it became a wavering thrum that sent the tiny pieces of rock and dust scattered across the ledge, skittering over the ground and the lip of the outcrop.

MacAlister finally dropped his eyes from the binoculars and turned to look at Emily. "I don't like the look of this one—"

He was interrupted by a new sound, like splintering rock. It flooded upward from the crater as the articulated legs suddenly flexed in unison as they heaved the giant, gray body of the ship out of the ground and then upward, revealing the full extent of the machine's size.

A shovel-shaped, curved "head" about the length of a football field was buried deep into the foot of the mountain on the eastern side of the crater. As it pulled free, masses of earth and shattered bedrock cascaded from it into the pit below. Emily saw the newly revealed front of the ship had a flat underside but the top was slightly curved and, given its massive size and distance, Emily estimated it must be at least four or five stories high.

For a moment the machine stood, its gray body reflecting the sunlight, then, one after the other, each leg began to move, grabbing at the ground as the machine hauled itself away from the pit. Each gigantic leg stretching forward as it nimbly, for such a massive mechanism, began to climb out from the huge pit along the side of the mountain. Each time a leg lifted and plunged back into the ground Emily felt the side of the mountain tremble, like dynamite blasting away at its face.

"Dear God, look at the size of that thing," MacAlister said, his voice filled with a raw mixture of awe and suppressed terror as he began to scramble his way backward along the outcropping, away from the ledge.

The machine moved in a fluid, distinctly organic manner, each leg rising and falling in a perfectly timed motion that propelled it along the foot of the mountain parallel to the ravine, its spiked feet coming down on either side of it as though it was following the path it had arrived from.

Emily could hear Thor begin to whimper and then bark as the machine thumped its way past the outcropping Emily and the other survivors had chosen as their hiding place. The noise of the machine's passing was stunningly loud, huge clouds of rock and dust were ripped from the ground as the legs lifted and then moved on, the main body blotting out the sun as it strutted across the landscape.

It continued to follow the base of the mountain then suddenly cut right and began to head south, moving out into the deeper jungle that had taken root and flourished in what had once been the open desert of Clark County bordering California. It picked its way almost daintily through the trees and thickets of the jungle; Emily could not see one tree uprooted, not one indication of any kind of disturbance or damage to the new vegetation. She was reminded of her father when she was a kid: he a keen gardener, she watching as he carefully maneuvered between the rows of cantaloupes, and tomatoes, and strawberries, and other vegetables, always wary of stepping on one of his prized plants. Yes, that was exactly it, there was a carefulness to the giant machine that seemed so out of place with its size and latent power.

As the machine grew distant, so the sound of its pounding mechanical legs faded only to be suddenly replaced by a louder, much more chaotic sound. The noise was coming from somewhere behind them, Emily realized. She turned just in time to see a stretch of the mountain above them crack and break.

Then, almost in slow motion, a massive slab of the mountain began to slide toward them.

"Run!" MacAlister shouted. Scrambling to his feet he sprinted across the ledge, his feet sliding on the loose gravel, and leaped off the side, landing roughly in the scrabble next to where Reilly and Thor had been waiting. But as Emily landed next to the Scotsman a second later, she could see Reilly already hightailing it away from the outcropping, dragging a reluctant, panicked Thor behind him. The malamute strained at the leash until finally, Reilly dropped it and continued on without him. Thor instantly began to run back toward Emily.

"Head for the forest," MacAlister yelled through panting breaths, his voice almost lost in the rumbling clatter of the avalanche of rock behind them.

It was impossible to run directly down the side of the mountain, it was littered with too many large boulders to trip over, too many chuckholes to slide a foot into and snap an ankle. The only way to maneuver with any safety or certainty was with a sideways lope, like a deranged crab.

MacAlister was just six feet ahead of her, Reilly was already halfway to the border of the jungle. Thor was leaping forward then back again, barking loudly not at but toward Emily and the source of the thunderous roar that sounded as though it was just feet behind her.

She chanced a quick glimpse over her right shoulder and in that fleeting moment she saw what looked to her like a wave of rocks and boulders flowing across the ground toward her, not more than fifty feet away. The shingle and rocks in front of the tsunami of shattered mountain bounced and shook as it flowed like water down the slope, sending up a plume of gray dust that billowed into a cloud, blotting out the sky. Tiny splinters of crushed and shattered rock flew through the air ahead of the wave, smacking against the back of her jeans and jacket. An inch-long piece sliced across her cheek but her panicked mind did not even register the pain.

Thor's rapid barking, barely audible over the roar as he sprinted ahead of her, his paws acting like a four-wheel drive on the treacherous terrain, drew her attention back to what she should be concentrating on: running for her life! She turned back just in time to see MacAlister throwing his hands out to his side as his foot slipped off a rock, he twisted to try to regain his balance but then fell and tumbled twice. She managed to leap over his rolling body, narrowly missing his head with her foot.

"I'm okay," he yelled as she flicked her head in his direction. He was already back on his feet and running dangerously fast to make up the lost ground.

"Mac! Look out!" she yelled as a rough boulder, shaped like a soccer ball and about six times the size, broke free of the main wave of rock, speeding through the air toward MacAlister. Instinctively, he ducked, just as the boulder flew past him, bounced off the scree a few feet ahead of them, then careened crazily down the remaining slope, crushing a row of freshly sprung saplings in the half-naked approach to the jungle, before stopping between the blood-red roots of an alien tree.

MacAlister, his eyes wide with fear, grabbed Emily's hand in his own as his longer legs ate up the distance between them.

"I can't make it!" she pleaded, even as she forced her legs to move faster, her breath a steamy hiss between the slit of her lips. MacAlister ignored her, his only response was to squeeze her hand even tighter.

But then they were on flat ground and able to sprint full bore for the safety of the jungle, Thor leading the way ahead of them. The giant trunks, thick chaotic tangles of roots, and walls of brush had never looked inviting until now, the jungle their only hope of escaping the rushing avalanche that seemed so intent on burying them here forever.

Shards of rock began to smack into the ground around them like meteorites, impacting with the sound of shattered china.

Mac hissed in pain as he grabbed at his left elbow, a bloody stain already forming around the torn jacket where a dagger of flying rock had hit. "Just keep running," he yelled as he dodged around the stump of a tree. "Don't look back."

The roar of the rock enveloped them entirely now, and ahead of them, Emily could see the fronds and leaves of the trees at the leading edge of the jungle vibrating and shaking. Reilly, with a hundred-foot lead, was already at the edge of the jungle. He looked back at them and Emily saw his eyes go wide before he climbed over a knot of black roots and disappeared past the tree line.

Emily's breath was coming in short, rapid bursts, her lungs fighting to suck in air even as they inhaled the choking dust pushed ahead of the falling debris. The ground seemed to pitch and heave as the pressure wave from the millions of tons of rock following behind them raced ahead of the slide.

The blue sky vanished, replaced by the red hues of the jungle canopy before Emily even realized she had made it to the jungle's edge. She leaped over a root, letting go of MacAlister's hand so she could keep her balance. Thor landed beside her, ducking under another root and heading deeper into the forest, his leash trailing behind him. *Oh, God, if that got caught on a root or a branch!* She pushed the thought aside and managed three more strides before the sound of snapping branches and splintering tree limbs added to the roar of thunderous rock.

MacAlister dodged to the left, then vaulted over a root that was as thick as his body. Emily propelled herself over the same root, landed awkwardly as she tried to avoid a second limb obscured by the first, and succeeded only in tumbling headlong to the ground. She scrambled to her feet just as a wall of white dust enveloped her. Half-blinded she staggered forward, her hands thrown out ahead of her trying to feel her way, choking and coughing as the dust stung her eyes and filled her nostrils.

The rumbling of crashing rock and splintering trees grew; it seemed to come from all sides now as she staggered through the white fog of pulverized rock, unsure even whether she was still moving in the same direction or whether she was running back the way she had come from.

She stumbled forward.

Ahead of her, a shape materialized out of the white curtain that had descended over her; it was MacAlister. He was lying on the ground ahead and staring up at her. She could see his chest rising and falling in rapid succession. From somewhere she found a reserve of energy, enough to sprint to his side. She grabbed his outstretched hand and began to pull him.

"Get up, Mac," she yelled. "Get up." He didn't move. She could see his lips moving but the words made no sense to her. She yelled again, tugging harder, "Get up . . . *please!*" she pleaded.

Again his lips moved, but this time she heard him over the buzzing pounding in her head and the plug of dust and dirt that had clogged almost every orifice of her face, including her ears.

"It's okay," he yelled. "You're safe. You can stop now."

Emily relaxed her grip on Mac's hand, although she did not let go completely, and turned around to look back in the direction of the mountain. The dust still wafted through the spaces between the trunks and vines and branches, but it was already beginning to settle like a drift of snow over the ground. Through her watering eyes she could see a few splintered tree boles, but the rockslide had stopped, slowed to a final halt by the jungle.

Emily sank to the ground next to MacAlister, coughing up and then spitting out the dust that peppered her tongue, lips, and throat.

MacAlister, his face as pale and coated as she was sure her own looked, reached out and wiped dust from around her eyes, knocking bits of gravel from her hair.

Before she could convince herself not to, she leaned in and kissed the Scotsman full on the lips. He tasted of concrete, and after a moment of shock he kissed her back, his hand cradling the back of her neck.

They broke away as a rustling from a bush nearby drew their attention. MacAlister began reaching for his rifle but stopped when Thor emerged, his coat a lot grayer than usual thanks to the coating of dust covering it. "Come here, you little bastard," Emily said, holding her hands out to embrace the malamute, who willingly accepted his mistress's affection.

A sudden twinge of panic overcame Emily and she grabbed for the camera around her neck. If she had lost the only evidence of the alien craft then their journey would have been for nothing. But it was still there, dangling against her chest.

MacAlister struggled to his feet. Blood streaked the right side of his face and his elbow, and his knuckles were skinned raw, his gloves in tatters.

"Hello?" Reilly's voice echoed through the trees.

"Over here," Mac yelled in reply and a few moments later Reilly appeared from behind the trunk of the tree they stood next to.

"Shit, are you two okay?" he asked.

Emily's eyes met MacAlister's and she felt a smile rise unbidden to her lips. "Yes," she replied, "we're just fine."

MacAlister returned her smile with one of his own, "Come on, let's go home."

CHAPTER 27

Despite their cuts and bruises, and having been almost buried alive by a couple million tons of rock, they made surprisingly good time on their journey back to the helo waiting for them at the Tacoma, buoyed in part by the knowledge that they had successfully completed their mission. It was a strange positivity, when Emily thought about it, but finally knowing beyond a certainty of a doubt what it was they were dealing with, that Jacob had been correct in most, if not all, of his wild theories, was a relief much like the relief she had heard some people experienced when they finally knew with utter certainty that they had cancer.

"You're sure you're okay?" MacAlister asked Emily for the fourth or fifth time since they had begun the long slog back to the hotel.

"I'm fine. Just a few bumps and grazes. How about you?"

He lifted the elbow that had been hit by the shard of rock up to try to examine it, but it was too awkward an angle for him to see. "How's it look?"

Emily stepped over a twisted root and leaned in to inspect the bloodstained slash that ran along the elbow of Mac's combat jacket. "The bleeding has stopped, so I doubt there's any chance of you bleeding to death just yet," she joked.

Thor gave a sudden deep growl, his hackles rising in response to some unseen threat ahead. He stopped mid-step and Emily froze too, causing Reilly to almost walk into her.

"Mac!" Emily called out, as low as she could. The Scotsman, midway through straddling a fallen streetlight, turned and raised his eyebrows questioningly at her.

She stabbed a finger at Thor. The dog was frozen in place at her side, the flews of his muzzle pulled back to reveal his teeth as his head swiveled from side to side as if he was trying to identify the location of what it was that was disturbing him.

MacAlister jumped down and stalked back to them, his head scanning from side to side, his finger pressed against his rifle's trigger guard.

"What's going on?" he whispered.

"Don't know. Thor just started acting squirrelly all of a sudden."

Reilly chimed in, "Come on, it's just a dog. He probably smells something dead or needs to take a piss. Let's get going."

"Listen," Emily said, trying to keep the annoyance out of her voice, "this dog has saved my life on more than one occasion. I've learned to trust him. If he thinks there's something to be worried about out here, then you should be real fucking worried too."

MacAlister's eyes had not stopped moving the entire time Emily talked. They scanned the depths of the jungle, constantly alert for any movement, any sign of a threat. "Okay, let's keep it as close and quiet as we can, we're too exposed here anyway," he said. "We need to find somewhere we can lay up for a while, until

Thor here tells us otherwise." He gave the dog a good-natured rub behind the ears.

The group began moving again, toward what had probably been some kind of store before the rain, but now looked like the entrance to a cave, covered in low-hanging vines and partly obscured by the trunk of a huge tree that had pushed its way up through the sidewalk in front of it.

Thor slunk along beside Emily, panting rapidly, his nose moving back and forth in the air as he again caught a scent only he could smell, his mood becoming increasingly jittery and nervous. Emily fastened the leash back onto his collar and held it loosely in her hand. They were almost at the entrance to the store when Thor gave a deep growl followed by three sharp barks and lunged at something in the foliage of the jungle. The suddenness of the movement pulled the leash from around Emily's wrist with a whip-crack as the dog sprinted off into the jungle, his barks resonating through the tightly packed trees.

"Thor!" Emily yelled after the quickly disappearing dog, but he kept on running. She stood transfixed for a second, unsure of what she should do. "Shit!" she sighed, then took off after her dog.

She could hear the boots of MacAlister and Reilly pounding after her. They didn't call out to her, and she became painfully aware that if there was anything threatening nearby, she had almost certainly alerted it to their presence. But she did not care, something had spooked Thor so badly that he was either running toward it or from it, she had no idea which it was, but there was no way she was going to leave her dog behind.

"Thor!" She yelled again, as she scrambled over a protruding explosion of roots, just in time to see the rear end of the malamute wind his way around the trunk of a particularly huge tree, leaping over the roots as though they did not exist. Emily had to slow and carefully maneuver over them. When she was on the other side she saw Thor disappearing around a bright purple bush with dark-red, gelatinous berries that hung like grapes in bunches.

"Thor," she called out again as she sprinted the fifty feet or so after him. This time it seemed to do the trick. The dog stopped, staring straight ahead, his tail down between his hindquarters, motionless, as though he knew he had done something wrong.

Emily picked her way past the bushes and tree limbs, then rushed to the dog's side. They were both panting heavily, the humidity robbing the air of oxygen. Sweat stung her eyes and she wiped it away with the back of her arm.

"Jesus, dog. What the hell is wrong with you? You about gave me a fucking heart attack." She threw a protective arm around his neck, grasping his collar tightly. Thor didn't seem to hear her, barely registering she was even there; instead, he continued to stare into the distance.

Another growl rumbled up from deep within his chest.

Emily's eyes slowly followed the direction Thor was staring. Despite the heat of the jungle, her breath chilled in her lungs at what she saw.

In a clearing ahead was a sight unlike anything she had seen before: three entities, humanoid looking, tall, with long, slender yet muscular limbs. They stood about eight feet in height, their oval, featureless heads swaying back and forth as they moved with balletic adroitness around the clearing on long, articulated lower appendages. Emily hesitated to call them legs, because the only resemblance they bore to a human limb was the elongated shape. Each "leg" seemed able to flex at any point along its length, even though she could see no sign of a joint, and where a human foot should be was a half-globe-shaped hoof that looked like an upturned dish. Each creature held an object in its right hand: a cube. Although holding was perhaps the wrong word; guided would be more accurate as the cube appeared to float about an inch above the outstretched palm of each triple-fingered hand, glowing with a faint green luminescence. Occasionally one of the three slender digits of the hand manipulating the cube would twitch, just the tiniest of flexes, and the box would change color, pulsing brightly before dimming again. They wore no clothes and appeared completely sexless. The creatures' skin had an almost metallic sheen to it, as though they had all been stamped from a single block of aluminum. Each looked identical to the other.

They moved with such grace, their long limbs shifting in smooth unison as they strode across the clearing, pushing the glowing cubes before them, or perhaps being guided by them? When the cubes stopped the creatures became completely motionless. So still were they Emily could have mistaken them for the petrified victims of Medusa if it were not for the occasional minute finger movement as they manipulated the cube-device floating before them.

They're not even breathing, Emily thought, watching the nearest being go about its work, not two hundred feet from where she and Thor crouched. It stopped momentarily, moving the cube up to a low overhanging branch of a ruby-red tree.

The cube throbbed, contracting in on itself and then expanding in a weird hall-of-mirrors distortion as it seemed to shrink then expand. Just for a second, in the weird prismatic bowl of light the cube had become, Emily thought she saw somewhere else, another place reflected out of that shimmering box of light. It was a fleeting glimpse into some place manufactured, certainly not the jungle that she knew lay beyond the alien-cube's operator.

The cube suddenly contracted back to its normal shape with a bright flash of orange and an audible snap. Emily felt a stabbing pain just above her eyebrows, as though she had been staring at a computer screen for far too long.

When she looked again, the branch the humanoid had been examining had vanished, leaving a black cauterized nub near the trunk.

The strange elegant alien moved again, stepping lightly through the few trees that lay between it and Emily's hiding place, the box's glow casting strange light and long shadows over the ground.

■ ■ ■

Thor let out another low growl as it moved closer to them, seemingly oblivious to their presence behind the bush.

"Shush!" Emily whispered, her lips level with Thor's ear as she cradled the dog to her. She could feel his muscles tense, taut with potential energy beneath his thick, gray fur.

A sudden crashing sound behind them made Emily swirl around, her heart in her mouth, just in time to see Reilly trip and almost fall as he stumbled over a tree's root.

"Fuck!" he yelled, but managed to recover his balance.

Emily hissed at him to be quiet, but when she turned back to the clearing all three creatures had stopped what they were doing, their bald, eyeless heads swiveled intently in her direction.

Then, as one, they began striding over the ground toward her.

"Oh, shit!" Emily yelled, unconsciously scuttling backward as the aliens—and Emily had no illusions that that was what they were, not created on this world, but from some other distant place—moved in that elegant, flowing gait toward her hiding place. As she moved backward, her grip on Thor's collar loosened momentarily and he was gone again, launching himself toward the silver figures with a snarl, drool flying from his lips as he raced at the three aliens.

"No, Thor. Stop!" Emily yelled, fear in her voice now. "Please stop."

She was in a waking nightmare, and she knew there was nothing she could do other than watch as her dog ate up the ground between her and these three humanoid intruders.

All three aliens stopped as they registered the dog rushing toward them. One of them raised its cube and, just as Thor launched himself at the nearest creature, it flashed red.

Thor yelped once and went limp.

Emily let out a strangled shriek of horror as she watched Thor's limp body crash to the ground at the feet of the creature.

"No!" she screamed in a voice an equal mix of anguish, fear, and rage. She leaped from her hiding place behind the bush and unshouldered her shotgun, quickly leveling it at the nearest alien as she stalked toward it. Her first shot disintegrated the low-hanging branches of a tree to the creature's right, her aim affected by the blur of tears that had suddenly filled her vision. She wiped one hand across her eyes and took aim at the alien again. The second shot caught it at the waistline, severing it in two. The top half toppled backward, the cube in its hand glowed brightly and stayed suspended in the air for a second, then turned to black and fell to the floor next to the twitching torso. The legs of the creature crumpled and collapsed next to the motionless body of Thor.

"Emily!" MacAlister's roar of concern was a distant whisper even though she knew he must be yelling. "For Christ's sake get back here," he called after her as she walked past the bifurcated body of the fallen alien.

She ignored him and racked another shell into the shotgun. Moving quickly now across the open ground toward the two remaining aliens, she raised the Mossberg to her shoulder again and sighted down the barrel at the next nearest creature just as it turned toward her, the cube in its outstretched palm pulsing rapidly.

"I'm going to kill all you fucks," she yelled, hot tears of rage spilling over her cheeks. "You're going back to whatever hellhole you came from. You hear me? Do you fucking hear me?" Her finger caressed the trigger of the shotgun just as the alien's cube seemed to explode brilliantly.

A numbing buzz surrounded her. It ran across the surface of her skin like static electricity and filled the inside of her head with a momentary flash of blinding light that pulsed through every synapse, penetrated every memory she had, filled each molecule of her being. Abruptly, she was disconnected from her body. It was as though a switch had been thrown, freezing all communication between her brain and her nervous system.

The only way Emily knew she was falling was because her eyes were still her own: She saw the red grass rushing up to meet her, and in the final second before she hit the ground, she saw Mac's distraught face as he rushed from the edge of the clearing toward her.

Then everything went white.

CHAPTER 28

Emily found herself suspended in a place between sleep and wakefulness, enveloped by a warm light that had no color, yet seemed to contain every shade and hue imaginable. It might be that place, she dreamed, that humanity had defined as the ever-so-thin line between life and death; limbo, if you pleased. Or perhaps it was the sanctuary which, as a child, defined the limits between life and dreams, and that as an adult, had seemed lost to her forever. No matter where she was, it was peaceful, quiet; she was finally at rest. The non-light tingled against her skin, its silk-like texture holding her securely in place, not against her will, but *because* she willed it to embrace her. It brushed against her skin, warming her like the first sigh of a mother's breath against her newborn's body.

Emily tried to remember everything that had come before this moment, but all she found was a blank slate; there was nothing but the now, and she reveled in the knowledge that she was an anomaly, brand new, an incongruity overlooked by the universe, both newborn and eternal, yet somehow, still an irreplaceable facet of a vast mechanism, comforted by her own anonymity, her own individualism, her own uniqueness.

Time passed, and after what seemed like a quiet eternity of serenity, from the nothingness a red spot began to form in the vast and narrow limits of her mindscape. Tiny at first, it quickly spread through the non-light like a drop of ink in water, pushing outward as it grew, pulling in everything that surrounded it.

Emily watched as if from a distance, with no hint of fear, only wonder and fascination.

More tiny dots of color, each unique as she, appeared, quickly spreading out across the canvas, merging and bonding with each other until a sudden rush of experience soaked her, drenching her in memory.

She sensed herself exhale a gasp of astonishment . . . followed quickly by pain as the tide of reality washed her ashore, and . . .

. . . Emily sat up, instantly regretting the move as every nerve in her body seemed to send a simultaneous signal to her brain, a flood of information and experience that overwhelmed her, setting every synapse on fire. She slumped back down again, and a low moan escaped her as she was overwhelmed by disorientation. When it finally eased, she rolled gently over onto her left side, fighting against the urge to vomit, dragging in deep gulps of air. Slowly, the spinning began to subside, and her senses and nerves began to return to normal. Still, her skin tingled with static electricity strong enough it made her want to scratch every inch of it.

She forced her eyelids to open. Slowly! Slowly! Unsure of how they might handle any sudden light.

She tried to remember everything that had happened in the past few . . . ? How long *had* it been? Hours? Days? She had no idea how much time had passed, or how she had gotten here; she had a hazy vaguely recalled memory of . . . an open field, beings that had no right to exist on Earth . . . and Thor!

Her eyes snapped fully open.

She was naked. She could feel a rapidly cooling liquid or membrane coating her skin and she suddenly felt chilled as it began to evaporate off her body. Ignoring the pain and disorientation she pushed herself back upright.

"Thor?" she called out, her voice a weak croak. Her vision swam for a few seconds with even this simple effort. A blur of swirling colors played in front of her eyes, gradually organizing themselves into shapes, which in turn coalesced into objects as her eyes adjusted to the dimness of her locale: curved walls, a ceiling of nothing but black above her still-whirling head, the hard shelf she sat upon, its surface smooth, slightly warm beneath the palms of her hands.

She was in some kind of a room, her senses told her. It was poorly lit but not dark, and, as her eyes were gradually adjusting to the twilight, she noticed she was not alone.

Three figures stood at the dimly lit edge of the room, hidden within the penumbra of shadow.

Thank God. "Mac? Is that you?"

Emily blinked a couple of times as she tried to focus on what lay at the boundary of her sight as the three silhouettes finally resolved from the darkness around them. She stifled a scream of confusion and fear at what stood before her.

Two of the figures were the same elegant aliens she had seen in the field. They stood unmoving, their blank oval faces staring—if that was the right word, they had no eyes after all—directly at her. But it was the third figure, flanked by the two aliens as though they were his guardians, their shadows cast across the shorter shape, that caused her heart to pound. There was something disturbingly familiar about the outline.

The middle figure took two steps forward into the light.

An abrupt intake of breath from Emily marked her recognition, then a name shattered the silence of the room: "Jacob?" she asked.

She stared hard at the figure, unsure of whether what she was seeing was true or a trick played on her by the shadows.

It *was* Jacob, free of his wheelchair, his legs apparently now fully functional as he took another step closer to Emily.

"Hello Emily," he said, his voice slurring slightly, as though he was still getting used to forming words with his mouth and tongue. "It is so very good to see you again."

Emily pushed herself across the shelf she sat on until she felt a wall at her back, her eyes darting around the room, searching for any way out of it and finding nothing. The walls were seamless with no apparent exit.

"You have nothing to fear from us, Emily. We are not here to harm you," Jacob said, a hand extended out in front of him, encouraging her to stop her nervous shuffling.

Us? We? Her heart skipped a beat when she thought back to the creature that had tried to take her and Simon's family in Stuyvesant. It *had* taken Simon and eventually Ben, turning the child into some *thing* that she had later killed, but not before the creature had used Simon, transforming him into a puppet to lure the children and Emily to it.

"What . . . what the *fuck* are you?" Emily asked, her eyes shifting constantly from Jacob to the two sentinels standing motionless behind him, then back to Jacob again. She could see no connection between the two silent creatures and Jacob, no black tentacles that would mean he was under their control. But that did not mean that he was not their thrall in some other way.

"Our creators gave us no name, but over the millennia, other species have named us. *You* may think of us as the Caretakers. It is the most appropriate, I believe."

"I know you're not Jacob, so, what are you?" she insisted.

"You are correct and incorrect," Jacob said, his eyes drifting down to his own legs, legs that had been useless when Emily had last seen him. "We are here to ensure the transition of the planet takes place as it has been designed. I *am* Jacob, perfect in every single way, minus his infirmities, but I am also a part of the others you see here and those of us stationed around this planet. And we are all connected to the change occurring here."

Emily felt rage begin to surge up from deep inside her, sublimating the confusion she felt listening to this *thing* try to explain itself.

"*You* are the ones responsible for everything that happened, aren't you? You're the ones that . . ." she could barely control herself at this point, the anger erupting from every cell of her body ". . . you are the ones that killed us. You destroyed our planet. Our civilizations, my family, my friends, my parents. You *murdered* us by the billions!" The last sentence was coated with such venom and hatred she half expected that the three creatures standing in front of her would disintegrate from its vehemence. But, of course, they did not. Instead, they remained as immutable as they had since she woke here.

Jacob seemed to ponder her accusation before answering.

"I understand your confusion, Emily, but *we* did not destroy this planet, we saved it. That is our task. The preservation of life. We have repurposed almost every biological entity on this planet to become more efficient, to ensure survival, to ensure growth. Nothing has been wasted."

"Re-fucking-purposed? What the fuck do you mean 'repurposed'? You took everything that I had that was precious to me and destroyed it, turned them into monsters. Monsters! Jesus Christ,

I killed a little boy because of you fuckers. I *murdered* a boy." She was on her feet now, closing the gap between Jacob, spittle flying from her mouth as the words, emotional gunshots each of them, exploded from within her.

Something warm and wet trickled through her fingers. Looking down at her clenched fists she saw a rivulet of blood leaking from between her fingers, nails dug deep into the heel of her palm.

"We are . . . aware of your emotional pain, Emily, but the end was near for our, your, species. Within a span of several hundred years, you would have been reduced to a statistically insignificant number. Your survival viability was . . . negligible."

"Then why not just leave us to wipe ourselves out?" she yelled into Jacob's face, all fear of him gone now. God damn them all to hell. "Why the fuck would you want to come in and destroy us now? Why not just let us do it to ourselves?"

Jacob returned her gaze unflinchingly, either unaware or uncaring of the rage that was directed at him.

He continued, his voice still soft, still low, as if he was talking to a child, "Because your species would not have been the only one to have become extinct. More than ninety-eight percent of this planet's species would also have been lost along with you. Given the high probability that the remaining two percent would also become extinct within a thousand years, we decided to act while there was still sufficient biological material available to ensure success."

"So what?" she yelled, her voice cracking from the strain. "So fucking what if we destroyed this world? It was our world to destroy, you fucks."

"This was *never* your world, Emily Baxter," Jacob interrupted, the first real hint of emotion entering his voice as he leaned in closer to her. "That was a delusion your species created to ensure its continued pillaging and self-destructive actions. If you could see what I see, Emily, if you had the knowledge that we have, you would understand. You would know that life in this universe is so very, very rare, so fragile. When we find a world like this one, we observe it in the hope that its occupants might correct their course. Inevitably, they do not. That is when we initiate our program. While there are still enough biological resources available to reverse the downward spiral."

Emily slumped to the floor, her legs folding beneath her.

"'Biological resources.' You mean people, right? People and animals and plants. My friends and my family." She flicked a dismissive hand toward Jacob. "Jesus, even you and the shit you put me through. They even used you."

"Your animosity toward me, toward who I *was*, is understandable, Emily. Both you and I are so very similar, we are both perfect examples of how badly life wants to try to exist. My memories tell me that I had to deceive you to ensure my continued survival, just as you have done so very much to ensure not only your own survival but also that of Rhiannon and your other companions."

"I am *nothing* like you," she screamed, pushing herself to her feet. "*Nothing!* You, whatever *you* are, are pure fucking evil."

This time Jacob smiled when he spoke.

"Your concept of good and evil is an outdated one, Emily, the product of a young, deluded species. The race that created us evolved past such emotions while your solar system was nothing more than a swirling mass of dust and noble gases. They had explored this universe and others like it and found *nothing* but darkness. The only light, an occasional gemstone of a living world. Being creatures of pure reason, they assumed the task of preserving that life where they could, and ending it for the greater good where they must. We are the tools they created to accomplish that task."

Emily slumped back to the floor. Its surface was warm, with an almost living texture and heat. It was repulsive and she shuddered, drawing her hands into her naked lap.

Jacob continued, "The life on this planet was used to feed and nourish the new life we have created: better, more efficient life that will ensure the continued viability of this planet."

"If your makers are so fucking omnipotent then how did I survive? Why did *I* survive?" Emily asked, her energy lagging now from the emotional outpouring.

Jacob crouched down until his eyes were at the same level as Emily's before he spoke. "There are always survivors from the original inhabitants. Always some who, through a natural immunity that we could never account for or cosmic luck, possess a resistance to the effects of the red rain, as you called it. It is always a statistically insignificant number. You, and the others like you, are an anomaly that, by virtue of being so unlikely, become a probability. That is why we send the Harvesters, to ensure the complete integration of any surviving life forms. But there are always those that manage to elude them."

Emily stared at the floor. "Harvesters? You mean the thing that killed Simon and Ben? That tried to kill Rhiannon and me? The thing I fucking crushed? Did you mean *that* Harvester?"

Emily laughed but there was no humor in it.

"So come on, use me for your great and wonderful fucking plan. Why waste more perfectly good 'biological material'? Just get it over with, for fuck's sake. I am so damn tired of listening to you talk."

"That is no longer necessary."

Emily slowly raised her head to Jacob's eye level. "You've got to be fucking kidding me, right? You're rejecting me?" This time a laugh that she could only describe as diabolical bubbled up from her throat.

Jacob did not seem to find it quite as ironic. His lips parted in a slight smile, the first hint of real human emotion she had seen from this Xerox copy of the original man. "There is no use for you now, Emily; the process of recreation is complete. It would be uneconomical to integrate you or your companions. But we do have another use for you."

"Let me guess? You're going to carry out more of your warped experiments on me? Turn me into one of your living machines? Is that it?"

"No, Emily," Jacob said, seeming honestly offended by her remark. "We need you to take a message back to your people and the others that will join you."

Jacob gestured with a hand and a map appeared in the air between him and Emily. It was so realistic she felt that if she wanted to she could reach out and touch the mountains and the coastline, run her fingers through the slowly moving waves of the ocean that washed over its surface.

It was a map of what had once been the southwest United States, red now, except for the occasional snowcapped mountain.

Then Jacob began to explain what it was he wanted from her, and with each word he spoke, Emily felt the anger begin to leave her.

■ ■ ■

"Do you have any questions, Emily?" Jacob asked when he was done explaining the message he wanted her to carry back with her to the other survivors at Point Loma.

"Why?" she asked finally. "Why would you do this?"

Jacob's lids closed. Beneath them, Emily could see his eyes moving back and forth as though he was deeply asleep. A slight smile crossed his face and his eyes snapped open again.

"Because, despite what you think of us, what you *believe* us to be, we are not monsters, Emily."

An opening appeared noiselessly in the curve of the wall to her left. Jacob stepped toward it, still flanked by the two aliens. "This way, Emily," he said, gesturing toward the doorway.

Emily stood, ignoring the pins and needles she felt tingling through her legs from being seated for so long, and walked through the doorway, the floor warm against her bare feet. Beyond it lay another, larger room. This one was circular, with an oval ceiling that spiraled up to a point far above her head. The room was empty except for one wall where multicolored liquids gurgled and oozed through a row of thick, clear pipes on the opposite side of the room. They merged into a single larger pipe where the liquids mixed together and flowed onward to whatever destination and design the aliens had for it. She did not want to think what that goo might once have been.

Another opening appeared in the opposite wall. This time, beyond the second doorway, Emily could see the gentle swell of a hill, covered in the red lichen, but otherwise clear of the tangle of jungle that seemed to have sprung up everywhere across the planet.

A ramp led from the edge of the wall to the ground.

Emily glanced at Jacob. He held her stare wordlessly until she turned away and walked nervously through the opening and out onto the sun-drenched hillside.

As she stepped from the ramp Emily heard a soft pop behind her. She had expected to find herself next to whatever alien craft she had been held in, but when she turned to look back, she was alone on the hill. There was no sign of the ramp or the room that she had just left. Shading her eyes against the glare of the sun,

Emily scanned the sky for any indication of a departing craft, but the air was empty of all but a few small clouds.

She allowed her gaze to follow the downward curve of the hill as it dropped away before eventually meeting and being swallowed up by the ubiquitous red jungle below. Beyond the jungle, in the distance, Emily could see the outline of what had once been Las Vegas. She had assumed that she had been within the aliens' craft, but the truth was, she now understood, that "room" could have been anywhere on the planet or off it. The aliens—what had they called themselves, the Caretakers?—seemed more than capable of manipulating space, bending it to their needs. Still, it was a surprise to realize that they had stranded her on the opposite side of the city from where they had landed.

On the ground near to where she stood, Emily noticed her backpack, clothes, shotgun, and other belongings, neatly deposited in a small pile.

She dressed quickly, then undid the flap of the backpack and pulled it open, searching inside for the two-way radio MacAlister had insisted she take. It was still there, thank God. She pulled it out and switched it on. A burst of static exploded from the radio. She turned the volume down and held the radio in front of her mouth.

"Hello? Can anybody hear me?"

The quiet soughing of an afternoon breeze moving through the distant jungle was her only answer.

Emily pressed the talk button again, repeating her question, "MacAlister, do you read me?"

Another burst of interference was followed by a momentary silence, then a familiar voice crackled from the radio's speaker.

"Emily? Emily, can you hear me?" He sounded amazed to be speaking to her, and a little relieved too.

"MacAlister! Yes, it's me." She found herself almost yelling into the microphone.

"Are you okay? Are you injured?" The concern in MacAlister's voice was touching. But it was a good question: Was she okay? She wasn't sure. Looking down at herself, there didn't seem to be any signs of injury, but her brain still felt fuzzy, almost as though she was drunk, but without the feeling of needing to throw up. She felt . . . different somehow.

"I'm okay," she said hesitantly.

"Where are you?" MacAlister asked, his voice all business now.

She looked around the top of the hill. The sun was well past its zenith, and heading toward the western horizon to her right and she could see the remnants of Vegas poking up from the jungle in the distance, but almost directly ahead of her.

"I'm on a clear hilltop, about six, maybe seven miles north of where we landed," she told MacAlister. She turned through 360 degrees. "It's pretty much the only place here not covered by the jungle."

"Just sit tight, Emily. We're coming to get you, okay?"

"Okay," she replied, feeling a steady pull of exhaustion begin to tug at her muscles.

She sat and waited.

Minutes later, as the afternoon sun beat down on the hilltop, the steady beat of the helicopter's rotors chopping through the air echoed across the Las Vegas valley, arriving long before Emily spotted the dark dot of the Black Hawk as it sped toward her. She pulled off her jacket and stood, waving it above her head with as much energy as she could still muster until she saw the chopper adjust its vector and curve gracefully in her direction.

The helo circled around the hilltop as MacAlister searched for a safe place to put it down. Emily shaded her eyes from flying debris as the Black Hawk descended, and then she was moving to the helicopter before the wheels had touched down.

The passenger door slid open and a shape leaped from within and bounded toward her.

"Thor!" Emily yelled, her voice whipped away by the noise of the Black Hawk's engines.

The malamute raced toward her, then hesitated and slowed, his head dipping down almost to the ground, but his eyes never leaving her as he sniffed at the air around Emily and let out a low half-whine, half-growl.

"What's wrong with you, mutt?" she said. The malamute had never hesitated with her before. "It's just me." There must be some residual smell or essence of the creatures she had encountered on the ship that was making him nervous. "Come on. Come here," she cooed, offering her hand out to her dog. He sniffed it once then licked it and that was enough. The malamute almost bowled her over, weaving around and between her legs, pushing up against her. She grabbed the dog by his collar and guided him back toward the waiting helicopter.

Reilly leaned out and yelled something that she couldn't hear over the roar of the engines, then Burris's head appeared over his shoulder as the two sailors beckoned her to get in.

Thor leaped inside the helo and Emily climbed in behind him. Reilly slid the door closed again. She could see MacAlister twisting in his seat toward her. He was mouthing something to her but she couldn't hear him, the engines still too loud even with the cabin door closed. He tapped the headphones on his head and pointed above her head. She reached for the set of headphones, slipping them over her ears.

MacAlister's voice filled her head, "—you okay? Emily, can you hear me? Are you okay?"

"Yes. Yes, I'm okay."

"What the hell happened? We thought we had lost you. I thought I had lost you."

"It's a long story, Mac," she sighed, her nervous-energy supply finally hitting empty. "Just get us out of here."

MacAlister reluctantly turned his attention back to the console and Emily felt the Black Hawk lift off and begin to gain altitude.

"Home," she said. "Take us home."

CHAPTER 29

The Black Hawk approached Point Loma just after sunset, the remnants of the day still smoldering on the horizon, spilling orange fire along its edge.

"So are you going to tell me what happened?" MacAlister said over the helo's intercom.

Emily shook her head, "No, not here. It's something everyone has to hear, and I don't think I want to tell it more than once," she told him. "Why don't *you* tell me what happened after I was shot?"

MacAlister reluctantly allowed the subject to switch to him and Reilly.

"When you shot that one alien—God, that sounds weird said out loud, doesn't it? Alien!—I thought maybe we'd be able to take on the others too, but then . . ." Emily heard a stutter in the Scotsman's tone, a quiver to the usually strong voice that betrayed the emotion the man was feeling. "Then you went down. I started to move toward where you'd fallen while Reilly laid down some covering fire—"

"I think I hit one too," Reilly chimed in.

"—but then you weren't there anymore. The aliens did something with those weird cubes they had and all of you just vanished. Poof! Disappeared. The aliens and their mate you slotted, just gone. It looked like bubbles popping. Scared the crap out of me, to give you the God's honest truth."

"Only Thor was left," Reilly filled in. "We were sure he was dead, but when we got close, I could see he was still breathing. Couple of minutes after you disappeared, he was up and about again. Bit wobbly on his legs, but he didn't seem none the worse for wear. Tough little fu . . . bugger. He's a tough little bugger."

"Why didn't they just kill us?" Emily pondered aloud. "I mean, why would they just stun us? Doesn't make sense."

"Maybe they didn't know what you and Thor were?" Reilly suggested. "Maybe they thought you were one of their creatures, the ones that came after the rain. Think about it: If they've gone to such great lengths to ensure this world was changed to be exactly the way they wanted it, maybe they didn't want to chance damaging one of their precious creations? Maybe that's why they only stunned you. Just a thought."

Emily thought it was probably an accurate one too. The aliens had been very particular in explaining why the change had overcome the Earth. This whole concept of massacring an entire planet's ecosystem to ensure the continued viability of that planet as a life-producing system was, well, about as alien a concept as she could get her brain around. It was as good an idea as any other.

"Or maybe they just didn't see you as much of a threat?" said Burris.

"She managed to blow one of the bastards in half. I'd call that pretty 'threatening' in my book," said Reilly, jumping to her defense.

They all laughed. It was the kind of nervous laughter that only comes from a shared experience that no one had expected to survive, shot through with a vein of uneasiness that would come back to visit them late at night for the rest of their lives, Emily suspected.

"So, then what?"

MacAlister picked the story back up: "We sortied around the area looking for you or any clues to where you might have gone, but there wasn't any sign of you."

"Sergeant MacAlister was all set to storm that alien ship to get you back," said Reilly. "I swear, if we hadn't—"

"Son," MacAlister interrupted, "if you don't want to become a paratrooper anytime soon, I'd suggest you shut it."

This time Emily's laughter was pure mirth, albeit injected with a hint of embarrassment at the revelation of the depth of MacAlister's dedication toward her recovery. "I'm sure Mac would have done the same for any of us."

Reilly grinned wildly from the seat across from hers. "Not bloody likely," he mouthed silently then said, "Yes, Miss. I'm sure he would have."

Mac and Reilly had combed the area looking for her, but even Thor could not pick up a scent. So they had made their way back to the helo and waited. The way back to the Tacoma casino had been even more treacherous in the few hours since they had descended. "That place is being chewed away like nobody's business. Won't be nothing left but dust soon," Burris had said.

There had been no argument from the sailors when Mac had told them they were going to be spending the night on the roof of the crumbling casino until he knew for certain what had happened to Emily. The plan was to wait until morning and then head out and see if they could spot any sign of her.

"Have to admit I was not looking forward to staying on that roof knowing there were all those creepy-crawlies below us," said Reilly. "We all breathed a sigh of relief when you showed up."

They had tried using the radio to contact her every fifteen minutes initially, but dropped to every thirty minutes to conserve power. They had been about to switch the radio off when her call had come in.

"We're just glad you're safe, Emily" was the last thing MacAlister told her before the cabin settled into a welcome silence.

Emily found herself nodding off, despite MacAlister's occasional attempt during the return flight to drag what had happened out of her or to ask again if she was all right; her fatigue was just too overwhelming and she soon fell into a restless, exhausted sleep.

. . . And she dreamed. Dreamed of a presence hidden deep within the shadowy folds of her consciousness that observed her, looking out through her eyes as someone might use a spyglass to observe the inhabitants of a distant island. But the harder she tried to reach it, the deeper the presence seemed to burrow into her mind, slipping from her view like water running through her fingers. And did she truly want to catch this elusive sense of other fleeing so elegantly from her? She was unsure, it felt as though catching it would be like a secret might finally be revealed to her, about her; a secret too painful to withstand the light of her knowing. But still she chased after it through the maze of her thoughts and memories, down into ever deeper, ever redder areas until . . .

Emily jerked awake, her eyes snapping open at the gentle shake of her elbow by Reilly, and his crackling voice in her ear that told her: "Wake up, Emily, we're almost home."

"Okay," she managed to say, as the memory of the dream itself slipped from her mind.

The Black Hawk circled over Point Loma, and through the dirt-stained cabin window Emily could see people far below caught in the dying light of the day.

They were all the family she had now, she thought as she watched each of them stop what they were doing and stare up at the helicopter buzzing toward them, craning their necks as they searched the sky at the sound of their approaching craft.

"Where the hell is that landing strip?" MacAlister asked over the intercom. The light was fleeing the world so fast it was becoming hard to make out the actual buildings of their camp from their shadows. "I don't want to have to set us down on Coronado, if I can help it."

As if they had heard his complaint, Emily saw three bright-red lights burst into life one after the other on the ground. Flares. Whoever lit them had tossed them down to form a triangle that was obviously meant to define their landing point.

"Starboard, Mac," Emily said into her microphone.

"Where? . . . Okay, got it." He swung the helicopter around and dipped it down toward the improvised landing pad. They descended and Emily thought she heard all four of them let out a sigh of relief when the tires finally touched down.

"Terra firma," Mac said as he cut the engines, then added with a grin, "The firmer it is the less bloody terror. Welcome home."

Emily could see the beams of flashlights around the edge of the landing pad; they were moving toward them now, bouncing back and forth as their owners ran to greet the returning group, the Black Hawk's rotor blades already slowing to a stop.

The door of the helo was opened from outside and Rhiannon's face appeared, ghostly in the orange glow of her flashlight. Thor sidled over and licked the girl's face, his tail beating against Emily's leg.

"Hi," Rhiannon said nonchalantly, as if they had just returned from a shopping trip rather than an exploratory mission to seek out new life and boldly go where no one had gone before, to quote Captain James T. Kirk. But Emily saw the girl's eyes flit from person to person as she made sure everyone was accounted for. The kid had a caring heart. It was going to be difficult for her to keep it in the world Emily knew lay ahead of them.

Now, as Emily unbuckled her safety harness and jumped down to the waiting crew, for the first time in what seemed like years to her, she felt a real sense of hope. A sense of belonging. She threw her arms around Rhiannon and hugged her, welcoming the one she got in return.

"You okay?" she asked the girl.

"I'm good. Did you find the spaceship?" The question was asked so innocently, as if hunting for crashed aliens was something normal, another reminder of how topsy-turvy the world had become. Spaceships and aliens and the end of the world. Oh my!

"Yes, we found it," Emily smiled.

"Cool!" Rhiannon said. "Come on, Thor." The dog gave a deep bark and chased after Rhiannon as she headed back to the camp and the welcome warmth of its security lights.

"Everything okay, Em?" MacAlister said as he climbed down from the cockpit and joined Emily on the ground next to the rapidly cooling Black Hawk.

"I'm going to need everyone assembled in the canteen," she said, ignoring the barrage of questions fired at them by the small group of sailors who greeted the four returning comrades. "Can we do that in about an hour?"

MacAlister nodded. "I'll make sure everyone's there."

"Thanks, Mac." She reached out and found his hand and squeezed it. "And thanks for waiting."

He gently returned the squeeze. "Anytime." Their hands lingered for another second then reluctantly drifted apart.

■ ■ ■

It took a little longer than the hour Emily had requested to get all the survivors into the same room together. But as the last stragglers walked in, Emily took a swig from her bottle of water and looked out at the rows of expectant faces staring right back at her.

When the last butt was in a seat, she stood and raised her hands to quell the hum of chatter.

Where to begin? Where to begin?

"I know most of you are probably only now coming to terms with the events following the rain. And I also know that most of you probably think I'm a little . . . nuts." There were a couple of knowing smiles from the crowd and a scattering of polite smiles. "But I would also hope that you would at least accept that what I've told you up until now has been proven correct, in as much as it's possible to prove. So, if you can give me the benefit of the doubt that I'm not completely crazy, it will make what I have to say next a little easier."

She took another long pull from the water bottle. It was room temperature by now but it still felt good against the scratch of the sandpaper that had suddenly coated her throat. How best to say what she needed to say next? Straight to the point would be best, she supposed.

Okay, here we go.

"During our expedition to discover what the object was that took out the ISS and crashed in Nevada, we discovered a spaceship. It had landed just outside Las Vegas, and during a . . . altercation . . . I was captured by the aliens that caused the red rain. I was taken somewhere, I don't really know where it was, and they explained to me why everything that has happened since the day the rain occurred."

God, that sounded ridiculous, but it was the truth.

There was a smattering of embarrassed laughter from the crowd, but mostly Emily saw blank stares or faces twisted with incredulity looking back at her. She couldn't blame them, of course; how would she react if she were in their place? How many kooks and crazies had she walked away from when she was working at the *New York Tribune* who insisted they had been abducted or seen a UFO? No, she couldn't blame them, but still, she had to convince them.

Truth be told, it did not matter what they thought about this part of her story, because what she had to say next was going to be even more unbelievable to them.

"I know, I know. It probably sounds crazy to you—"

"Probably?" one of the sailors said from the back of the room. His remark was followed by a scattering of snickers.

"Hey!" MacAlister said, rising up from his seat at the front and turning to face his crew. "Give it a rest."

Emily began to explain how she had woken in the ship, how she had met the aliens calling themselves the Caretakers, and the explanation they had given her for why they had chosen Earth. When she was done a heavy silence settled over the crowd of sailors.

"We've still got a couple of nukes in the bay," a sailor Emily thought was named Cooper said finally. "I say we drop one on the bastards and see how they like that."

Captain Constantine spoke, "Wonderful idea, Mr. Cooper, and then what? There are God knows how many more of these ships around the world, so how would you suggest we handle it when one of them decides to take a shot back at us? That's assuming our nuke even has the possibility of hitting them. For all we know, they could lob the thing right back to us. Or detonate it before it even left the launch tube. No. There won't be any nukes."

"Do you have the photographs?" Emily asked.

Mac nodded. He had found a printer in one of the unused offices and run off enough copies of the photographs Emily had captured for everyone.

"Pass these along," he said, handing a stack to the first sailor in each row.

There was a chorus of curses and expletives as the photos were passed from hand to hand.

"That is what we are dealing with," said Emily when the last of the men had the image in his hand. "And Commander Mulligan mentioned there were more, seven in total we think, that landed around the world besides this one. Still think it's a good idea to nuke it?"

The mood of the crowd had become less cynical since they had been handed the photographs, Emily thought, and a little more receptive, so she pushed on.

"But that's not all they told me," she continued. "They also gave me a warning that I should pass on to all of you."

The chatter that had broken out among the crew faded to silence again.

"They told me that they would allow us an area of land extending twenty miles out from Point Loma. That we would be left to our own devices as long as we stayed there, but if we or any of the other survivors they say are out there try to expand beyond that area, well, then we would be 'dealt with,' to use their words."

"'Dealt with'? What the fuck does 'dealt with' mean? Fuck!" This from the same sailor who, minutes earlier, had suggested they nuke Las Vegas.

"Use your imagination, Cooper," MacAlister hissed this time. "What do you think an alien race that's capable of eliminating an entire planet of eight-billion people and then setting up home there as easily as we go on a camping trip is capable of doing? Hmmm? Jesus Christ, if there was a navy left to complain to I swear I'd be asking them to check you for fucking brain damage."

This brought a smattering of laughter from some of the other sailors. Cooper flushed scarlet with embarrassment. "I was only asking," he mumbled.

"Yeah? Well let me spell it out for you, for all of you. I've seen this ship up close. I've stood not fifty feet away from these aliens, so hear this from me: If we stray outside the cordon these Caretakers have set aside for us, they will fry our arses. There. Is that clear enough for you?"

Cooper nodded.

"Good. Emily, please continue."

"While they never directly said anything about frying anyone's asses . . . or arses, they did make it clear that there would be severe repercussions if we strayed outside the boundaries they set for us. What's more important is that they were very specific in their insistence that we are not the only survivors left alive. There are others and we have to find them. There are how many of us left? Thirty-five. That's nowhere near enough to maintain a viable community, not if we want the human race to become something more than just a footnote on this planet's history. We have to track down these other survivors. It's our only chance at a future."

When Emily finished speaking she looked across at Captain Constantine. "That's it," she said.

"Alright, well, thank you Emily. Does anyone have any questions?"

A sailor at the front raised his hand.

"Go ahead, Stevens," said the captain.

"But what happens in the future, what happens if these other survivors join us and we survive and we grow?"

All eyes turned back to Emily again.

"While he didn't use these exact words, the alien I spoke with effectively said we are on probation; behave ourselves and they will leave us alone. Start any trouble, and they'll deal with us accordingly."

"What happens if we run out of room?" another voice asked.

"Again, it's going to depend on our behavior. But at some point in the future, the Caretakers will judge us; if we meet their standards, I think we might be given room to expand."

"And if we fail?"

"It's up to *us* to make sure we *don't* fail. It's the responsibility of every one of us left to ensure that we, and every generation that comes after us, understands what is needed to survive on this new planet. We won't be allowed to meaninglessly squander resources or life anymore because we're no longer at the top of the food chain; something with a lot more intelligence, a lot more power than we could ever imagine, runs the show now. But all they are asking is that we learn a little humility, a little respect for what we have."

Emily paused and looked around at the faces looking back at her, the last of humanity gathered here in this one little room. "Because if we choose not to listen, they can take it all away. And the next time, there won't be anyone left to make a difference."

CHAPTER 30

Emily knew she would never grow tired of hearing the waves breaking against the shoreline around Point Loma. The constant susurration of white-capped rolls of ocean slipping up the sand and pebble-strewn beach was the closest she would ever come to the chaotic symphony of the great city she had loved so very much . . . only to lose forever.

But that loss no longer hung over her with the same heaviness.

In the eighteen months since she and Mac had returned from Las Vegas, Emily had resigned herself to being one of the final witnesses of that old world, an anachronistic memory, destined to become part of a myth, woven into the fabric of humanity's story. It was a surprisingly comforting thought to know that she was one of the last of something that would never, *could* never, exist again. It made what she still had left from that old life, and the things that she had gained, seem all the more precious to her.

She walked the beach as she did every morning, lost in her thoughts, the sleeves of her cargo pants rolled up to just below her knees, flip-flops kicked off long ago and carried in her hand as she followed the gentle curve of the beach for a mile or so away from the settlement, her feet tingling as each new wave broke over the wet sand, squelching between her toes.

It was the same beach that she and the other survivors from the Stockton Islands had first set foot on in this strange new continent, familiar in so many ways, yet changed forever. It was also the same beach where, just ten months earlier, MacAlister and she had spoken their vows together. She smiled at the memory as she passed the spot where Mac had taken her hand in his own and promised to be hers and she had vowed to be his. Captain Constantine had officiated over the ceremony, a simple affair; two survivors, happy to be alive and both amazed that with their species dangling over the precipice of extinction, love, much like life, had managed to find a way to survive.

In the time between then and now, Emily's view of this world had . . . adjusted.

In almost every novel she had read, every movie she had watched that pitched the end of the world as its theme, it always seemed to pander to humanity's fear of what would be lost rather than what could be gained through the birth of something new. Birth was a messy business, she knew that from firsthand experience, but the end result was, well, something magnificent.

Binoculars hung from a strap around her neck; she raised them to her eyes for the fifth time in as many minutes and scanned the open sea for any sign of their new arrivals.

Captain Constantine had told her over dinner one evening that before the rain had come there could have been upwards of fifty or more submarines plying through the world's oceans on any given day. That meant there could be thousands more survivors out there, safe beneath the waves, isolated in their hermetically sealed tin cans. That was the day she had started to reach out to potential survivors via the radio.

In the weeks and months after that first broadcast Emily had managed to make contact with four submarines. Two of those subs—one French, the other Argentinian—had chosen to join them at Point Loma, adding a further three-hundred-and-twenty souls to their growing community of survivors.

There had also been failures. A German sub and a Russian vessel had chosen to ignore her warnings about settling outside the Green Zone. They had headed back to Europe and their home ports. The German crew had lasted two days at their new location before all radio contact was lost, the Russian crew just under three days before their radio communication abruptly ceased.

Neither group had been heard from again.

It was impossible to estimate how many more vessels might be out there, or how many had even survived the tumultuous red storm that had brought such dramatic changes to the planet, but after this length of time, supplies onboard would be all but exhausted, and time would be quickly running out for their crews.

But the terrible loss of the two crews had at least provided the Point Loma settlers with some valuable information: There seemed to be a window of opportunity, albeit just a matter of days, before the Caretakers would fulfill their threat of retribution to any human who strayed and stayed outside of the zone they had assigned to the remnants of the human race. It also appeared that if a submarine stayed beneath the waves and kept moving, they were not seen as a threat. Maybe the Caretakers could not detect them? Maybe, as long as they kept on moving, the aliens did not care? Emily had given up on trying to fathom their inscrutable motivations.

Today, however, was an extra-special day. Today, somewhere out *there*, beneath the rolling blue waves, was a US submarine heading home. And, while Emily welcomed the cosmopolitan mix of accents and attitudes that had sprouted up around the camp, it would be nice to be around others from her own culture.

She had begun to think that she and Rhiannon were the last survivors of her country. But just a few weeks earlier they had made contact with the *USS Michigan*, a ballistic missile sub that had ridden out the storm anchored off of the Arctic, much as the crew of the *HMS Vengeance* had done at the opposite end of the world. They had a full contingent of almost one-hundred-and-thirty-two personnel onboard as well as a number of scientists they had rescued from Arctic research stations similar to the one she and Rhiannon had fought so hard to reach in the Stocktons. The knowledge and skills those scientists and engineers possessed would prove invaluable to the group and their efforts to survive and thrive here at this Southern California refuge.

They were out there right now, Emily thought, her eyes drifting over the sea, searching for any sign of the new arrivals. She knew she was getting ahead of herself, allowing her excitement to get the better of her; the last time they had made contact with the US sub they were still a good eight hours out, but still, she was looking forward to the promise of new faces, fresh personalities, and new stories to be heard.

"Hey, you! What you up to?" The familiar voice came from behind her so she did not flinch when she felt a strong hand on her shoulder. She turned and kissed her husband, then pulled back to arm's length.

"Aren't you supposed to be doing your boss thing rather than creeping around on the beach accosting innocent women?" she asked MacAlister.

"The boys have a handle on it. Besides, what's the point of being the boss if you can't take an extended break or two every now and again, eh?" He slipped his arm around her waist as they walked along the shorefront.

Mac headed up one of the clearing crews tasked with keeping the ever encroaching alien flora as far away from their doorstep as possible. It had been a slow, painful, and at times dangerous daily task to clear out the vegetation that seemed as intent on claiming Point Loma as the survivors were on keeping it. The remnants of San Diego, out across the bay, had disappeared in much the same way as Las Vegas, quickly disintegrating into nothing as the alien vegetation ate it away in the space of a week. So, if they wanted to keep this small spit of land they now called home their own, it was going to take a continual effort to hold back the wall of red.

The task of hacking down and burning the plants was grueling, backbreaking work, but rather than have a single group deal with it, it became a shared responsibility for all able-bodied souls. That responsibility had become far easier with the arrival of the newcomers, and multiple groups now took on the task of keeping the camp clear of infestation. Each group worked one day clearing the vegetation with chain saws, fire, and machete. They had managed to reclaim and hold a two-mile perimeter around the base, clearing out the homes, offices, and other buildings on their stretch of the peninsula.

Even with so much of the area directly surrounding Point Loma cleared, the vast majority of the survivors had chosen to remain within the fenced security of the main base, but a few brave (or dumb, Emily still wasn't sure which) individuals had set up home in one of the many vacant residences beyond the security fence, in anticipation of the base becoming overcrowded as new arrivals joined the group. They had their choice of the prime homes, and so far, fingers crossed, there had been no mishaps or loss of life.

In his off time, Mac worked with Parsons and a small team of fellow engineers trying to figure out how to provide a permanent link to the nuclear reactor of the *Vengeance*. A reliable source of electricity would be needed quickly to help supplement their dwindling supply of diesel. In the meantime, they had managed to jury-rig a couple of wind turbines located during one of the camp's weekly scavenger hunts that helped ease the load a little.

It was a start, and Emily had every faith that they would accomplish their goal.

She, on the other hand, had somehow found herself in the roles of unofficial mayor, public liaison officer, diplomat, and welcoming committee all bundled into one. On the six days she wasn't working one of the cleanup crews, she was manning the radio station where she tracked and spoke with the other submarine survivors, usually trying to convince them that they should join her group. When possible, she steered clear of explaining why they should not land any farther north than Los Angeles, afraid that she might cause them to run in the opposite direction really, really fast if she told them about her encounter with the Caretakers and their warning. That was a conversation better left to a face-to-face meeting when she could have Mac and the rest of her group vouch for her veracity.

And when she found herself bored of listening to nothing but static or of repeating the same question for the hundredth time or of trolling through the ether listening for any radio chatter that might lead her to a new group of survivors, there was always *something* that needed to be done around the base. Rhiannon was happy to step in and take over the radio duties, but she had taken on a major role herself.

As the group of survivors grew, so too did the drain on the meager resources they had managed to scavenge locally. A few quick sorties into the surrounding areas in the early months, before what was still left of the old world had vanished completely, had bolstered their supplies, but with the total annihilation of the planet's subsistence crops, a long-term food source was needed. Tentative experiments with some of the new plant life had identified several roots and shoots that could sustain a person almost indefinitely if push came to shove. It was just a pity, Emily thought, that no matter what was added to the alien plants by way of spices or garnishment, it still tasted like shit. Most people couldn't even keep it down. Attempts to fish the ocean proved only that it seemed empty of all but the lowliest of life.

And that was another reason people were so eager to welcome the USS *Michigan* and her crew home. One of the rescued scientists onboard, a biologist, had mentioned the existence of a seed-bank facility built into a frozen cluster of islands north of what had once been Norway. The archipelago of islands lay close enough to the North Pole to have survived the great changes and might hold the key to humanity's survival.

The Svalbard Global Seed Vault, according to the biologist, lay in a massive bomb-proof underground bunker cut into the frigid rock of Spitsbergen, the largest of the Svalbard archipelago. Safely stored away beneath the permafrost of the island, the seed vault had been created to guard against the unthinkable happening.

Well, the unthinkable had become an everyday occurrence.

So, a plan was being formulated; it was a risky one, no doubt, and would involve taking one of their collection of submarines to the frozen island in the hope that *maybe* its precious reserve of Earth-born seeds had survived.

Emily glanced across at Mac, sitting next to her on the beach. His beard was fuller these days but better kept than when she had first met him. He had added a pair of neatly trimmed sideburns.

"Makes you look like Abe Lincoln," she told him, rubbing the tip of her finger across the oblong of hair on his cheek.

"Abe Lincoln? Wasn't he a singer with one of those eighties bands?"

She nudged him playfully with her shoulder, then leaned in close, her head against his shoulder, linking her hands around the crook of his knee. Mac's eyes were focused on the far horizon but every now and again he plucked a handful of the coarse yellow sand and allowed it to sift slowly through his open fingers.

"No sign of them yet?" he asked, pressing his cheek against the crown of her head.

"They're still a couple of hours out, I guess. But they'll be here soon and everything will change again." They sat in peaceful silence for a while, allowing the pleasure of each other's company and the breeze rolling in from the sea to envelop them.

"Well, duty calls," Mac sighed eventually, unaware of Emily's internal conflict. He turned and kissed her lightly on the lips, untangled himself from her grasp, and pushed himself to his feet.

"Help me up," Emily said, all thoughts other than the love she felt for this man fading from her head. Mac pulled her to her feet and she took his hand in her own. "I'll walk with you. Rhiannon's probably wondering where I am anyway."

They strolled back toward the camp slowly, reveling in the time they had been allowed. Behind them their fresh footprints and the indentations in the sand where they had sat quickly filled with the incoming tide and then vanished, leaving the beach as pristine as before they had arrived.

EPILOGUE

Thor greeted Emily at the door of the apartment, tail wagging enthusiastically, tongue lolling from the side of his jaw. They used the term "apartment" loosely around camp; it was actually part of a smaller office building that had been sectioned off into quarters for married or partnered couples. It wasn't what you would call fancy, and certainly no comparison to her apartment back in Manhattan, but still, it was home and she smiled every time she walked through the door. Of course that smile could also be credited to the love that was waiting for her each time she set foot inside.

"Missed me, eh?" Emily asked, rubbing the dog behind his ear as he pushed up against her legs, escorting her inside. "Where is everyone?" she called out.

"We're in here!" Rhiannon shout-whispered, her voice floating in via the living room. Emily followed it into the bedroom.

Rhiannon looked up from a chair in the corner and smiled at Emily. "Look," she murmured to the tiny form bundled in a blue blanket held tightly in her arms, "Mama's home."

"Hi, Baby Boy," Emily cooed as she reached down and took the child from Rhiannon and cradled him to her chest. She looked down adoringly into the face of her son and he stared back, wide-eyed, reaching a tiny hand out to his mother.

They named him Adam. It seemed fitting given the circumstances. He was the first child born into this new world and had quickly become a symbol of hope for every one of the survivors at Point Loma. This unexpected gift had, at first, shocked then lifted the spirits of their fledgling community. And since his birth, Emily knew of at least four more pregnancies.

Emily placed her lips lightly against her boy's forehead. Adam gurgled his pleasure back at her, smiling in that odd way of his, as though he wanted to speak something to her but his body was too young to form the words he needed to say.

Emily sighed and pouted at her boy. This was going to have to be just a short visit; just to see her son, just to make sure that he was real, that she had not dreamed him up. She often found herself finding an excuse to pop back to the apartment and check on him, but she had work that she *had* to get back to, preparations that still needed to be made before the new arrivals showed up, so she would have to return the boy back to his auntie Rhiannon for the rest of the afternoon.

"How's he been?" Emily asked as she walked around the bedroom, rocking the boy gently back and forth, cherishing every moment she could.

"Fine. He just woke up from a nap, so he's a little hungry. I was about to feed him." Rhiannon gestured to a bottle of baby formula sitting next to the chair.

"I'll do it," Emily said. She moved a fold of blanket from the boy's body and looked adoringly at her son. To say that he was a miracle was an understatement. She clucked at the boy and he smiled awkwardly back at her, squirming gently in her arms, both hands now reaching out for her, lacing around her outstretched finger. *He is just perfect*, she thought.

He had Emily's same high cheekbones and nub of a chin (*although not my ears, thank God for small miracles*) and the same shock of hair and slender lips as his father. But it was Adam's eyes that truly set him apart; they followed his mother's face with innocent interest, his ruby-red irises sparkling like stardust, responding to the tiny scintillations of red that dotted Emily's own eyes, glowing with their own faint luminescence. And, in that briefest of moments, Emily sensed the unbreakable connection that existed between her and her child. She sensed him reaching out with his young, inquisitive mind, exploring, and from around the planet she heard a chorus of other voices answer, welcoming him to their strange new world.

ACKNOWLEDGMENTS

Well, here we are again. As always, there are a few people I would like to thank. It should go without saying that I owe a debt of gratitude to the 47North team, who continually amaze me with their creativity and precision.

To my editor, Jeff VanderMeer, cheers, mate.

And, of course, I want to thank you, the fans and readers of Emily, Thor, and her new compatriots. Hopefully this book has answered some of the burning questions you have emailed me since the release of *Exodus*.

I had always envisioned Emily's journey to have taken up three books, but she has taken on a life of her own and demands that I tell more of her tale. And as we all know, you don't mess with Emily, if you know what's good for you. So, there will be more books to come in her universe.

Make sure you check out my website at www.DisturbedUniverse.com or join my Facebook page, www.facebook.com/pages/

Paul-Antony-Jones/150633681672260, for news and updates on her new adventures.

Paul Jones
November, 2013

ABOUT THE AUTHOR

A native of Cardiff, Wales, Paul Antony Jones now resides in Las Vegas, Nevada. He has worked as a newspaper reporter and commercial copywriter, but his passion is penning fiction. A self-described science geek, he's a voracious reader of scientific periodicals, as well as a fan of things mysterious, unknown, and fringe-related. That fascination inspired his first novel, *Extinction Point*, and its first sequel, *Extinction Point: Exodus*. Emily Baxter's adventures will continue in future installments of the series. Join the author's mailing list at DisturbedUniverse.com.